THE NAPUS

Borgo Press Books by Léon Daudet

The Bacchantes: A Dionysian Scientific Romance
The Napus: The Great Plague of the Year 2227

THE NAPUS

THE GREAT PLAGUE
OF THE YEAR 2227

LÉON DAUDET

Translated by Brian Stableford

THE BORGO PRESS

MMXII

CLASSICS OF
FANTASTIC LITERATURE

NUMBER FIVE

THE NAPUS

FIRST EDITION

Published by Wildside Press LLC

www.wildsidebooks.com

THE NAPUS

CONTENTS

INTRODUCTION
by Brian Stableford

Le Napus, fléau de l'an 2227 by Léon Daudet, here translated as *The Napus: The Great Plague of the Year 2227*, was originally published in Paris by Ernest Flammarion in 1927. Although Léon Daudet had published a previous satire with a biomedical theme in *Les Morticoles* (1894), and was to go on to write two further novels involving innovative scientific speculations in *Les Bacchantes* (1931; tr. as *The Bacchantes*) and *Ciel de Feu* [Sky on Fire] (1934), *Le Napus* must have seemed to Daudet's readers in 1927 to be a radical departure from the vague pattern established by the twenty-eight contemporary and historical novels he had published between 1895 and 1926. It is, however, very much a product of its time, being one of a number of ambitious futuristic novels published in the decade following the end of the Great War of 1914-18, reflecting on the historical significance of that war by projecting its lessons forward in hypothetical time.

By the second decade of the twentieth century, the observation that "the only thing that anyone ever learned from history is that no one ever learns anything from history" had become an accepted truism, albeit a fairly dubious one, and various further aphorisms had been spun off from it, including the rule that "those who fail to learn from history are condemned to repeat it," and the later addendum "first as tragedy, then as farce." It is within that context of thought that almost all the speculative novels attempting to deal with the lessons of the Great War operate, and such was the nature of the lessons involved that novels dealing in tragedy and farce—more often combined than sequential—inevitably did so in terms of deep tragedy and black farce. *Le Napus* is one of the most striking and one of the most ambitious, in both its depth and its blackness, and it remains one of the most bizarre works of futuristic fantasy ever penned.

Works reflecting on the legacy of the Great War by attempting to imagine what future wars might be like were produced in various countries in Europe, and also in the United States of America, and in broad terms they all reflect the particular experiences that the various nations had during the war. America, involved in the war belatedly and at long distance, not only suffered relatively lightly in terms of casualty figures, but came out of the war with its economic situation on the world stage vastly improved, possessed of an economic hegemony that it would not lose for at least a century in spite of the Wall Street Crash and the Great Depression. Britain came off much worse, both in terms of political economy—losing a hegemony that it had previously enjoyed and beginning a long slide into irrelevance that similarly lasted for more than a century—and in terms of sacrificial slaughter. France, however, suffered even more than Britain, by virtue of providing a large fraction of the terrain in which and under which the war was actually fought, having the whole sorry affair crushing it for four long years. To make matters worse, the war broke out when the nation had not yet fully recovered from the economic aftereffects of the Franco-German War of 1870, which was still smarting in the memory of its older generation and its literature. Given these difference, it is not surprising that British future war fiction of the 1920s is much blacker than American future war fiction, and that French future war fiction is the blackest of all.

In the USA in 1927, in fact, futuristic fiction in general had just passed what can be seen in retrospect as a landmark in the history of that genre. In 1926 Hugo Gernsback had founded *Amazing Stories*, the "magazine of scientifiction," from which the marketing genre of "science fiction" eventually sprang, slowly building a huge edifice of ideas and images in which, for the most part, dark events only featured as interims, unfortunate preludes to new progressive dawns. Future war became a significant theme almost as soon as "scientifiction" was born, but its tragic and farcical aspects were given short shrift, and the heroes of scientifiction were not only in those wars to win them, but to do so spectacularly, with the aid of shock and awe. In 1928 two significant future war stories appeared in the same issue of *Amazing Stories*: "Armageddon 2419 A.D." by Philip Francis Nowlan, which introduced the science fiction genre's first archetypal hero, Buck Rogers—whose adventures were extensively continued in the nascent comic strip medium—and the first episode of *The Skylark of Space* by Edward E. Smith, which blithely took the future of humankind, including warfare, on to a vast galactic stage ripe for adventure, colonization, and conquest, those three items being viewed as a natural sequence of development.

In Britain the situation was very different. Britain had already had a thriving genre of future war fiction prior to 1914, initially launched into popularity by George Chesney's alarmist account of *The Battle of Dorking* (1871), which drew stern lessons from the Franco-Prussian War, and given a spectacular boost by George Griffith's extravagant account of world war waged by heroic Terrorists, *The Angel of the Revolution* (1893). Most such fiction took it for granted that the next war would not be long in coming, and that the most likely enemy by far was Germany, but almost without exception, and quite naturally, the authors looked forward to a resounding British victory. In a sense, they were right; the next war was imminent; Germany was the enemy; and the British did end up on the undefeated side—but the victory anticipated in fiction did not resemble the actual victory at all, which turned out to be ruinously expensive and exceedingly hollow. In the run-up to the actual war, the fictitious anticipations had billed it as a war to end war, and a war for the salvaging of civilization, but it was acutely obvious by 1918 that it had been nothing of the sort: that it had, in fact, not only been disastrously costly in human and economic terms but had achieved nothing in terms of making future wars less likely. Indeed, people possessed of clear sight could see that it almost certainly made a future war on an even larger scale inevitable—a result that added a blackly ironic absurdity to its manifest tragedy.

In those circumstances, it is not surprising that futuristic fiction, and the ideas that it had celebrated, suffered something of a backlash in Britain. The briefly-thriving genre of scientific romance, which had been spun off from the future war genre in the 1890s, was dragged down with its parent into suspicion and ignominy. It never disappeared, but it lost the precarious popularity that it had briefly enjoyed and became esoteric. It also became, in the main, deeply and bitterly pessimistic. Such future war novels as *The People of the Ruins* (1920) by Edwards Shanks, *Theodore Savage* (1922) by Cicely Hamilton, and *Ragnarok* (1926) by Shaw Desmond were all tragic and frankly apocalyptic, and they all had a brutal ironic edge. In 1927 the entire genre of futuristic fiction was still in the doldrums in Britain, but it did contrive a comeback of sorts, and a new burst of energy after 1930, when the edge of bitter irony in the treatment of future wars became more pronounced, sometimes extending all the way to black farce, in such novels as *The Seventh Bowl* (1930) and *The Gas War of 1940* (1931) by "Miles" (Stephen Southwold, better known as Neil Bell), *Tomorrow's Yesterday* (1932) by John Gloag, and *Gay Hunter* (1934) by J. Leslie Mitchell.

The French genre of the *roman scientifique* had also undergone a boom of sorts in the 1890s, when it also featured a good deal of future war fiction of a markedly jingoistic and ultimately triumphalist stripe, but the prior evolution of the genre and the subgenre had been markedly different, and the parentage was the other way around. French speculative fiction had first emerged in the context of the Voltairean *conte philosophique*, so an ironic, skeptical and satirical dimension was built into its historical foundations, and it re-energized Utopian fiction as well as giving birth to its skeptical counterpart, which took a long time to acquire the label of "dystopian fiction." French *roman scientifique* also received an extremely important inoculation of black farce at a relatively early date when the writer and illustrator Albert Robida published *La Guerre au vingtième siècle* (1883; revised 1887; tr. as *War in the Twentieth Century*), whose grotesquely exaggerated machines of war colored the imagery of French future war fiction even for writers who had no sympathy at all for Robida's determined pacifism.

Robida was the fastest writer out of the blocks in publishing a reflective imaginative response to the Great War in *L'Ingénieur von Satanas* (1919), but others inevitably followed his lead. In France, remarkably, future war fiction of a sort had even been produced during the war, apparently as a deliberate propagandistic strategy, albeit within controlled circumstances that did not permit satirical hostility or any thought of ultimate defeat. Thus, such novels as *Rouletabille chez Krupp* (1917; tr. as *Rouletabille at Krupp's*) by Gaston Leroux also helped lay groundwork for the post-war backlash, by introducing imaginary superweapons that could not be used, but nevertheless gave a hint of awesome possibilities to come. The potential destructive capacity of such superweapons was rapidly displayed in such extravagant post-war novels such as Henri Allorge's *Le Grand cataclysme* (1922; tr. as *The Great Cataclysm*).

The most striking and significant reaction to the Great War cast in the form of bitter futuristic fiction was Ernest Pérochon's *Les Hommes frénétiques* (1925; tr. as *The Frenetic People*), and it its possible that it was that novel which prompted Daudet to write *Le Napus*, not as a copy but as a political correction, Pérochon having strong socialist and pacifist principles, while Daudet was at the opposite end of the political spectrum, as one of the leading lights of the strident right-wing periodical *Action Française*. Pérochon had the advantage of a certain philosophical consistency in his work that Daudet did not have—it is far easier for a pacifist to represent war as a thoroughly bad thing than for a man committed to uncompromising toughness to make out a case for high-tech war being something with which people simply have to get used to living—but that only made the latter's task more interesting in imaginative and narrative terms, and encouraged a further tipping of the balance between tragedy and farce.

It is not an exaggeration, nor is it uncomplimentary, to say that *Le Napus* is the most farcical of all the future war novels of the 1920s. Modern readers will might well find it a deeply troubling book in terms of its political slant, especially its crude and now-discomfiting racism (the publisher who issues most of my translations declined to publish this one on the grounds that "Léon Daudet was not a nice man"—a principle which, if universally applied, would slim down the literary tradition considerably), but that does not detract from its historical significance, nor from its remarkable bizarrerie. Daudet had no sympathy at all for such *avant-gardist* literary movements as surrealism, but *Le Napus* makes it clear that he was not uninfluenced by surrealism in his choice of motifs and his methods of deploying them. Like all unique books, it deserves some attention by virtue of that fact alone, but there is also much in its arguments—especially the absurd ones—that is worth taking seriously, if only to strengthen disagreement and disapproval by virtue of dynamic tension.

Along with most of the writers of future war fiction in the 1920s, Daudet suggests that the very nature of war had undergone a fundamental shift during the war of 1914-18, presaging the inevitability that future wars would involve whole populations rather than armies, and that long-range weapons would be routinely used against both military and civilian targets. He names that new kind of warfare after an anecdote first related by the Classical satirist Lucian, who claimed (more than three hundred years after the event) that during the Siege of Syracuse by the Romans in 214-212 B.C., a Roman fleet had been destroyed by a kind of heat ray devised by the city's most famous son, the great engineer Archimedes. Later writers who mistook this obvious item of fiction for earnest historical truth (a not-uncommon problem with Classical writings viewed from a Medieval standpoint) suggested that Archimedes might have used a parabolic array of metallic mirrors to focus the sun's rays on the ships, thus setting fire either to their sails or—more likely—the tar with which their hulls were caulked, although modern attempts to perform such a feat have all failed. The point is, however, that Archimedes' "heat ray" entered the mythology of warfare, and assumed a new importance in the early twentieth-century imagination, when the discoveries of X-rays and radium made the idea of "ray guns" of various kinds exceedingly fashionable in speculative fiction.

In *Le Napus*, a German writer named von Herzius is said to have written a book called *Archimedes*, setting out a prospectus for future warfare in which enemy nations can be devastated by various kinds of innovative long-range weapons, including ingenious projectiles—missiles and bombs—and scientific devices for causing, earthquakes, floods, violent storms, and so on: a prospectus enthusiastically taken up in the novel by a resurgent German Empire, in spite of the extremely high cost of such weapons. The great bugbear of the era, in terms of actual anxieties, was poison gas delivered by air fleets, but that only plays a minor role in Daudet's expansive scheme, which is more various as well as more grandiose, also involving economic warfare of an ingeniously ludicrous variety.

Superweapons had long featured in French speculative fiction, which had begun to take aboard in the 1850s the notion that technological progress would eventually permit the invention of weapons so powerful that making war would become "unthinkable." It is, however, very noticeable in hindsight—and must have been obvious even in the 1920s—that notions of what might constitute a weapon so dreadful as to make its use in war "unthinkable" were forced to undergo a considerable melodramatic inflation as actual weaponry advanced in its destructive potential. Daudet was by no means the first person to realize that there is, in fact, no conceivable weapon so destructive that military men would not eagerly deploy it, even at the cost of destroying civilization, the human race, or the planet, but he was the first to assume that such deployments would eventually become routine, only restrained by their enormous cost and the fact that, being untestable before use, the weapons in question would always be likely to misfire, at least to some extent.

Fortunately for Daudet, that last point dovetailed very well with his general attitude to science, which had been permanently soured in the 1890s when he was thwarted in his first career plan, to become a physician. Although he passed all the necessary examinations, he did not survive his initial training as an intern, being thrown out for a theoretical unorthodoxy that his superiors considered as blatant and gross insubordination (he was a fan of homoeopathy and did not believe that diseases are caused by "microbes"). Following his famous father into a literary career was a fallback position, and although he developed that career very successfully, he never lost the rancor that his initial setback had generated, nursing it so affectionately that it eventually grew into a fully mature obsession.

Le Napus, in building of a future in which scientific knowledge has continued to progress, takes it for granted that much of that science will be intellectually bankrupt, and that the fraction that is not will be largely deleterious to the quality of human life. It is one of very few science-based speculative novels to assume that much contemporary theoretical knowledge is seriously mistaken, and that the theories that replace contemporary ones will be just as arbitrary and liable to supersession. In the world of *Le Napus*, it is not only the Archimedean super-weapons that routinely misfire—while still doing enormous damage and inflicting serious mortality—but all the efforts of scientists, especially and most importantly in confrontation with the Napus itself: a new and utterly mysterious "plague," which adds an extra dimension of complication to the war.

If the world featured in the novel is perverse to the point of paradoxicality, so is the narrator through whose eyes we see it: the result of an experiment in selective breeding that was supposed to produce idealized humans but—inevitably, in this context—went awkwardly awry. As heroes go—and his notion of himself as a modest hero is by no means entirely mistaken—Polyplast 17,177 is certainly peculiar, but only an unreliable narrator in an unreliable world could stand any chance at all of acquiring a measure of paradoxical reliability. There is a sense in which his is the ideally perverse viewpoint from which to obtain a measure and grasp of the perverse society in which he lives. Even readers who cannot sympathize with him, let alone identify with him, might nevertheless find a certain interest in his gradual evolution towards a more humane humanity—as, indeed, they should.

The specific technological anticipations featured in *Le Napus* now seem very primitive, but that is inevitable given its date. In 1927 telegraphy was still mostly wire-based and radio broadcasting had yet to begin. Medicine was still largely ineffective; the first antibiotic, penicillin was not discovered until 1928, and although vaccines had been in use for a century their development had not yet been systematized and their utility was still dubious. Aviation was still relatively primitive, and so was the cinema. Daudet realized that much more technological development was to be expected from *ondes* (waves) and the electromagnetic equipment involved in their generation and control, but his vision of those possibilities was inevitably vague, and when it became specific, doomed to be mistaken.

These factors should not detract, however, from a proper rational appreciation of the effort involved in writing a futuristic novel in 1927, or from a proper esthetic appreciation of the devices that Daudet "invented" in his imagination. Most of those devices never actually came to be, but they are interesting nevertheless. His notion that there would be a fusion of cinema and text, so that in the world of *Le Napus*, which has no television, people can read "*cinébouquins*" (cinebooks) with moving illustrations complementary to the text, is particularly intriguing. Such ideas, which have been sidestepped by actual history, have recently begun to acquire a certain literary charm as the substance of "steampunk" fiction dealing with obsolete versions of yesterday's tomorrows, and of all the antique novels to have been retrospectively reclad in a steampunkish gloss, *Le Napus* is one of the quirkiest. If it is not as steamy, or as punkish, as the author's subsequent novel *Les Bacchantes*, it makes up for that deficit by virtue of its much greater extravagance, which is a far more important aspect of steampunk style and ambition.

Le Napus could not have been written in America in 1927, and if, by some freak of chance it had, it could not have been published or appreciated there; it is not surprising that it has had to wait nearly a century to be translated, and if political correctness were an excluding factor, that time would never have arrived at all. It would, therefore, be entirely inappropriate to look at *Le Napus* as if it were a "science fiction" novel and to try to wedge it belatedly into the historical canon of science fiction. It has much closer affinities with the tradition of British scientific romance, but the French tradition of the *roman scientifique*, although vaguer, was far more prolific, sophisticated and robust than either of the parallel English-language traditions, and it would be more reasonable to view the English works in the composite genre as eccentric offshoots of the French canon rather than the other way around. To be properly appreciated, *Le Napus* needs to be seen not as something faintly reminiscent of works with which English readers are already familiar, but as an example of something truly and intriguingly alien.

This translation should not, therefore, be viewed as a belated and eccentric contribution to the genre of science fiction, or even that of scientific romance, but rather as a twisted classic, of sorts, of the gloriously exotic *roman scientifique*: a book that, although carrying forward an evident tradition, and extending many of the fibers of thought holding that tradition together, is nevertheless a book like no other, a unique entity. It is, in consequence, potentially precious to all those pataphysically-inclined readers who prefer to study exceptions rather than rules, and delight in the unfamiliar rather than the familiar, especially when it is provocatively uncomfortable rather than soothingly soporific.

* * * * * * *

This translation has been taken from a copy of the original Flammarion edition. It poses the usual problem of translation applicable to antique futuristic fiction, in that the terminology subsequently developed in the real world to describe the technologies anticipated in the book is markedly different from the terminology that the author was compelled to invent, but I have resisted the temptation to substitute the real-world terminology even when it would seem appropriate to a modern reader, thus avoiding such terms as "radio," even though its omission might now appear odd, in the interests of attempting to preserve the eccentric flavor of the original.

PROLOGUE
THE APPEARANCE OF
A NEW DISEASE

First, I shall tell you what happened to me on the third of May 2227, in the thirtieth year of my terrestrial existence. Afterwards, I shall tell you who I am and why I am writing these memoirs. Don't be impatient. Don't skip a single page— nor a line, nor a word. Everything is connected, in such a way that, after having read me attentively, you will be in possession of a whole host of new and refreshing conceptions, useful for the guidance of life. Afterwards, you can do with them as you wish.

So, on the third of May 2227, which marked the debut in France of the terrible disease, I was going up the Avenue des Champs-Élysées on my own, heading toward the former location of the Arc de Triomphe, which had disappeared in the earthquake of 2150 after being badly damaged by the aerial bombardment of the Franco-German and European-Asian wars of the year 2000. The sky was blue; the air exquisite; life, so far as I was concerned, was good.

As I arrived at the crossroads where avionnettes used to be stationed in the days of non-magnetic aerial transport, I perceived, coming toward me, a tall, handsome old man with a white beard, who was holding a little girl by the hand, flanked by her Chinese governess. The child appeared to be about two or two-and-a-half years old, like a pink porcelain angel under her blonde hair. She was laughing and pulling obliquely ahead of her grandfather's stride, with a graceful gait.

Suddenly, I heard a dry click, and the old man disappeared completely, as if snatched away by a supernatural force.

"*N'a pus,*"[1] said the girl, spreading her dainty arms wide.

The face of the Chinese woman had become immobile and grave, like that of a conjuror's assistant witnessing an unknown trick. Numerous passers-by, witnesses to the event, began to tremble, like me, in all their limbs, recognizing, in that adventure, the first coup of the mysterious disease that the press had been reporting for a month, which had first become manifest in Chicago. Half a dozen cases had been cited, followed by three more in Berlin.

"*N'a pus, a grand pé a pati, n'a pus,*" repeated the child, elated by the annihilation of her grandfather and the accumulation of fear and stupor that had formed around that redoubtable absence.

A policeman arrived as we were getting a grip on our emotions. I gave him my name, number and occupation—Professor of Cellular Energy at the Aristotle Foundation—and was asked to write "Polyplast" myself in his notebook. He was as astonished by my name and the number attached to it as by the unusual phenomenon. Gripped by an abrupt need for mystification that is one of the axiomatic reflexes, I added that the old pedestrian had succumbed to a new disease, the "*n'a pus*" or Napus, which was beginning to be discussed among scientists.

"Is it catching?" the representative of public order asked me, with an anxious expression.

I assured him that it was not—that the symptom-free disease, which was exceptionally rare, was episodic and not conta-

---

1. *Pus* is the past historic of *pouvoir* [to be able], so the phrase as rendered can be construed, approximately, as "it cannot be" or "impossible," although it seems more likely that the child is mispronouncing "*n'a plus*" [is no more] or even "*n'a pas*" [is not] and is simply indicating absence, in line with her more elaborate comment "*a grand pé a pati*"—i.e. *grand-père a parti* [grandpa's gone].

gious. Then the worthy fellow signaled to a vehicle and had the Chinese woman and the little girl climb into it with him: "a matter of informing the family and the commissariat."

It was agreed that I would be called as a witness, the case being extraordinary, unusual and, all things considered, bewildering. What was no less bizarre was the difficulty we found, as co-spectators of the event, in going our separate ways and leaving the location of the tragic miracle of sorts. It had created a bond of solidarity between us comparable to a sympathy that did not entail any amity—a necessary of community. Our feet were stuck to the ground.

We exchanged visiting cards, and vague considerations regarding the unknown quantity surrounding us and the future of humankind, henceforth very hazardous. Some thought that the new thunderbolt would remain in a state of rarity, in view of the excellence of our temperate climate; others believed, on the contrary, that it was the beginning of a plague.

The latter, of which I was one, were correct. The worst is virtually certain.

With the general system of waves, the event quickly became known. Half an hour later, the entire world knew of the arrival in France, on the Avenue des Champs-Élysées in Paris, of the new disease of the total and abrupt disappearance or acute aphanasia popularly known as the Napus. The little girl had thus baptized the annihilation of her grandfather.

And now, before continuing, it's necessary that I tell you who I am.

I belong to the group of international "witnesses," the outcome of the international interbreeding of the year 2007, which succeeded the six year war in which thirty million people of all nations were killed. It was then thought that universal peace might be obtained by numerous Franco-German, Franco-English, Franco-Italian, Italo-German etc. marriages, and the forenames of the semi-artificial products that my grandparents thus became were replaced by numbers. We call ourselves "Polyplasts," which signifies "formed of several" and I am known as 17,177. It's perfectly ridiculous, but there is nothing I can do about it.

I will add, though, that the multiplicity of my origins has only increased in me the quality and evidence of current Frenchness and stimulated my patriotism. It is the same with all the Polyplasts spread throughout the planet. We are also interested in military inventions, as if the confused sources of our violent blood were continuing their antagonism. Psychological chemistry is as ironic as the majority of human inventions, which rapidly turn against human beings after having served, in an illusory fashion, for their comfort and pleasure.

CHAPTER ONE
AT THE ARISTOTLE FOUNDATION

The Aristotle Foundation, due to the specific legacies and the generosity of a number of Australian and American bankers, is somewhat analogous to what the Institut Pasteur was three centuries ago—with the difference that the latter was devoted to the study of the microbes (as one said then) that were believed to assault the human organism from without, and the juices, or sera, capable of curing the diseases caused by those microbes. Since the advent of the theory of cellular energy, itself creative of benevolent and harmful microorganisms, neither independently nor by means of products and chemical extracts, but by virtue of the new force named *cyton*.

The Aristotle Foundation is devoted to the study of all the forms, variants and transformations of cyton—of which the history is rather unimportant now, in view of the criticisms to which it has been subjected. These repeated criticisms, some of which are well-founded, have weakened our theoretical studies and laboratory work with regard to cyton to such a extent that we can no longer do anything, so to speak, except discuss between ourselves the events of the day, new armaments and methods of combat, and the rivalries—economic or otherwise—between nations.

A gossip-mongering bear-garden, that is what our venerable institution has become. It is the same for all the foundations of the same category in Europe and America, whose decrepitude and decay have been the object of numerous discouraging theses.

When I arrived the next day at my laboratory—or, more exactly, my talking shop—my male and female colleagues where all discussing the exciting aphanasia of the Avenue des Champs-Élysées, which filled the papers and wireless broadcasts. I was surrounded and bombarded with questions, to which I replied as best I could.

The term Napus delighted them, and the female doctors made faces, mimicking the infantile appellation and the fateful phrase: "*a grand pé a pati, n'a pus.*" There was talk of a further event of the same order, which had occurred in the Faubourg Saint-Antoine and had "blown away" a foreman at a furniture factory, as well as an epidemic of threes cases in Marseilles affecting a family of Greek cockle-fishers. We were well-read people, Polyplasts for the most part, and hypotheses were being produced in abundance.

"It's the beginning of the end of the world," asserted my cousin 17,178, knowing nothing about it. He was the product of a mixture of Germanism and mysticism that had caused him to be baptized Görres, the name of a celebrated turner of German heads.[2] He claimed that the affair had been predicted by a Moldavian monk in the twelfth century and that Nostradamus had made allusion to it in a *centurie*:[3]

---

2. Joseph Görres (1776-1848) was a leading member of the German Romantic Movement whose activities as a journalist made him a leading critic of Napoléon, who thought his *Der Rheinische Merkur* a particularly significant ideological enemy. He also became a significant Catholic mystic, publishing a five-volume account of *Christliche Mystik* between 1836 and 1842.

3. The prophetic quatrains published by Nostradamus in 1555 and divided into ten "centuries" were greatly elaborated after his death, although most fakes did at least observe the four-line format that is neglected here. In the same way, the most famous set of prophecies credited—falsely—to a twelfth-century monk were attributed to the Irish Saint Malachy, not to a "Moldavian" (Moldavia had not yet come into existence at that time), so Daudet appears to be deliberately playing up the falsity of the entire prophetic tradition.

When the seventh, preceded by a double third,
Will have broken the Ardent of august Sex
And powder expends with nothing found outside.

"The first line," my cousin affirmed, signifies 2227, the number two being repeated three times. The "august Sex" signifies the little girl, whose courage—the Ardent—was broken by the sudden pulverization of her grandfather, who disappeared without leaving a trace."

My lovely laboratory assistant Henriette Tastepain, however, who had discovered a new magnetic center in the cell, remarked that the lines of the famous *centuries* were contrived in such a way that one could always find meat and drink therein.

At that moment, Polyplast 14,026 arrived—the issue of a series of alternating Franco-American and Franco-Hungarian interbreedings crossed with negro, whose physiognomy is like a mosaic of those various nationalities. His erudition is extraordinary. He knows almost all the languages spoken on the planet, the majority of mathematical and biological sciences, and can cite, in bibliographical matters, the abstracts of all the periodicals that have appeared in France, Italy, England and Germany in the last ten years. The little fellow, who is also sensitive and even passionate, is an ambulant index. We asked him what he thought the explanation of the phenomenon might be. He reflected for ten minutes before answering, in the fashion of a prodigious calculator, and then his strong, cracked voice set forth the following:

"The disease, epidemic today, is, in my opinion, very ancient, having probably appeared in uncivilized countries and in a sporadic form. Complete disappearances that occurred before witnesses were recorded in Patagonia a hundred years ago. There have been others more recently in New Guinea. In the deserted part of Ireland, where the uninterrupted civil war has only left a few buildings standing, an observation mistaken for a legend—which is quite frequent—has established the sudden and total disappearance, about thirty years ago, of three members of the same family. I believe I remember, though, that Marco Polo, in his account of his journey to China, had already...."

The laboratory door opened to admit my Lyonnais laboratory technician Mouillemouillard, who has the face and accent of Chignol,[4] minus the "*sarsifie.*" He was both alarmed and terrified.

"The hourly wireless broadcast has announced that two other people have just disappeared from the Rue de Rivoli, while they were trying on shoes in a store. The young woman who was assisting them with the shoehorn is half-mad."

We burst out laughing—which finished widening Moulemouillard's pale gray eyes. The bizarrerie of the Napus, in the early hours, simultaneously excited an easily comprehensive fear and a kind of bizarre rictus, which must have been that of our earliest ancestors before the invention of fire or the appearance of the mammoth. In addition, scientific curiosity mingled with it. Stuffed with theories to the point of nausea, it was a veritable feast for us to get hold of a raw, undeniable and patent phenomenon. That is why amusement was associated in our souls with anguish.

Although it carried people off without any warning and sometimes prematurely, aphanasia at least offered the advantage of avoiding the formalities and embarrassments created by bodies, and, as Bossuet put it, "unfortunate residues." With that, no more coffins, no more funeral processions, no more cemeteries. It had no deleterious effect on religious beliefs—on the contrary, in fact: corporeal disappearance could be considered as the acme of spiritualism, giving free range to all certainties of a mystical order, which are in any case the least unsteady.

---

4. Various characters of this name featured in French literature trace their origin back to one of the stock figures of the Théâtre du Guignol de Lyon, a marionette theater related ancestrally to the Italian *commedia dell'arte* and in terms of its descendants to British "Punch and Judy" shows. The word "*sarsifie,*" approximately equivalent to the English slang term "sauce" [pugnacious impertinence] was invented to describe the particular character of his irreverence.

It reinforces the belief in the miraculous that inhabits even the most materialistic among us, if they care to reflect that everything down here is miraculous, beginning with the fact of their existence.

"Messieurs," said Professor Ailette, "there is no doubt that, in the general disarray procured by the appearance of a new plague—for doubt in that regard is, alas, no longer possible—the public will turn to us and demand explanations. Let us therefore get to work and seek the cause, or the causes. Then we can think about the means of combating it. At first glance, however, it doesn't seem very convenient."

The general hilarity was increased by this speech, officious in appearance and in conformity with the specialty of Professor Ailette, who has a dry tone, small, pale and hairy features, and a mania for holding forth endlessly about any subject whatsoever, and making speeches over any tomb whatsoever. Everyone was thinking that the Napus would cut off his speech at source and deprive it of its ritual and preferred exercise. In any case, on what could we base research into the cause, or the causes, of a destruction followed by the scattering of being in the ether?

The terrible plague brought us all, ignorant and knowledgeable alike, back to the "subjection without understanding" that likens human and terrestrial discipline to the strictest military discipline. That was what Professor Sidoine, a brown-haired giant, stolid and hirsute, expressed very aptly:

"My dear Ailette, I'd like nothing better than to work, with you and our colleagues in the Aristotle Foundation, to combat this frightful disease. It is, however, still necessary for me observe a case with my own eyes—for after all, it might be a myth, or a illusion on the part of our eminent comrade Polyplast 17,117, or a communal hallucination propagated by the press and the wireless.

"Remember, in fact, that a little more than three centuries ago, one of our most illustrious predecessors, Professor Charcot—who flourished, its true, on the crumbling soil and in the unsteady light of democracy—described and named a non-existent disease, hysteria, of which no specimen has ever been seen since, in three hundred years. I have in my library, however, works—which have become rare after a long period of oblivion—in which women are observed twisted into all sorts of attitudes by that implausible and improbable malady. Professor Charcot was certainly neither a visionary nor a liar. He believed that he had seen what he described. He had projected a phantom, a mirage."

Thus put on the spot, I reiterated the account of the grandfather and the little girl, the testimony of the persons present, the new cases reported in the newspapers. I added that I had not put into it any kind of authorial or journalistic distortion; that it was possible that I had participated in a mass hallucination, of the sort created by the famous and imaginary trick of the fakir who caused a rope to stand up and then climbs it; I proposed that we wait, that we allow ourselves to be guided by events—advice which, although being only timidity, generally passes for wisdom.

We separated on those good resolutions—but I was certain that we would come together again before long, and that the malicious demon of aphanasia would not rest there.

Indeed, forty-eight hours after Sidoine's exceedingly reasonable observations, as if by a sort of irony, it was at the Aristotle Foundation itself that a further disappearance by Napus occurred, in circumstances that would not have left St. Thomas himself any room for doubt.

One of the luminaries of our establishment, who had contributed a great deal, fifteen years before to the since-overtaken theory of cyton, was Madame Grégeois, the divorcee of the late Professor Grégeois precisely because of their disagreements on the subject of the magnetic centers of the cell. The husband claimed that they were two in number, the wife that they were three, neither having anticipated the fourth center discovered by the lovely Tastepain. Madame Grégeois was ugly, shrewish, peremptory and interfering, and had been decorated with every possible award of every nation of the inhabited earth, which formed an impressive multicolored display on her semi-masculine costume at official receptions. She detested Tastepain, of course, not only because of the cyton but also because of her charming physique.

Now, the supreme council of the Aristotle Foundation having met urgently, we—a few Polyplasts, Professor Ailette, Grégeois-la-Grège,[5] as we called her in jest, and half a dozen other leading lights—were in Sidoine's laboratory. The harpy was in the process of expounding her opinion on the probable origin of the Napus, which was attributable, according to her, to the spots of Jupiter acting of their own accord on sunspots and rendering them cytocidal, fatal to human cells. Suddenly, the little dry click that had remained in my ears since the old man of the Champs-Élysées was heard, and nothing more remained of Grégeois-la-Grège than the memory of her slanders, her ugliness and her genius.

The professors went as pale as effigies of fresh plaster. We Polyplasts, of harder composite formation, had difficulty holding back the convulsive laughter I mentioned before. Ailette was already twitching his goatee under the triple bony projections of his cheekbones and forehead, commencing the funeral oration of our vanished colleague. The habit he had of making speeches over graves and commemorative monuments caused him to dive right in, listing in his wooden voice the merits and achievements of the unfortunate Grégeois, thus returned to the impalpable ether after having sustained the cause of the triple magnetic center of the cell all her life. He even went so far as to classify the annihilated—"our great annihilated"—among the scientific martyrs of the twenty-third century, which was exaggerated. A pickpocket, a doorman or an ambulant seller of chestnuts or dates could just as easily be subject to the Napus as the King of France or the President of the Britannic Republic.

I ought to add, in order to maintain the historical veridity that is the greatest attraction of memoirs, that the disappearance

---

5. Grégeois-la-Grège translates as "raw Greek fire."

of that Megaera of the laboratory caused general delight at the Foundation. Mouillemouillard, whom she harassed and even slapped on occasion, if he had mislaid a retort, trembled with joy. He never ceased repeating: "What a blessing, Lord Jesus, what a stroke of luck, damn it!" As for Henriette Tastepain, she could hardly believe in such good fortune, and it was necessary to show her, through a doorway, the grave and contorted face of Ailette the speech-maker to convince her of the napusification of her enemy.

The news media and technical press generally lag behind, the former by ten years and the latter by ten months, with regard to the true status and scientific value of personalities who die, with or without leaving mortal remains. Thus, fifty years after the microbial doctrine had been abandoned by the institutes, the Academicians and even the Universities of America and France—the two nations most attached to their scientific fetishes—and the great dailies contained to entertain their readers with the bacilli of typhoid, tuberculosis and syphilis, and other phantoms and fancies of a similar stripe. For a week, the concept of cyton and its derivatives alimented the necrology of the "excellent Grégeois," universally missed and mourned, especially in the glorious establishment where she and her illustrious husband "had brought it to the perfection in which it is seen today."

These well-informed publications were sure that the study of the new plague would be taken to the extreme by the scientific personnel of the foundation, and that it would be mastered before long. It was decided that a national subscription would be opened for the erection of a statue to the Grégeois household, so perfectly disunited, in the central courtyard of the dwelling that they had made to resound, for many years, with the din of their learned conjugal disputes.

In the following week, however, ten cases of Napus were duly observed in Paris and its suburbs, five in Lyon, twenty in Marseilles, seventeen in Lille and three in Nancy. It was thought that rural areas might be spared, until three aphanasias of classic form appeared in Nièvre, five in Brittany, and twenty-two—a frightful figure—in Auvergne, around Clermont-Ferrand and Brioude. At the same time, England, Switzerland, Italy, Germany and Sweden appeared to be afflicted even more rudely, with figures whose mounting progression sent shivers down the back. The little dry click, the announcer of the disappearance, was perceived everywhere. Some witnesses of the fatal phenomenon thought they had perceived a smell of burning, similar to the one our distant ancestors attributed to the arrival and departure of the Devil.

Once the initial moment of stupor—and, for us Polyplasts, of merriment—had passed, a great activity was manifest in all the institutes, academies, universities and scientific foundations in the world, in the form of correspondence, communications, discussions and controversies regarding the origin of the unprecedented plague. Human intelligence, much more restricted than is generally affirmed, even in the most elevated and penetrating minds, has a tendency to imagine, for such a phenomenon, some unique cause, and only admits a multiplicity of cases with difficulty. The explanation of the damned Grégeois by reference to the Jovian spots left the world along with its enunciator, but the following theses were successively envisaged:

Firstly, the liberation of an unknown force, which enthusiasts for the defunct cyton did not fail to suppose to be the issue of the human cell itself, in certain atmospheric and meteorological conditions as yet unsuspected. Professor Ailette rallied to this supposition and devoted a three-hundred-page volume to it, with diagrams, which he naturally had one of his pupils write, who delegated it himself to a laboratory assistant—hence the extremely vague character of the work, which was immediately crowned by the Académie des Sciences and rewarded with a prize of fifty thousand francs, of which the laboratory assistant received a hundred, the pupil five hundred and Ailette the rest. He had considerable expenses to meet, maintaining, in spite of his advanced age and being as ugly as sin, a nineteen-year-old dancer.

Secondly, partial electrical discharges, veritable lightning-bolts of prodigious amplitude, due to the abuse of waves of every sort, which are running around the planet in all directions at all hours of the day and night. Professor Sidoine became the champion of this ingenious, even plausible idea, to which he soon attributed a character of certainty and evidence such that he flew into a rage if the slightest doubt were emitted on the subject of what he called his "doctrine." The aforesaid doctrine was soon to have terrible consequences, in the form of clashes between the nations of Europe, America, Africa, and Australia, which had reached different levels of electrical sophistication and exploitation.

Thirdly, a slow and clandestine wastage of the tissues—a cancer without cancer—provoked and accelerated by certain violent hereditary images accumulated over several generations. This hypothesis, due to Professor Eustache, was itself divided into two sub-hypotheses, one envisaging only the toxicity of internal images, the other bringing into consideration the diffusion of "cinetexts," or books with moving images.

Fourthly, the formation, because of overly frequent ethnic interbreeding and excessive naturalizations, of a race with tissues in unstable and, so to speak, ephemeral equilibrium. The adherents of this final explanation unleashed violent anger in the camp of the Polyplasts, to which I belonged, and almost provoked civil war by virtue of the epidemic character generally attributed to the Napus. I did not participate in these vain furies.

Soon, the rumor having circulated, falsely, that the Aristotle Foundation had discovered, as a consequence of explanation number two—the Sidoine thesis—an electrical vaccination against the Napus, a host of people from all walks of life presented themselves at the doors of our establishment, begging us to immunize them. It was no banal spectacle, the sight of all those panic-stricken individuals forming a queue for hours on end as if at the door of a bakery in a besieged town, only to hear that the news was premature and that several "preservatives"—that was the term of choice—were being studied but that nothing definite had yet been determined. The meager and minimal reserves of pity and charity subsisting among the Polyplasts, other than our friend 14,026, were used up and exhausted by it.

Nothing is more amusing than experimenting on oneself with the distillation of the last drops of the charitable emotion that all humanity experienced after the sacrifice of Our Lord Jesus Christ. I firmly believe, for my part, after having analyzed myself very thoroughly, that the exclusive scientific development of the human mind ended in that extinction of the two sentiments that stimulated admirable works, today almost incomprehensible to Polyplasts and laboratory workers in general. Laughter, in us, has dried up the tears that once passed for a relief, for a veritable anesthetic.

The progression of cases of "death without remains" in Paris, the suburbs and the provinces ensured that the multitude of supplicants thus evinced was augmented in disquieting proportions, at the same time as apprehension rendered them noisy and stormy. The convened authorities addressed themselves to the Foundation and urged it to find some means of calming minds and preventing the anguish of the plague from degenerating into riots, like those already produced in America, England, Germany and Italy.

Sidoine offered the opinion that all high- and very-high-tension electrical installations, as well as all wireless communication, should be suspended over the entire extent of the nation's territory, even at the cost of the greatest economic, financial and commercial disturbance. It was a big decision to take; the Crown and its Ministers demanded time to reflect, all the more indispensable as the question was international, and, by virtue of the conflict of interests subordinate to wealth in electricity and waves, risked provoking grave diplomatic complications.

Super! the Polyplasts immediately thought. *There's going to be a scientific war! Victory will go to whomever, having discovered the secret of the Napus, can apply it to military operations.*

Spurred on by the Ministry of Hygiene and the promise of a signal decoration to be worn in the middle of the thorax, Professor Ailette, for his part, immediately fabricated a cellular, or cytoplastic, broth at three francs a gram, composed of the mesenteries of young pigs and the lymphatic ganglia of previously-ionized veal-calves, with three additional doses of ultraviolet light and two doses of electric eel phosphorescence. According to him, no one who had ingested the remedy would be any longer susceptible to the Napus. He was running no risk of failure, no proof being possible that anyone who died without remains had taken the antiaphanasic broth or not. There was an urgent debate in the Council of Ministers as to whether to make the mixture obligatory for everyone in France, but the same whimsy that had presided over the manufacture caused the legal project to be set aside.

Suitably watered by the budget for so-called beneficial publicity, the press made a remarkable fuss of the "Ailette brew," and fifty thousand hundred-gram bottles of it were sold within a week, which generated a very tidy profit for the Foundation, for Ailette and for the dancer (who immediately bought a comfortable residence overlooking the location of the ancient Arc de Triomphe devoted to the battles of the First Empire). It was a fine example of the naivety of the public, in which no one made the perfectly simple reflection that it was a matter of sucker-bait, like the powder that prevented flies from laying eggs that was all the rage in the twenty-second century, if one can believes the chronicles of the epoch, or the concoction of dog-dung launched as a general antiseptic and elixir of longevity by the Russian scientist Metchnikoff in 1909 or thereabouts.[6]

6. Élie Metchnikoff was a leading researcher at the Institut Pasteur, who received the Nobel Prize in 1908 for his studies of the immune system and the activity of phagocytes. The scornfully sarcastic reference is presumably to his commercial promotion of an ointment of calomel (mercury chloride) as a prophylactic against syphilis. The use of mercury to treat syphilis—which, if it ever worked at all, was severely undermined in its utility by horrid side-effects—fell into disuse after the discovery of better antibacterial treatments, eventually capped by antibiotics.

The Americans have always done things excessively, with a sort of intellectual and economic gigantism, as if by contrast with their predecessors the Aztecs, a small race who minimized everything. It was soon evident that the explosion of the Napus was three times as powerful beyond the Atlantic than here, and that its progression there was geometric rather than arithmetic, as in Europe. Undoubtedly, though, there was some exaggeration in the claims.

The Asiatic Napus, notably in Chins and Indochina, was accompanied by a dull thud, which was thought to come from the ground, and left a rather odorous residue, comparable to a piece of the sole of a foot shriveled into three lobes, somewhat reminiscent of a human doll. We asked for specimens, but the coolies on land and sea refused to handle them, claiming that one could catch the Napus by contact with them.

That etymological persistence of the term "Napus" through languages very distant from one another demonstrates the degree of terror and mental anxiety attached to the plague, such that people clung superstitiously to its initial denomination. The Chinese ideogram created with that intention, which the Japanese copied, represented it by a grid composed of three vertical strokes on the right. Introduced to a manuscript or a prayer-wheel, it was equivalent to the doubt arising from the sudden extinction of the personality, without one knowing into which part of the invisible the Dragon has carried it and hidden it. Commercial travelers in the Far East let it be known that the Sons of Heaven, to protect themselves, were chewing the sole-shaped residues, after having crushed them into a sort of disgusting powder.

That means was no more ridiculous or arbitrary than Ailette's brew, but the members of the Aristotle Foundation were thrown into great perplexity by the fact that there now existed two forms of the Napus, one total, the other with a residue or relic. Electromagneto-radiant installations being less numerous in China and Asia than in Europe and America, Sidoine's theory acquired a certain prestige thereby, which did not take long to complicate affairs.

With the blissful or artificial optimism characteristic of the ignorant, the most widely-circulated newspapers, which are the ones that provide the most inaccurate news—for the masses abhor truth as nature abhors a vacuum—had started out by declaring that the disease would not be generalized. On the contrary, it would become a rarity, or, at least, a temporary accident, due to obscure causes, and would disappear one day just as it had arrived. Far from taking that course, however, the Napus soon appeared as a new and unexpected catastrophe, firmly-established, which, threatening bodies to the extent of annihilating them, resounded in all the domains of the intellect.

It is true that ordinary death, death "with remains," lies in wait for everyone from birth onwards, and all poets, preachers, and philosophers have embroidered beautiful and sometimes grandiose variations on that theme—but the threat of the new death, the death without remains, appeared to be something more redoubtable and more atrocious, in that it disturbed entrenched habits and extended depopulation even to the cemeteries. It was called the "blank epidemic," and also the "empty epidemic." In all the dailies, the necrological section was doubled in size, and necrology, properly speaking, became napusology. For example, one could read in the *Vingt-troisième Siècle*, in *Le Figaro*, and in *Action Française*—which had become, by force of circumstance, the official newspaper of the monarchy—news of this sort:

> *The Disease* (with a capital D, because after two months one did not even say Napus any longer) *has claimed another victim in the person of Monsieur d'Estampille, former Undersecretary of State for Finance, who disappeared yesterday at five p.m. at the corner of the Rue de Rivoli and the Place de Rohan, in his fifty-fifth year. God has his soul! The commemorative service will be held at Saint-Philippe-du-Roule next Tuesday at ten a.m.*

Or:

> *We record with regret the decease by the Disease of Mademoiselle Mahaufret (Élodie), disappeared in her property at Étampes,* Les Clochettes, *on Saturday the 14th at 3 p.m. God has her soul! The religious service will be held, etc....*

Or even:

> *It is with veritable dolor that we learn of the total disappearance of Professor Chestenèfre (Adhémar), which occurred during his lecture at the École de Médecine on Thursday last, in the large amphitheater at five p.m. The laic Astonishment will be held tomorrow, Saturday, in the courtyard of the Écoles in the Rue Monsieur-le-Prince at noon. No flowers or wreaths.*

The ceremony of "laic Astonishment" consisted of a sort of punch of honor dedicated to the memory of the deceased, in the course of which each member of the audience raised his eyes to the President of the Astonished and made the sign of the amazement caused by the sudden annihilation. I had the opportunity to be present at the Astonishment of that brute Chentenèfre, one of the last representatives of the scientific materialism of yore, in company with my cousin Polyplast 17,178, and I cannot describe the state of hilarity into which that baroque ceremony plunged us.

Some people boldly declared that, of the two faces of Death, they preferred the neater one, the one that boldly gave the lie to the celebrated axiom that "nothing is destroyed, nothing is created"—but the majority stubbornly refrained, out of superstition even from pronouncing the word "Napus," and changed the subject if the topic arose in conversation.

The Disease, which had begun by striking old men or adults, went on from there quite rapidly to adolescents, notably of the female sex, and then to children, even nurslings, which suddenly disappeared from their mothers' arms, leaving the breast bare. It seemed that the plague was thus re-climbing the slope of life from bottom to top. It was also remarked that it preferentially attacked perfectly healthy individuals, although that was not an absolute rule. Lunatics, ataxics, the tubercular and the syphilitic were in the front line in the statistics of hospitals and the private clientele.

As a member of the Aristotle Foundation I easily acquired from the municipal council the placement of a marble plaque at the location of the first case of the Napus officially recorded, with the date 3 May 2227. It was a historic and scientific souvenir of the first order. When it came to the inauguration of the plaque the following July, however, there was a superstitious retreat. I solicited, successively, the Ministries, the Constitutional Bodies, the Académie des Sciences, the Académie Française and the Académie de Médecine, but in vain. Everyone found a pretext to refuse me his collaboration, and I foresaw the moment when I would have to conduct the ceremony on my own, with the groundskeeper and the man with the lifting-tackle. At the last moment, however, a few highly-placed individuals, fearful of ridicule, changed their minds, including an immortal by the name of Bachelard, who had written a small treatise on the metaphysical significance of "the Disease." A podium had been set up on the very place where the little girl had pronounced the famous phrase: *"a grand pé a pati, n'a pus."* I had ordered a brass band, which was to play one of those military marches of which we Polyplasts are so fond.

Then something implausible happened: at the moment when Bachelard, dressed in green like a giant frog, unfolded his notes and opened his mouth to begin his speech, a dry click was heard...and the Academician disappeared.

"Impossible to show more tact," said the lovely Tastepain, who had lost a fiancé the same way a few months earlier. The discovery of a fifth magnetic center in the cell had rapidly consoled her.

I like Catholic Theology a lot. It is the only science that does not vary and its centuries-old subtlety puts to shame the sketchiness of the other research to which our intelligence has devoted itself. The rumor went around that the appearance of the Disease, which no mystic had foreseen, disconcerted the austere and religious scientists who had saved—once again—humanism and civilization two hundred years before. Not trusting the rumormongers, who are the dust, and then the mud, of life in society, I resolved to clarify the matter.

I went to see Père Estève in his convent at Richefort in the Cévennes. The great Benedictine received me with his customary generosity and affability. He knew nothing about the Napus except what he had read in the newspapers. None of his monks had disappeared—but had such an event occurred, it would not have caused him any more emotion than a death with remains.

"Death, my dear boy, is still death, and if Providence has decided that this new form of cessation of life should exist, it's evidently for our greater good."

"But Father, one can be surprised by the Napus outside of a state of contrition."

"It's the same with any kind of sudden death. As for the absence of remains, that might either be an artifice of the Demon or a privilege of Providence, and it won't be long before theologians and synods can issue a reasoned opinion on that delicate point. But tell me what effect this unexpected event is producing on the Century, and how it is being taken and accepted by the frivolous and by scientists?"

I told him what I knew. Père Estève did not know the origin of the word "Napus." He laughed wholeheartedly on learning it, and made the remark that once again, an innocent child had been the first witness of the prodigy. "For it is indeed a prodigy, which might lead to extraordinary changes. I can't remember any similar upheaval of ideas or habits. But tell me, my boy, what impression you felt before that extraordinary annihilation, comparable to the extinction of a fire?"

I was obliged to confess that the impression had been primarily comical, and that the majority of Polyplasts had reacted and were reacting to the Napus in the same way. The issue of successive interbreedings, and destined, in the ideas of the legislators, to propagate the ideas of peace and humanism through our shaky societies of the twenty-third century, our reaction had been the inverse of the one expected of us. The complexity of our temperaments had given one of them—the national—sway over the others, and reinforced the warrior instinct. Under the cover of pure science, we were dreaming of domination and battles, and that psychological inclination combined with the economic and industrial inclination that pushes ever harder for the intensive manufacture of improved arms, gases, heavy artillery, electrical weapons, and so on.

While I was speaking, Père Estève shook his head, doubtless ruminating the words of *Ecclesiastes*: "Vanity of vanities, all is vanity...."

CHAPTER TWO
THE FORCE OF IMAGES

It was about the year 2100 that popular libraries of "cinetexts" or "cinebooks" with moving images were established. Immediately before that era, a certain number of scientists, notably in Japan, had attracted attention to the psychopathic modifications made to the human mind, particularly in young people, by the immoderate usage of the old cinema. It is alleged today that the toxicity of high doses of alcohol, opium and peyotl—and, in general, all substances capable of poisoning the intelligence, vision or will, as well as hearing and touch—involved the uncoordinated release of images. Each of them, in fact, has an organic and cellular respondent; and the state of judgment and reason, which is that of the equilibrium and order of images, is also that of the health of our tissues. In the same way, the state of disequilibrium or of unreason, raging from simple light-headedness and the partial collapse of common sense to characteristic alienation, has its physical correspondences and symptoms.

What is an internal image? It is a phantom, or, more exactly, a fragment of a hereditary phantom, of that which we call a *personimage*.[7] Do we not say that we "evoke" an image, just as

---

7. I have transcribed this neologism directly, as the author would have used a different term had he wanted to signify the equivalent of the English "personality" or "self-image." Daudet was fond of improvising new words from Classical roots, and the reader will encounter several more in the course of the text.

we say that one "evokes" a phantom? Whether it comes from within, from the depths of ancestral memory, or from without, an image is never indifferent, but it is much more active when it is artificially provoked.

Desirous of taking account of the influence of the cine-book on our organism and evaluating the thesis of Professor Eustache, I went to the municipal library during the initial ravages of the Napus and asked for two works: the account of the battle of the Marne in 1914 by Dominé, with moving illustrations by Courtille, which is a masterpiece of that particular genre and whose establishment in 2200 required the expenditure of three million francs; and the cinebook of Shakespeare's *Othello* featuring Cawfort and Helen Harvey. I will tell you now what I experienced, and what any individual, even a Polyplast, handling those two admirable successes of cinetypography, would doubtless have experienced too.

The first moving image in Dominé's classic work represents an episode, reconstituted in bookish film, of the famous retreat of Charleroi, when the French armies recoiled, harried by the German troops. There is a long file of infantrymen, artillerymen, field pieces, ammunition boxes and wagons, in the landscapes of the Pas-de-Calais, the Somme and the Oise, which have obviously not changed since the last Franco-German War, and which have recovered their ancient character after so many devastations. There is the same life, the same confused, tragic, ingenious life of the retreat and its alarms.

There results, in the spectators of all these faces and horizons, an exaltation that cannot be procured in any fashion by the immobile illustrations of old, which now seem like dead things, desiccated leaved, regardless of the artistry of the illustrator. When one thinks that even the prints and etchings of a Rembrandt have taken on a cadaverous aspect!

Yes, but when five or six animated plates have passed successively before my eyes, nervous fatigue intervenes, an oculo-cerebral fatigue of a particular quality, in which it seems that the entire intellectual system is impoverished by the articulation or conjunction of the illustration and that which it invokes. The mental depression is the same as that of a runner who, having prepared for a jump of several meters, has only to surpass sixty centimeters in one bound. That is because the illusion increasingly ceases to deceive us as it becomes stronger.

If such an impression grips me, habituated as I am by science and the laboratory to resist all kinds of shocks, what must it be like for simple folk, or people who are young, and therefore excitable and malleable! There is nothing extraordinary in the fact that after some four generations—from 2100 to 2227—these defects of personality have led to an internal corrosion, susceptible to degenerate into aphanasia, or death without remains, if one adds to it the effects of electromagnetic wear and tear alleged in parallel by Sidoine.

With regard to the cinetext of Shakespeare's *Othello*, the fatigue or nervous corrosion procured by the contemplation and mediation of that fine work is of a more complex type, doubtless even more redoubtable. In fact, the convoluted composition that is characteristic of Shakespearean genius had embodied in the settings and dialogue of that celebrated drama passionate seeds that had not borne all their flowers and fruits until the moment when the art of the cinetextualist permitted them to develop.

There is no doubt in my mind, especially since the mental shock of recent events, that the acting, already so subtle, of Cawfort and Helen Harvey is further multiplied in efficiency and depth by the transposition of their attitudes and physiognomies into the films of animated illustration. We grasp all the perfidy of Iago, all the voluptuous tenderness of Desdemona, all the roots of the cruel jealousy of the absurd Moor—but that perfection of the rendering, that restitution and renaissance, in our souls, of the overwhelming imaginative labor of Shakespeare—a demon posed at the intersection of centuries and the mysteries that surround us—all raises us to a height where we lose our breath, and from which we fall disabled and exhausted.

In other words, before the invention of moving illustration, the eye only gave the mind a excitation in rapport with its tonus or capacity; instead of which, since the advent of cinetext, the eye informs the mind superabundantly, to the point of making it exceed its limits, which are rather narrow in the common run of mortals, especially in young people and children.

Once again, I grasped the falsity of the principle—which has become a dogma—by virtue of which every scientific advance is necessarily beneficial. Humans have adapted, over the ages, to a certain proportion of ignorance and a certain variation, or variance, of knowledge, which cannot be exceeded without damage, either in one direction or the other. All we terrestrials are, in a certain measure, the barrel of the Danaides; as novelties, complications and so-called progress fill us on one side, we empty on another; and that which flees from us, or through us, is often more important that that which we acquire. Then again, in the domain of acquisition, there may be excess and abuse, even without ulterior particular toxicity, and then it is the mental machine itself that gives way, dragging the corporeal machine with it.

At least, that is my opinion, ripened in the society, or confronted with that, of my colleagues.

While I was at the cinetext library I saw an amorous couple arrive, young and well-matched, doubtless fiancés, who asked for a copy of *Manon Lescaut*, with the moving engravings of Valruve d'Agen. I pretended to be absorbed in the study of the battle of the Marne, after having returned *Othello*, the choice of which would have put them on the alert.

In writing his masterpiece long ago, amid a host of unreadable novels, Abbé Prévost had had a multitude of amorous images within him, regulated according to a certain cadence, which, giving the impression of sensual fatality, gave rise to the exquisite merit of his book. Beneath those images, and the words designed to render them sensible, there were others—as in Shakespeare' *Othello*—supporting or accompanying them, which the mobile illustrations of Valrive d'Agen render manifest and gripping to us. It is as if the poem of love were enlarged and vivified beyond its written and printed disturbance. That augmentation of a work already beautiful appeared in the gazes of the two lovers, who sometimes contemplated the delicate and nuanced films and sometimes sought one another and exchanged glances charged with a renewed ardor.

I waited curiously to see what would result from such a nervous tension: an abandonment to the excessively intoxicating book, as in Dante's immortal verses, or a drowsiness, or a quarrel. It was the soporific effect that carried them away. After having looked at four or five figures, which restored for them the burning and bitter life of the inconstant beauty and her cavalier, their faces leaned over the table, doubly radiant by virtue of their features, and what their mutual love added to their features, and they went to sleep in delight beside one another.

The librarian said to me, smiling: "It's not the first time that's happened. I certainly won't wake them up. They're enjoying the dreams of gold; the dreams of lead will come soon enough."

I asked him, laughing, if he was personally familiar with all the treasures of his animated library. He gave me this typical reply: "Certainly, when I first came here, I had a great curiosity regarding the cinetextual works of which I heard so much talk, and as soon as library closed—at six o'clock in summer and four o'clock in winter—I took out a book and started the illustrations moving. What delight! But I soon perceived that my pleasure, which sometimes approached happiness—yes, Monsieur—was having a deleterious effect on my health. At night, I dreamed that the figures were dancing once again before my gaze, and by day, they were superimposed on the external spectacle and even upon my humble reflections—I mean those related to my job. Soon my lassitude was such that, after the passage of a vitalized engraving, I remained as if petrified, incapable of closing the library or of preparing my meal. That's why I stopped...."

As he pronounced those final words, I heard a little click, similar to the click of a badly-greased lock, which was unmistakable once one's eardrum had registered it. At the same time, the amorous young man disappeared, as if snatched by avid eternity in the midst of tenderness.

"Oh, oh, oh!" said the librarian, in three different tones, which ranged from surprise to terror.

The young woman woke up, thought that her companion had left her there, in front of the exemplary movement of the perfidious Manon, and went pink with shame—but a pink like the flower. The sparse expression on the face of the worthy librarian gave her no suspicion of an event that she had never experienced before. She got up with an adorable gesture of confusion and simply said, but with an intonation quite different from that of the little girl in the Champs-Élysées: "He's gone. That's not polite...."

At that moment I imagined that she was about to start searching vainly in all possible directions, alarming family and friends, for someone she would never see again; that she would consume her young and delicate existence in the alternation of hope and despair—and thought that it was not permissible for me to conceal from her a truth that the librarian also understood, to judge by his distressed features. The latter, who was not a Polyplast, and thus subject to the dream of destruction, witnessing a Napus for the first time, experienced a disturbance of grimacing form that altered his features in a particular way.

"Mademoiselle," I said. "I'm Polyplast 17,177 of the Aristotle Foundation. That title, which might not mean anything to you, is that of a biologist specializing in cases of aphanasia, or Napus. Your friend has just disappeared. We witnessed it, this gentleman and myself."

"Disappeared...?" she said. "But how? And what do you mean by *aphanasia, or Napus*?"

I was taken aback in my turn; it was difficult for me to conceive that the fuss made about the new plague had not reached the ears of a person who, to all appearances, belonged to an excellent family. The cinetext librarian seemed as astonished as me by that blissful ignorance.

I tried to explain briefly to the poor child what the death

without remains was. She doubtless mistook me for a madman, because, in the middle of my explanation, she ran away on her agile legs, leaving behind an odor of carnation and jasmine. It might be that at the time of writing, she is still searching for her gallant canoodler—unless she has found another.

I was preparing to leave the library, but the functionary drew closer to me, as if to impart a confidence. "Since you are from the Aristotle Foundation, Monsieur 17,177, I will confess to you that I would prefer, after what has just happened, to exchange my present uniform for the coat of a technician in your laboratory. It seems to me that I'd be safer. These things attract the lightning...."

His trembling finger indicated the cinebooks—which, on their gilded copper shelves, had indeed taken on a threatening aspect. He had certainly caught wind of thesis number three, attributing the Disease to extreme erosion by internal and external images, multiplied by moving illustration.

In order to reassure him and discourage him at the same time, I told him about the case of Mère Grégeois, napusified before my eyes, even though she was a pillar of our institute and a leading member of the prophylaxy committee.

He repeated, with a somber expression: "I sense that, if I stay here, it will end up happening to me."

Personally, I was not very reassured either, for I observed that this was the fourth case that had occurred in my presence since the beginning of the epidemic. Was there, then, something about me that attracted the Faceless Death? I promised the librarian, however, that if my faithful Mouillemouillard should happen to disappear, by virtue of normal death or the Napus, I would take him on as the brave Lyonnais' successor.

As he handed me my hat and cane, he said: "I'd also like to ask you, my dear Maître, what you find so funny about the total disappearance of a living being? I was struck by the fact that you laughed when that poor young man....and yet you have a good heart, in your capacity as a scientist."

Among the people, everyone is convinced that every man who

works, especially in Science, has a good heart, while all idlers with private incomes are wicked. It's a relic of Romanticism. I refrained from explaining to my interlocutor that ethnic confusion atrophies sensitivity, even the sensitivity of Polyplasts. I talked to him about nervous laughter, an insurmountable tic that desolated my existence—to effectively that he gradually lost his suspicious expression and resumed the attitude of great veneration that is the rule with regard to the depositories of Knowledge with a capital K.

On this subject, it's necessary that I tell you an anecdote that illustrates a social condition.

One of the most inventive Polyplasts of our Foundation was also a poisoner, of rare perversity. It seemed that his criminal instinct was a function of his medical genius, or *vice versa*, for each of his discoveries corresponded to a crime bearing his hallmark, such that neither the police, not the magistrates, nor a jury could have any vestige of doubt. He was sentenced to death six times, but pardoned and set free every time, because people in high places wanted him to resume his occupations, so useful to suffering humankind. It was calculated that he had killed, amid his admirable endeavors, a hundred individuals of the two sexes. Now, he encountered on his path a saintly man who made him ashamed of his crimes, led him to repentance and even to perfect contrition, with the result that he renounced his phials of toxins and devoted himself to charity—for he had accumulated great wealth with his remedies and pharmaceutical specialties. Yes, but from the day he ceased poisoning people, he also ceased to invent, as if the two wellsprings, the benevolent and the malevolent, had dried up at the same time.

It appeared to me that the napusification of the reader of *Manon Lescaut* was the kind of thing that would interest Professor Eustache, to whom I paid a visit in his magnificent town house in the Rue de Monsieur, filled with fake Old Masters and antique furniture forged by skillful cabinet-makers.

Pale and glabrous, the scientist in question, to whom we owe the most beautiful studies of the "corporeality of images" and hereditary memory, received me eagerly, and became totally livid—in him, a sign of anxiety—when he discovered the objective of my visit. He had a long nose, thin lips and a high forehead, somewhat reminiscent of Dante. He was reputed to detest Polyplasts, but he gave no sign of it to me.

Naturally, in his view, Professor Ailette's cellular explanation was untenable, as was Sidoine's electromagnetic explanation. He had been told by the Prefect of Police, his nephew, that thirty per cent of cases of Napus had been produced in habitués of the municipal library and the Bibliothèque Nationale—which is to say, cinebook readers—but I found out subsequently that the nephew had massaged the statistic in order to please his uncle, a bachelor on whose inheritance he was counting.

Eustache told me that a great debate was about to take place at the Académie de Médecine, in which he would participate, along with Ailette, Sidoine, a German professor named Murmelthier, an English professor named Morrow, an American professor named Harold-Feller, a Spanish professor named Ladilla, a Japanese professor named Kasavigata, a Russian professor named Broussoloff, and an Italian professor named Salvibianchi.

"Just as long as the death without remains doesn't choose that fine meeting to exercise its ravages," I said, innocently.

That simple remark had an extraordinary effect on my eminent colleague. In fact, by virtue of studying images and their action on the organism, he had developed an unusual sensitivity to any mental representation translatable into words. Large drops of sweat formed on his forehead and ran down his cheeks and nose. He was extremely pale, like the fresh "roughcast" plaster that masons apply with a trowel. He was having difficulty breathing. I wondered whether he might be about to furnish me with another example of aphanasia right there and then.

"Do you think," he said to me, in a halting voice, "that the fact of occupying oneself medically with the Napus is capable of favoring the appearance of the Plague among those who study it? That comes within the scope of my studies of imaginative pathology. It's a question I'm asking myself."

I explained to him that I had observed, some weeks earlier, the first authentic Parisian case of death without remains, and that I had witnessed several others—but that I was still here, and even, as the slang term has it "all there."

"That's because you're also a Polyplast, and thus especially armored against the aggression of images," the Master replied, with a sigh, "for I don't believe in either a particular fragility of your tissues or an exceptional metabolism of your cells. But if there were the least presumption of such a risk, I'd immediately call off the Académie debate. Shall I admit to you that I have no fear of any malady, old or new, colonial or metropolitan, epidemic or otherwise, contagious or otherwise—but that aphanasia scares me? It's unexpected, it's annihilation, it's the void, the desert, the inexplicable—in brief, it's frightful."

In saying that, the professor, celebrated for his harshness with regard to humans and animals, the pitiless vivisector, who had every right to bear the name of a knife,[8] had adopted the expression of a fearful and quivering Dante, menaced by all the demons of the infernal "bolges."

Wiping away the salty stickiness of his sudoriferous glands, he continued, in a more confident tone: "Would you ever have imagined that a man like me, who doesn't believe in anything except the force of images—the annotator of Lucretius, the figurehead of the New Materialism—would light a candle at Notre-Dame des Victoires to deflect the plague away from me? That, however, is what I've done. Yes, my dear chap, I went, secretly, to beg for my survival, for the few years that remain for me to drag my package of cells around down here, with their magnetic centers and their congenital impressionability. There was an enormous crowd in that ancient church, before the flickering candles, as, I suppose, there was in the year one thousand, since the terrors of the millennium have come back

---

8. In French, "*eustache*" is a slang term for a clasp-knife or a cut-throat razor.

again—but seriously motivated this time. I'd undoubtedly been seen, but I made myself scarce. The important thing, for me, is not to dissolve into nothing at all after that little click...oh, what horror!"

I thought that I ought to make the observation that practitioners do not catch all the ailments of their clientele, and that many reach a ripe old age, after having consigned to the grave a multitude of invalids of both sexes.

He answered me volubly: "Disillusion yourself, my dear Polyplast 17,177, and ask your comrade Poly 14,026 to inform you of the very curious statistics that he has compiled on this subject. The more time goes by, the more susceptible a man who cares for others becomes to the afflictions of those for whom he cares.

"Two hundred years ago, specialists in malignant tumors only developed cancer in a proportion of one in a thousand, which did not permit any distinction to be made between pure coincidence and contagion—but today, by virtue of the accumulated and somatic penetration of images"—he emphasized the word *somatic*—"the proportion is ten per thousand, which is becoming disquieting. It's the same with diabetes.

"So, is it permissible to ask, before a disease as sudden, unexpected, and overwhelming as the Napus, whether the mere fact of occupying oneself with it, of being impregnated by the thought of it, might not predispose one's tissues to the instantaneous disaggregation that it signifies?

"As for that fool Ailette's preventive cellular broth, you can take it for granted that it's as effective as Perlimpinpin's powder or the serums of the 1920s. Oh, that Ailette would take the gold off a chair-leg or a tear from an orphan, as they say where I come from."

I knew that Eustache was an enthusiastic collector, a great lover of reproductions of tapestries, copies of paintings, pseudo-antique silver and supposedly-precious furniture, and I tried to guide the conversation on to that terrain, in order to give him a chance to get a grip on himself, but he interrupted with profound sighs the questions I asked him about the fakes, knick-knacks, curios and items of bric-à-brac that crafty merchants had sold him, or the supposedly twentieth-century sideboards, the Goyas fabricated in Montrouge and the fifty-franc Pissarros that had been "a steal" at forty-five thousand.

Emerging from the house of that Prince of Medicine slightly weary of my scientific colleagues and comrades, I headed for the Palais de Justice, which today takes up the entire area between Notre-Dame and the Louvre, by reason of its formidable growth, due to the extension of courts and tribunals.

The Place Dauphiné has become an interior courtyard, the Pont Henri IV an interior bridge—the Seine passing through the Palais—and the buildings destined for the use of the legal profession resume on the right bank, extending as far as the Rue de Rivoli. A small electric tram links the various sectors of that gigantic caravanserai, which is nevertheless twenty times smaller than those of New York and Sydney.

The number of advocates and judges has multiplied tenfold since the year 2000, in proportion to that of trials and quibbles of every sort and the superimposition of electrical, magnetic, industrial, commercial, economic and international Codes, extending almost to infinity the thorns and thickets of procedure, in spite of the attempts at simplification made by ingenious jurists.

I was able to observe, as soon as I arrived among the wigs and gowns, busily employed or standing around in groups chatting, that the great topic of conversation was the terrible Napus. In this realm there had only been some sixty victims thus far, but prominent ones, including three presidents of the Court of Appeal and eight counselors of the Court of Cassation "blown away" in the course of hearings, seventeen preliminary magistrates and assessors, and three examining magistrates. The Bar had been spared thus far, hence the dictum that it was necessary to await the Disease standing up rather than seated. It was said, however, that the Public Prosecutor was already more dead than alive and that the King's Prosecutors were in a bad way before the trembling of their chief. The result of that was an immense confusion in matters pending, which had spread to the clerks, the judiciary identity services, the judiciary police and the special police—to such an extent that thefts, murders and other violent crimes were multiplying in cities in the most disquieting fashion, overwhelming the local commissariats and the services of the Sûreté in general.

But these consequences were trivial as yet, compared to the upheavals that the death without remains had brought to jurisprudence and legislation—principally in matters of inheritance and certifications, civil and otherwise—which had not been foreseen, with good reason. That was what old magistrates with the heads of eunuchs or gorillas, their eyes obscured by cataracts, were rabbiting on about, surrounded by young lawyers, like lumps of rotting meat by buzzing flies, as far as the eye could see.

Some kept their arms in front of them while others held them behind their backs, inflating the sleeves of their robes as in the drawings of the great Daumier and Forain, which have traversed the centuries without growing old. Some burst into forced laughter, above their bulging briefcases. Others, putting on grave expressions, drew colleagues away by the shoulders as if to make them some important confidence—but the secret in question was bunkum or the produce of Mr. Punch, which would return to him. Yet others could be seen leaning on walls, legs buckled, shaking their heads like waiting horses in the days when horses waited. Circles of discussion formed, a few paces from other sordid circles, formed by the delinquents of common law, descended from police-vans, who were also talking about the Thing in low voices, as if they feared awakening and attracting upon themselves its blind rage.

As soon as I was perceived by some of my former comrades and neighbors from the École de Droit I was recognized and grabbed. I had acquired a certain notoriety of late, not because of my work at the Aristotle Foundation, nor my situation as a Polyplast, but by virtue of the fact that I had been a witness of the first authentic and verified case of the Napus. I was obliged to recount, for the hundredth time, the exclamation of the little girl who had baptized the death without remains, the disappearance of Mère Grégeois and that of the young man of the cine-texts. It was necessary for me to explain, briefly but precisely, the theses of Ailette, Sidoine and Eustache and reply to various objections raised by those quibblers, accustomed to splitting hairs into eight or sixteen and arguing about terms.

The announcement of the international debate at the Académie de Médecine caused a sensation.

One might imagine, in fact, that various opinions set in deliberation, might resolve a difficult better than the solitary ripening of a single opinion—but that is contrary to the truth. When it is a matter of finding a median between different, and sometimes opposed, texts and articles, a congressional debate might perhaps have some utility, but if it is a matter of an immediate, menacing reality and a frank and prompt resolution, that can only be the affair of a single individual who imposes his point of view on others when it is time to act.

A president of an initial tribunal, very knowledgeable and artful, by the name of Palemon, made the observation that it would be easy for murderers and accomplices to get rid of someone, dispose of the body and then come to testify to his death without remains. "We now find ourselves, Messieurs, in the presence of a capital danger, of an encouragement to murder such as has never been known before. What is more redoubtable than aphanasia itself is the simulation of aphanasia."

The circle approved, and everyone racked his brains in search of an appropriate solution—but no one could think of one. The optimists insisted that everything would settled down and that the first historical epidemic of the plague or cholera must have been far worse. The pessimists riposted that the Napus had a mysterious and universal character that exceeded the proportions and the level of an epidemic, and that the fate of the entire human race was at stake. Everyone agreed in regretting that the protective penetration of human intelligence had not grown in proportion to the evils unleashed by the mechanical inventions of that same intelligence. There was a continual reversion to the formula: "It's a pity that the qualitative has been allowed to be overtaken by the quantitative."

There was a sudden stir among the lawyers; it was the Minister of Inventions, Tonqueloque, who had come to visit the Public Prosecutor, evidently with regard to the Napus.

Tonqueloque belonged very evidently to the quantitative genre, being primarily a mathematician, and as such accustomed to seeing everything from the viewpoint of the absolute, even though everything terrestrial is relative and that which is biological is malleable. Physically, he was a short stout man with neatly-brushed hair that might have been mistaken for a wig, a stammer and a squint that were irritated and confused by the slightest objection. I knew him well, having dealt with him on numerous occasions with regard to the inventions—ephemeral, I must admit—that inevitably emerge from the Aristotle Foundation, and which our envious rivals have baptized "five-minute discoveries." Our characters were not compatible.

"Bonjour, Monsieur le Ministre."

"Bonjour, my dear Poly 17,177. Do you have anything new with regard to the treatment of the Disease? What is the effect of Professor Ailette's broth?"

That question had the effect of making the advocates and magistrates present—and Palemon most of all—laugh heartily. Tonqueloque adopted an irritated expression. "I don't see, Messieurs, that there's anything particularly cheerful about the present situation, and I must confess that it seems to me that serious questions ought to be treated seriously in the Palais de Justice."

"Excuse me, Monsieur le Ministre," said an old advocate by the name of Levert, who had a reputation as a joker. "We're laughing at human impotence in the face of the new abyss that has opened beneath our feet. There's no hilarity more philosophical."

"It has occurred to me," Tonqueloque said, without further

insistence, "that there might be considerable scientific interest in recording the points at which the unfortunate aphanasics disappear and linking these points by a line on an appropriate map. One would thus obtain a curve that would not lack interest."

That baroque idea, well worthy of a mathematical mind, increased everyone's gaiety. Several put down their briefcases stuffed with files in order to dilate their rib-cages more easily. The clerks coming from all parts of the Palais to investigate the reasons for that joy already imagined that an irresistible means of combating the Disease had been found.

The Minister was bewildered. In order to say something, he added: "It might be the case that some kind of cellulo-explosive phenomenon, comparable to a limited tornado, is circulating on the surface of the planet, selecting its victims in accordance with a determined asymptote. That too is calculable."

This time, the members of the audience split their sides. There is nothing more amusing than a individual behaving entirely in accordance with his character or temperament, in circumstances in which neither his character nor his temperament is apposite. That was the case with Tonqueloque.

He darted around a suspicious all-encompassing glance— that of a schoolteacher to whose back the pupils have attached a placard and is wondering which one to punish. Then, abruptly shrugging his shoulders and snorting, the Minister of Inventions headed for the Bar.

"Another case, Messieurs, another case!"

A plump and short individual, a clerk in the Court of Cassation, came toward us giving signs of terror. He explained, breathlessly, that Counselor Bienmanié had just disappeared, at the moment when he was sitting down at his table—the second on the right of the fourth criminal chamber—and reaching out for a file.

The new produced a certain emotion. Bienmanié had been charged, the previous day, with compiling a report on the juridical implications of the Death without Remains. The question that preoccupied Eustache was visible in every face: Does occupying oneself with it expose one to becoming subject to it?

"Oh, the poor boy"—Bienmanié had been seventy-five, and the term *boy* hardly suited him—"was reluctant to take charge of that dossier. Did he foresee what has happened?"

"No, it's pure chance."

"There is no chance."

Click! At the very moment when the sturdy magistrate, by the name of Capechard, emitted that by-no-means original aphorism, the sound of the "detonator" resounded, and the speaker vanished into thin air without a puff of smoke, without a whiff of odor, without *anything*.

The case was magnificent and clear, but I did my best to suppress my desire to laugh, which would have further increased the terror of all those lawyers.

Now, by virtue of an antithesis that Victor Hugo—over there on the right—would have loved, four centuries earlier, who did we see coming down the steps from the Court of Cassation, in his robe as well as his fresh and blood? Bienmanié in person—Bienmanié, whom all his colleagues had already begun mourning, and whose aphanasia had just been announced to us: Bienmanié returned, like a coin in the hand of a conjurer, while Capechard disappeared in the same fashion.

The idea of an exchange imposed itself on all of us, and one magistrate, who was particularly keen on being decorated, ran after Tonqueloque, the involuntary joker, in order to bring him up to date with that marvelous substitution. It was the raw material for a new curve.

Then an improbable scene took place. Bienmanié, informed of the clerk's error, abused the latter roundly, calling him a cretin and a fool, without the slightest regard for the minute's silence generally accorded to the spirits of napusified individuals. It was a very amusing spectacle: the modest functionary, harassed by that black ape, who seemed ready to devour him and was accusing him of having sought to bring misfortune down upon him.

Superstition was manifestly entering into everyone's soul.

At the same time as superstition, however, a new sentiment and a great tenderness invaded me.

Little subject until then to the assaults of amour upon my rational carapace, in my quality as a Polyplast, I felt that aberration opening up to me under the new threat of the Napus. I began to look more attentively at the pretty girls passing by in the street. If the lovely Henriette Tastepain was late at the laboratory, I became anxious about her, and her footsteps behind the glazed door caused my heart to beat faster.

I had previously read descriptions of that weakness in ancient and modern authors, which had seemed to me to be baroque and incompatible with the dignity of a seeker of knowledge; now, that opinion of my youth came to seem baroque, and I thought about making up for lost time.

I confided in my friend Poly 14,026, who, to my great surprise, admitted that he too felt internally modified since the advent of aphanasia, and had begun to wonder whether the most reasonable use of such a brief and precarious existence was the one we were making of it.

If we men of the laboratory were in that situation with regard to the blonde goddess to whom Lucretius had dedicated his poem,[9] it is easily imaginable that the rest of the nation had preceded us, and gone further. Never had the bonds between lovers been more tender than since they had been threatened by rupture by the Napus. Never had the symphonic song of the nightingale, the little winged conductor of the orchestra that he constitutes all by himself, appeared so delightful to the ear when it rose up at the advent of night above a field of perfumed lilies. Never had the scent of roses, assembled in a host on a rose-bush like red fireworks, surprised the sense of smell with such heady effluvia. Never had the slightly bitter perfume of lavender on Provençal hillsides carried lads and lasses to the land of carnal dreams in a more sparkling chariot. Never had a

---

9. The reference is to *De rerum natura* [On the Nature of Existence], the classic of skeptical Epicurean philosophy, which begins with a dedicatory invocation of Venus.

young man in love sitting on a strand, in a hollow between the rocks, beneath the emerging stars, enjoyed more voluptuously the vague silhouette of the object of his love dangling her little feet in the lukewarm salty water of the tide, gradually and unsteadily coming in.

The martial thoughts that haunted us as a consequence of the mixture of polyplastic bloodlines and the laborious contention of the laboratory—for tense analytical thought embodies a battle—began to give way to these strange impulsions..

In brief, we were softening.

One strange and sweet day was the one that Henriette Tastepain and I spent in the woods at Meudon toward the end of July, three months after the debut of the plague.

In the belief of the ancient urbanists of the early twentieth century, and their predictions, since recognized as false, the continual westward development of Paris through Passy, Auteuil, the Point-du-Jour etc. ought to have annihilated and absorbed the forested region that extends from Meudon to Villebon and beyond, where great rural properties had been built in the seventeenth century. On the contrary, however, it was toward the east and the north that Paris had developed after the great industrial and rural development of the twenty-first century and the legal limitation of non-electrical and non-magnetic factories. In the direction of Sèvres and Meudon, the sinuous snaking of the capital had, in fact, retracted somewhat, the ugly buildings and hangars of the factories on the banks of the Seine between Sèvres and Saint-Cloud giving way to charming villas and "follies" recalling those of the eighteenth century, while general farmers reappeared in an new guise.

So, the sun was shining and the blue of the sky caused strollers to forget, in the immediate chamber of the mind, the quotidian preoccupation with the terrible menace. The progression was still accelerating, but the newspapers, on our advice, had adopted a palliative strategy and again announced a discovery of a particular kind, permitting the plague to be driven back.

Henriette was wearing new clothes, which made her and her

supple, well-proportioned body into a parcel of harmonious enchantment, superimposed on nature. It seemed that we could hear a distant song, emerging from an irrational hope, as there is behind the simultaneously desolate and confident themes of the immortal Beethoven.

We followed the bank of the river—or, to put it better, the most spiritual river in the world—the banks of which form the so-called Île de France, a trifle cold in the Occitan parlance that is now so widespread again, but delightfully sinuous and sober. She and I were talking about the desiccation to which the overly-exclusive pursuit of the infinite and indefinite problems of science leads, and about the necessity, for the sake of equilibrium, of the free development of natural sentiments.

I would never have suspected, on the part of my brilliant assistant, such resources of fantasy, such a placid and serene vision of earthly things, or such a youthful generosity. It was a delight for me. She joked about our friend 14,026 and his uniquely book-based and documentary conception of the universe, all the Polyplasts of our acquaintance, and all our professors—the Ailettes, the Sidoines and the Eustaches. She mimicked their tics, their accents and their manias. I learned to experience a laughter that was no longer grating, which was not that of the recognition of human fatality, but which liberated the soul by traversing it with its mocking arrow and dragging it out of the icy regions of pure understanding.

I had not come to the woods of Meudon since my bleak and studious youth, by reason of the intensive labor to which Polyplasts are subjected. Our professors of geology had taken us there to the limestone quarries that contained, before the Deluge, specimens of flora and fauna classified, declassified and reclassified twenty times over according to contemporary geologico-biological hypotheses—but the old forest with its six-hundred-year-old trees belonged to lovers that day.

Hidden behind vast trunks enflamed by solar rays, lovers kissed with open mouths, in such a fashion that their faces disappeared, as if swallowed up by their kisses. Others pecked as they went along, arms around one another's waists in the fashion of peasant-women, or held one another by the little finger while walking a few steps ahead of their distracted parents, waiting to give them the slip in order to exchange their saliva avidly. They could be seen in the depths of thickets, looking one another in the eyes, without touching, with glowing and eager faces. They could be seen, intimidated by the entirely new sensation of reckless kissing replacing language, holding timid but heated discussions.

Here, a fiancé told a blushing fiancée how things would work out, when he had a job with a salary, and what the sump-tuous menu of the wedding-feast would be. There, lying on the ground, each chewing a twig in order to make themselves look cool, a blond and a brunette were laughing because they were finally together in spite of the malignity of gossips, having the day to themselves. Some became sulky, but only briefly, in order to make up and be closer bound together. One girl extended a slender ear, like a little pink sea-shell, to receive a confidence, while another wagged a menacing finger, doubtless in response to a *risqué* suggestion, the risk of which was nevertheless exqui-site.

The game of blind man's buff over to the left, in the clearing sown with yellow roundels, with a simpleton whose eyes were bandaged, seemed the very image of amorous pursuit; while the game of tag that the children were playing permitted the brush of hands and fingers that is the Devil's first temptation.

Such an atmosphere and such sights were well-calculated to induce desire in Henriette and myself. The plague was far away. Another scourge, this one adorable, was soliciting us, making our hearts beat in our bosoms and causing our desires to quiver like leaves in a warm breeze.

I took hold of the young woman's round arm and held it tenderly against my own. She let me do it. I drew closer to her.

Half a dozen couples, similarly occupied and busy with the great business, who surrounded us, served better than solitude to conceal that nascent joy. We confronted the pulsation of our arteries and our lips came together, touching, at the rapid velocity of thought, like two swallows flying in the open air toward a common goal and confusing their wing-beats. I must confess that never had such delights presented themselves to me, even distantly, during my scientific research. Don't tell me that it's a matter of opposed orders of meditation; the organism is one and does not react in a different fashion to the curiosity of intelligence and that of the flesh.

After that experiment, beneath the decreasing fires of the day, we didn't say a word. The eternal speech of lovers, with its first person singular, was itself postponed until later. We were reciprocally astonished to have waited so long—long months in daily contact—for the birth of an admission. I recalled certain ironic glances on the part of Mouillemouillard, certain joking allusions on the part of 14,026.

At the end of a sloping path, in the form of a kind of leafy country inn, the classic tastes of the environs of Paris solicited us: a glass of cold, light beer, a lightly-seasoned sausage, of which it was sufficient to remove the skin to dispel the ashy taste analogous to that of dull existence; and a hunk of fresh bread with a slight scent of wheat, although it was a crusty child of the immediate suburb. While the blissful discoverer of the fifth magnetic center of the cell employed her beautiful teeth I observed the charming oval of her jaw, well-articulated by hunger, laughter and love, delightedly.

We decided to dine in one of the small inns that have fortunately replaced the insipid palaces of old and honor the immutable dishes of the Parisian region, such as entrecote with "melted apples"—which don't melt—and fish in the vinegary and incomparable Bercy sauce, surmounted by a pat of odorous butter. With love and the love of food—the only true ones—we had conquered the world at a single stroke.

But it has to be said that the day did not end without hiccups. As we set forth again, chatting about things of no consequence, to which we would not have given any thought the day before, we suddenly perceived a group of walkers who had stopped at the corner of a path in front of an object that we took at first for a hut.

It was a monstrous mushroom, three meters high, with the inflated foot of the edible mushroom and a cap under which a dozen people could have taken shelter from a storm.

An old warden explained to me that the phenomenon had grown there in the space of a single night. He added that, according to the "messieurs" from the botanical laboratory at Bellevue who had come to examine it the day before, it was a question of the same mysterious force that was making people disappear without trace. At that revelation, a black veil passed over the beautiful gilded dusk. Lovers of both sexes, as if sobered up, gazed at the sinister cryptogam in a melancholy fashion, which, obtaining its advantage from the same mysterious power that annihilated humans, had been turned into a giant by the Napus.

"Don't get too close, Mesdames et Messieurs! It's said that it's not contagious, but all the same—one never knows!"

A dozen children, boys and girls ran up, laughing and jostling one another. At the sight of the fungal giant they became ecstatic, uttering cries of joy; then, holding hands, they started an infernal round-dance around its immense foot, to the rhythm of a popular song. The doubtless-philosophical warden hesitated momentarily as to whether to prevent them from mocking the monster, then reflected that the napusic explanation was doubtful and let the innocents have their way.

But the explanation was sound.

We soon learned, in fact, via telegrams sent from all points of the nation and various countries of Europe, that cryptogams of colossal size were appearing in various locations, accomplishing their growth overnight. There was no great harm in that, while it was a matter of edible mushrooms, although people hesitated nevertheless to cook them, for fear that their exorbitant dimensions might nauseate the most determined gourmets. As soon it was question of fly-agarics or amanitas, however, and the redouble spectrum of ink-caps, the fear was that the enormous receptacles of poison might poison, as they rotted, the ground in which they were growing.

In addition, clumps of these phenomena, attaining four or five meters in height and ten or twelve in circumference, appeared in places where it was not usual to encounter them, principally in the suburbs. Bourg-la-Reine, Clamart and Pantin were the worst-afflicted locales, in proportions such that the inhabitants had difficulty negotiating certain streets, which were completely obstructed.

Samples of these giants of the vegetal world were, of course, sent to the Foundation, where we analyzed them conscientiously, without discovering anything abnormal from a chemical or anatomical viewpoint. Ailette saw them as a reinforcement of his cellular hypothesis, Sidoine as support for his electromagnetic thesis. Eustache asserted that the two strange phenomena were completely unrelated—but it was evident to any mind deprived of prejudice that the relationship was close, and that the Napus, which was inimical to humans, stimulated growth and magnification in cryptogams.

That was an impenetrable mystery—and what else was going to happen?

For several weeks great botanists were seen running from one side of the country to the other: mysterious and manic individuals who were neither numerous not communicative, who usually toyed in silence with the Latin and Greek names that they applied to all the species of the vast vegetal realm. Their explanations did not differ sensibly from those of physiologists, cytologists and others, and were no more satisfactory to the intelligence.

As for the propagation of the Napus, it was neither relented nor diminished by that hypertrophic deviation, and the curve that we tracked on a daily basis, with scrupulous statistical care, continued its ascendant progress.

CHAPTER THREE
A FINE ACADEMIC DISCUSSION

It was on the fifteenth of September 2227—the first year of the Napus—that the great debate on the death without remains opened, before the combined academies and delegations from foreign institutes, which put the most celebrated parliamentary sessions of the nineteenth and early twentieth centuries in the shade. It was quickly evident therein that medical preoccupations with life and death, mingled with scientific quarrels, had set foot on the old seesaws of socialism, collectivism, egalitarianism, internationalism, humanitarianism, etc. that had once unleashed countless massacres and depopulated the planet under the pretext of pacifying it.

So far as my dear Henriette and I were concerned, we had divided our existence into two parts since we had discovered our reciprocal love: one consecrated to pure sentiment, from which would emerge one day, after the projected marriage, a little Polyplast destined to continue the arduous research of his Mama and Papa; the other dedicated to methodical labor at the Aristotle Foundation.

The conference sessions were held in the vast palace constructed on the site of the old Académie, at the end of the bridge formerly knows as the Pont des Arts. Four hundred armchairs had been set out, some of which were discreetly pierced in view of the great age of the conference-members and the possible relaxation of their smooth muscles. The places reserved for the public only numbered a thousand, and were retained by people of the highest society, attracted by the curiosity of all those old carcasses. The committee comprised the president, two vice-presidents and five secretaries, with half a dozen stewards and technicians attending to the apparatus automatically recording the speeches.

Due to take part in the debate, apart from Ailette, Sidoine and Eustache, and immediately after the funeral oration of Mère Grégeois, were the foreign representatives of the problem of the Napus, eight in number—one of whom, van Sleegen, simultaneously represented Belgium, Switzerland, Sweden, Norway, Holland and Rumania. The others were Murmelthier, Morrow, Harold-Feller (for America), Ladilla, Kasavigata, Salvibianchi and Broussoloff. There was a vestige in the debate of the uses and customs of the old seesaw of the twentieth century called the League of Nations, which had given us the last two Franco-German wars as well as the recent conflagration of the Orient against the Occident, and then *vice versa*.

But the first thing of all was solemnly to welcome a deputation of negroes partly whitened—and not annihilated—by the Napus, to present what promised to be a most interesting communication regarding the protective virtues of dirt and the danger of cleanliness and hygiene in the face of the plague. As for the cryptogamic gigantism, it had suddenly retreated, as suddenly as it had arrived, from the mushrooms of the Parisian region, only to appear in the countries of the north and the Landes region, where it was literally stifling the pine forests.

There were eleven thick-lipped and flat-nosed negroes with dark and beautiful gazes, who had come by dirigible from the now-overpopulated banks of the Tanganyika in order to enable us to admire the partial whitening of their epidermis, with regard to the face, the arms and loins. The rest of the body was an indecisive shade of dark brown. That abrupt transformation had also commenced on a date corresponding to our third of May 2227 and was, without a doubt an attenuated form of the Napus.

One of them was carrying in his hand the corpse of a tiny

elephant sixty centimeters long, an immediate diminution of a pachyderm six meters long and four meters tall. Thus, the Disease, which greatly magnified European mushrooms, minimized African elephants, and—thus far, at least—left near-normal proportions to the rest of creation.

The facility and rapidity of communication had not brought about any change in the intellectual impermeability of races and nations with regard to one another. The negroes imagined that the white men were about to furnish them with a rational explanation of an epidermal event that they considered, themselves, to be a consequence of the wrath of the gods. Their guide explained to us that they experienced a kind of baroque pleasure in these divergences of opinion with regard to causality. They had all immediately made a fetish of the Napus of their climate, and sacrificed children and young animals to it, with all sorts of intoxication, drums and dancing.

While these details were being furnished to the conference-members and the public, the off-white men contemplated the women, rolling veritable ocular billiard-balls of concupiscence and laughing as they pointed at the tiny elephant. Ailette invited them to calm down and behave decently, and the interpreter explained to them that the white men knew no more than they did and wanted to know their opinion, however infantile it might be, of the problem that was preoccupying the world. "For," he added, "we're all in the same boat."

These final words were not to the taste of the American Harold-Feller, from Boston, who had been giving signs of a violent disgust during the discussion with the negroes. He stood up abruptly in his magnificent yellow leather boots and declared in English that there could be no question, for civilized individuals and "people of color," of being "in the same boat." Such an expression giving the impression of constituting a criticism of the legislation of the United States and essential moral law, he preferred to shake the dust from his fifty-dollar footwear over such a degenerate conference.

This time, Sidoine and Eustache rose to their feet together

to protest against the awkwardness of the stammering and confused Professor Ailette, and to give a assurance that they would establish all the necessary difference between the poor river-dwellers of the Tanganyika, no matter how overpopulated they might be, and a professor of physiology from Boston.

Harold-Feller did not seem convinced, however. "I demand the arbitrage of Maître Claude Bernard," he said, in French.

It was explained to him that Claude Bernard had died in 1878—which is to say, 349 years ago—and not only had a lot of water passed under the bridge, but a lot of glycogen through the liver, since then. That observation seemed to appease him without humiliating him.

Professor Sidoine observed that, the black men having been immunized by the change of coloration, against death without remains, there would come a time, as the plague continued its ravages, when they would come to repopulate Europe. That prospect brought grimaces to the charming faces in the gallery. Then the interpreter was invited to take away "these sympathetic African specimens," while making sure that, if one of them died during his sojourn in Europe, his skin would be taken to the Aristotle Foundation for histological examination. As for the cadaver of the shrunken elephant, it was decided that it would be sent to the Museum.

The following communication brought to the podium a hairy, bearded, shrill and gesticulating individual of repulsive dirtiness, without underwear, who was nevertheless an authority on new or bizarre diseases, principally of colonial origin: Professor Pafenier. He had devoted a large part of his already-long life— he was approaching sixty—to combating the excess of hygiene: baths the employment of soap, massages, perfumes, improved toilet facilities, all sewers, and all supposed public health measures in general.

Pafenier had noticed that cases of longevity had appeared, since the remotest ages, in rural milieux where toilets are unknown and hygiene neglected or forgotten. He preached by example, not having washed for ten years. Since the appearance of the Napus he had been studying the social and hygienic situation of the victims of aphanasia and he had, he insisted, been able to verify the excellence of his thesis. Those people who, like the Eskimos, lived in a veritable matrix of dirt, were free of the implacable Disease.

The affirmations and explanations, as well as the sight and astonishing odor of the orator, excited the hilarity of the audience, which the president and vice-presidents had to call to order several times.

Pafenier, excited by his success, proposed to render himself as naked as a worm, in order to demonstrate the thickness of his protective carapace, but the committee rejected the proposal. He withdrew, cursing and thumbing his nose at the steward. Harold-Feller, as clean as a newly-minted dollar, whom that communication had scandalized, got up again and promised a reward of fifty thousand dollars to anyone who provided proof of the napusification of an incontestably disgusting dirty individual.

On that note, the session was suspended for a quarter of an hour and the secretaries had the shrunken and warped elephant passed around the ranks of the Academicians. Then the whitened negroes were examined at close range, as people at a circus, during the interval, go to consider the clever animals and chat to the brightly-costumed and heavily made-up clowns.

Almost no one had retaken their places when my friend Polyplast 14.026 gave the savant post-mortem—or, more exactly, post-napusum—eulogy for Mère Grégeois. Who, in any case, was interested now in controversies about cyton, as obsolete as the sera of the twentieth century? While Poly 14,026 was reeling off dates and figures, I observed the indifference of the few Academicians present, and noticed that many of them, although they were specialists, had been unaware of, or had forgotten, the resounding achievements of our defunct colleague. My dear Henriette, much rebuked by the harpy, and very unjustly, was well-avenged.

On the resumption, it was necessary to submit to a tedious

lecture by Ailette, enunciated in his feeble and hoarse voice, composed of interminable references. This fastidious enumeration was followed by a bitter, even polemical, and thoroughly-documented speech by Sidoine, who advocated not merely the limitation but the suppression of all the electrical, magnetic and wave-transmitting installations throughout the European nations.

If indignation makes poets, Sidoine appeared in the eyes of everyone as a lyricist of a particular sort, prophesying on an anti-electric Sinai. He depicted the force—in sum unknown, although it was presumably the issue of the rupture or clash of atoms—gradually destroying the universal equilibrium, disharmonizing human tissues, more fragile and complex than those of even higher animals, and, in the final count, ending up annihilating them by virtue of a sort of secret superincandescence.

Sidoine, who was also claimed to have been belatedly touched by love, was not only a scientist; he was an artist, who, unlike Ailette, observed a remarkable gradation in his lectures. Nothing is harder than exciting the attention of old men laden with honors, uniquely occupied with themselves, some of them close to senility, who can only, even in the absence of any napusiform threat, calculate with anguish the moment of their final departure; Sidoine, however, achieved that tour de force. Veiled or vitreous gazes, with recently-treated cataracts and crumpled eyelids, and wrinkled foreheads devoid of eyebrows, turned toward him while he vaticinated, in a powerful voice, with a poignant expression and his prominent features feverish and radiant.

Henriette whispered tremulously in my ear: "He's a strapping fellow, there's no denying it." That remark filled me with jealousy.

"Messieurs," said Sidonie, by way of conclusion, "I have explained my point of view, which is explicit, with total frankness. I do not conceal from myself for a moment the gravity of the extraordinary measure that I am proposing to all the legislatures of Europe and America, at the expense of all our finances.

But it is the existence of the civilized peoples that the frightful Napus threatens. You have heard, just now, the valiant representatives of the black world, spared, save for their coloration, from the plague. Do you want to disappear, *en bloc*, from here, in a matter of years or months—the latest statistics are terrifying—and make way for the sons of Ham? Then you have only to continue making use of the apparatus that is undermining our organisms and dispersing them, at a given moment, in the ether. The Baconian tables of presence and absence are implacable and inflexible, and they indicate the Cause, inexorably. Suppress that Cause and you will live. Allow it to act, and you will die."

Unanimous applause greeted this impatiently-awaited conclusion—although Eustache pinched his lips, for the difficult task was incumbent on him of contradicting a fellow like Sidoine and incriminating, without any great plausibility, the cinebook.

Then, however, an incident occurred of extraordinary gravity, which neither Henriette or I had anticipated.

Scarcely had Sidoine left the podium than the German delegate Murmelthier, known for his work on vegetal alimentation and the parametabolic dispersal of cellular plasma, succeeded him. He was a fat beer-drinker, whose face looked as if it had been rubbed with carmine, endowed with a formidable Teutonic accent, who imagined—quite wrongly-that he could speak "Gallic" fluently. His lips were like draught-excluders, his nose bifurcated the extremity of a pig's hind trotter. His arms were short and he wore sparkling improved spectacles, which he pushed up mechanically to his forehead when he wanted to produce an oratorical effect.

Murmelthier did not speak; he roared.

"Colleague," he said, indicating Sidoine, "your audacity is great to bring here such a diabolical proposition. What is, in fact, present civilization if not wave-transmission and electromagnetism in general, and how has social unrest been vanquished if not by the well-being of domestic power and universal energy distribution? I declare"—and he extended his short arms and stubby fingers—"that Germany will never accept such a proposition. I add that it will be considered as a manifestation of hostility. In addition, and from the viewpoint of method, is it certain that the negroes of the Tanganyika are ignorant or negligent of electromagnetic systems? Is it certain that it is that ignorance and abstention from wave-transmission, or the cellular quality of their skin, that has spared them from the Napus?"

The interpreter repeated these words, to which the negroes replied calmly that, sixty years ago, the river-dwellers of the Tanganyika had renounced electricity and magnetism, their vanities and works, and had returned to prayers, supplications, sacrifices, daces around fetishes, which were judged to be much more effective and much less dangerous. "No shocks, no killing, no explosions, no Napus."

Sidoine was exultant, and took his neighbors and colleagues as witnesses to the perfect common sense of the coffee-colored gentleman with the green stripes.

Van Sleegen, cold, tranquil, imperturbable, and compassed, declared in the name of Sweden, Norway, Belgium, Switzerland, and Rumania that he would adhere, without any reservations, to Sidoine's proposal, and that the scientific committees of those various nations would impose this wise view on their respective governments.

The Japanese delegate Kasavigata said yes with a rapid nod of his handsome yellow head. Numerous cases of Napus had recently appeared in Japan, which had also been subjected, in a hundred years, to eighty earthquakes and as many volcanic eruptions—but the prolific valor of that intrepid people, who offer the sternest resistance to blows of that sort, did not seem to have had any effect. For three hundred and fifty years they had been preparing to wage a naval war on the United States. On the scientific side, they presented the particularity that they continued to concoct sera, as in the distant times of the Institut Pasteur. The dogmas of that Institut had been confused in Japan with the national religion, and the sera in question, henceforth deemed ineffective with regard to humans, were reputed there to be agreeable to the gods.

More timorous that his colleagues, the English delegate Morrow asked for time to communicate with London and the government of the Britannic Republic before offering formal support to Sidoine's antielectric motion. But the British government, composed of Conservatives and fearing, in consequence, upsetting the Liberals and the Labor party, as well as the Dominions, also asked for a delay before giving Morrow a firm response. Now, it happened that neither the Liberals nor the Labor party had a clear view on the question, and that both feared bringing about a political, economical and financial upheaval by subscribing to a universal prohibition of electricity, magnetism and waves. As for the Dominions, notably Canada, the authorities were reluctant to bring about a rupture with what had, until then, been considered as the very emblem of progress. All these tergiversations, gradually revealed to the conference, indisposed the majority with regard to the English delegation, and England was falsely accused of covertly favoring the Napus as being "capable of depopulating Europe to the advantage of the less-afflicted British Isles."

However, while Morrow—who belonged to an excellent family that had furnished several peers and two bankers—remained glued to the telephone and replete with embarrassments, the Spanish delegate, Ladilla, held forth with extravagant gestures, arguing in both directions. Having received a solid philosophical education at the University of Salamanca, that plump, dark-haired man with a highly-colored complexion, had a passion for pros and cons, and destroyed an argument as soon as he had given it weight. He expressed himself in a mixture of Castilian and French, which was very picturesque but difficult to follow.

"Do you know, Monsieur, that this question is not one of those that a good solution can be suddenly brought against. If you extirpate electricity, could be that you will not extirpate the Napus. In that manner will have thrown into misery a considerable number of persons, workers and others, who will go from there to revolution, to subversion, to rioting, to carnage, to massacre. What an unpheaval! What a disaster! What universal desolation!"

The more thunderous Ladilla's accent became, sometimes emphasizing the penultimate syllable in the Castilian fashion, sometime the antepenultimate in the Catalonian, the more the audience in their armchairs and the public seats felt a strong desire to sleep, yawning, stretching and closing their eyes. The indefatigable orator took up an antithesis after every thesis, and a synthesis after every antithesis, accompanying his periods with supple gestures, as if steeped in oil, which further augmented the torpor. Deprived, to their good fortune, of parliaments, courts, forums and so on for three hundred years, the most loquacious of Spaniards seized and made the most of the opportunities offered by conferences and other debates. Woe betide anyone who opened those floodgates!

After having listened to that oratory monstrosity for six hours, the scientists and onlookers were no further forward that at the start. Everyone was harassed by exhaustion, as if they had become somnolent in the middle of a military band principally composed of brass instruments. The session was suspended until the following day...*hasta la mañana*. Everyone went to get a good night's sleep, after a meal, with a horrible and nauseous headache—as often happens at those kinds of feasts.

Still to be heard were Salvibianchi, the Italian delegate, and Broussiloff, the Russian delegate, Italy and Russia had suffered from the Napus more than any other nation for a month, by reason of the density of their populations, and they were inclined to accept any method of combating the plague, however harsh, that seemed to have a chance of success.

Salvibianchi declared, enveloping his opinion in numerous polite formulas, that Sidoine's speech and statistics had not convinced him completely, but that, given the doubt, he preferred "not to abstain" and that his vote was for de-electrification.

Broussiloff voted for it too, for a trial period limited to ten years. Everyone knew that, equally divided between revolution and autocracy, both tyrannical and devoid of nuance, Russia had adopted the alternation of white terror and red terror every ten years. During each decade the "good citizens" deported, shot and tore apart the "bad citizens" of the previous decade. The important thing for what the Academician de Vogüé[10] once called "the Slav soul" was that the state of terror did not diminish, or else the most serious consequences were to be feared. That explains the range of Broussiloff's vote; he also requested, by way of an amendment, that any derogation of the international antielectric laws should be punishable forthwith by death.

Before passing on to the vote, it remained to hear Eustache, who posed the preliminary question of napusification by images and the consequent erosion, notably by cinetexts—but the lassitude was such that the worthy fellow's speech, stuffed with ingenious observations and demonstrations of moving depictions of war and peace, left the assembly cold and distracted. Eustache, perceiving this, was disconcerted, hastened his delivery and became almost incomprehensible.

Everyone's position was taken. Soon, the vote on Sidoine's proposal was passed, in the midst of great agitation, and transmitted to the committee of jurists charged with polishing it, formulating it and codifying it. From there, it would pass to the committee of technicians charged with applying it, by force if necessary.

As soon as he saw that that the cause was lost, the German delegate Murmelthier had left the conference hall, proffering vague threats. He did not go far. As he pushed the door of the building with an angry hand, a dry click was heard and the discontented man disappeared. The event was witnessed by my laboratory technician Mouillemouillard and a very worthy Academician, Père Lepoil of the Académie des Beaux-Arts, whose emotion was so intense that he died twelve hours later,

---

10. Eugène-Melchoir, Vicomte de Vogüé, author of *Le Roman russe* (1886).

but with remains. The tragic consequences of the Boche Napus would be seen later.

Enthusiastic applause greeted the result of the vote. Before separating, the conference-members decided to hear a second communication of great importance from the Japanese delegate and the reading of a note from Polyplast 14,026 concerning losses of memory during the period of threat known as "pre-Napus."

Kasavigata therefore reappeared, holding a bizarre object— a kind of tripartite sole that was giving off a frightful odor. The members of the audiences blocked their noses, with their fingers or a handkerchief, and sometimes with both hands, one pinching the nostrils and the other the partition above. The ears, left free, heard that the "sole" was the remains of a napusified Chinaman—for in China, unlike the rest of the world, the Napus left that malodorous residue.

Kasavigata added that discussion was going on throughout the Middle Kingdom, increasingly cut off from the Occident, as to whether or not the residue in queestion was contagious. It was certainly so in Formosa, depopulated in two weeks, which had become a desert "strewn with footprints similar to this one."

The orator indicated by means of a gesture that he was ready to pass the "footprint" around the audience, as the shrunken elephant had been circulated, but no one took the redoubtable object, as much because of its stink, causing desperation and disgust by the intensity of its putrefaction, as the terror of contagion. People observed the revulsion and retreat of Ailette, Sidoine, Eustache and all the Japanese delegate's neighbors, who laughed at the sight of that Occidental panic.

"Among us," he said, "death is of no account, and, all things considered, the Napus is less cruel than hara-kiri."

"Neither hara-kiri nor Napus, that's my motto," murmured Henriette Tastepain cheerfully.

How I agreed with her!

As luck would have it, at the very moment when Kasavigata was brandishing the reeking remains, a second case of aphanasia occurred, this time in the Academic armchairs, leaving one of them empty in the blink of an eye. It was a member of the Académie Française by the name of Baptiste, very old, who had once written a pamphlet on the historical transformations of the locale of the Institut. The loss was minimal in itself, but it stimulated terror, which reached its peak when Kasavigata maliciously placed the Chinese relic on the marble of the podium a few centimeters away from Ailette. The Maître recoiled reflexively, which provoked muted hilarity on the part of the Japanese.

"Take that horror away!" said Eustache to an usher.

"I have a wife and children, Maître—I daren't!"

Eustache turned to another usher, who replied impolitely: "Why not take it away yourself?" It was rude, but logical.

It was the turn of Polyplast 14,026, my friend, to talk about the pre-Napus, but that erudite individual, who had been thought to be brave, was livid, and appeared undecided as to whether to brave the "footprint" of what had once been a human and a Chinese. I can still see him at the foot of the podium, declaring comically that "it was out of the question."

The situation was becoming awkward.

Sidoine had an inspiration. "Have the negroes and their interpreter gone yet?" he asked, loudly.

The answer was no—they were playing cards in the basement, their dirigible having been grounded until the following day for urgent repairs.

"Fetch one of them for me!"

Three minutes later, a tall gray-black man, striped by pale green bands—which indicated the passage of the Napus without decease reserved for those fortunate folk—appeared in the hall. He understood French well enough.

"Take that away!" Sidoine ordered.

"It doesn't smell good. It stinks."

"That's precisely why I'm asking you to take it away, and quickly."

"But where do I put it when I've taken it away?"

"In the dirigible, and once over the sea—over the sea, you

understand—throw it to the fish."

The negro shrugged his broad shoulders, as a sign of doubt regarding the utility of the mission, took the sole of the dead man and calmly stuck it in his loincloth, where it looked like one of the sculls that oarsmen sometimes employ. The audience marveled at the sight of that great dark and pale green man taking away the little yellow doll. Sidoine was surrounded by his colleagues, delighted by that elegant solution. The contents of Polyplast 14,026's communication remained unknown.

The last two days of the conference were dismal, devoted to the so-called "pre-Napus" period, about which no one knew anything. The public, weary of speeches, became sparse, and the immediate neighbors of the late Baptiste, terrorized, no longer attended the sessions. Historians, critics and philosophers are in agreement on the point that, in the order of servility and cowardice, the member of our five Académies, with the Académie Française at the head, come immediately behind the counselors in the Court of Cassation, who cynically put into practice the *ruere ad servitutem* of Tacitus.[11] That is understandable, if one considers that those "honors" are generally the result of an incalculable number of acceptances, abandonments and appeasements in respect of the public authorities, and various major and minor villainies.

Meanwhile, scarcely had the vote on the Sidoine proposal regarding the suppression of all electrical, magnetic and wave-transmitting installations been made known abroad than the German ambassador in Paris, Herr von Tschuppe und Werdenschapf, been instructed by the government in Berlin to make remonstrations on that subject and all reservations of rights.

On top of that had come the explosive news of the death without remains of Murmelthier, considered as the foremost scientist beyond the Rhine and an intractable gallophobe. It was

---

11. In his *Annals*, with reference to the accession of Tiberius, Tacitus advises everyone in subservient situations to flee; the quote is usually rendered as *ruere in servitutem*.

claimed that he kept the stuffed remains of four French soldiers in his home, from the last two Franco-German wars, each of which, as everyone knows, had been followed by an attempted Franco-German alliance.

The rumor spread, stimulated by Boche opinion, that the insufferable individual in question had been surreptitiously murdered between the double doors as a punishment for the opposition he had mounted to Sidoine. That rumor took on further substance because of the death of Père Lepoil, attributed to his horror at the murder of the German scientist.

In my capacity as a Polyplast, a laboratory head at the Aristotle Institute and, most of all, witness to the first Napus, I was summoned to the Ministry of Foreign Affairs, to the office of Monsieur de La Renaudière, who was rightly reputed to be one of the finest servants of the monarchy. He was an upright man, perfectly loyal, informed about everything, and as firm as his predecessors in democratic periods had been soft, stupid and seemingly spineless. He was neither a socialite nor a liberal. He saw and judged things as they were and people as they presented themselves. He knew the Germans and their centuries-old chicanery. Physically, he was a Talleyrand with nostrils less open and flared, and less distance between his nose and upper lip—a Talleyrand who had no respect for revolution nor any appetite for betraying the confidence of his sovereign.

Von Tschuppe und Werdenschaft was tall, well-proportioned, infinitely subtle and a liar. He was an aristocrat of the rural Pomeranian variety, to whom the career of a Baron von Stein or a Bismarck beckoned. As soon as he came into the office on the Quasi d'Orsay, I judged by his expression of concentration that the matter was serious. The prospect of war would have made me smile two months earlier, before I was in love with Henriette, as dictated by our cross-breeding, which had been intended to turn us toward peace, attached to the olive-branch and the dove. At that moment, however, the prospect sickened me.

"Monsieur le Ministre," von Tschuppe began, with the

European accent, a hoarse and rhythmic mixture of English and German, that is common in diplomatic circles, "I have the great regret of having been instructed to coming here by the President of the Council of His Majesty the Emperor, Herr von Haym. Please consider me not as a friend or a neighbor but as a chargé d'affaires."

"Sit down, my dear Monsieur," the Minister replied, in a cordial but official tone, "and have a cigarette. May I introduce to you Monsieur le Polyplaste 17,177, who is particularly well-informed on the question of the Napus, being a member of the Aristotle Foundation, who was present at the conference on the day of the disappearance of the illustrious Professor Murmelthier."

I bowed. Von Tschuppe responded with a military salute, for he occupied a high rank in the German army. I added that the witness to the event, Mouillemouillard, who was present when the "accident" occurred, was my laboratory technician, and an impeccably honest Lyonnais.

"Undoubtedly," said the ambassador. "There are, however, two regrettable coincidences. The first is that Murmelthier disappeared immediately after a vehement criticism of Monsieur Sidonie. The second is that Academician Lepoil died after the scene in the doorway, between the two sets of doors. It is precisely to these two points that I am instructed to draw your attention. It is being said in Berlin, where the emotion is considerable, that the Napus is a good scapegoat."

Still smiling, La Renaudière, was toying with his paper-knife. His serenity was perfect, although a little muscle in his clean-shaven chin had a slight tic. He pointed out that the discussion on the subject of the Sidoine proposal had not exceeded the limits of decorum, nor even those of reciprocal courtesy, and that the supposition of the murder of a eminent conference-member was, in the circumstances, utterly implausible."

"The truth can sometimes...," The Boche riposted, not without delicacy.

I proposed that Mouillemouillard be heard, which was

accepted. The minister telephoned the Aristotle Foundation and ordered that he be sent immediately. In the meantime, we talked about the antielectric obligation, which the ambassador judged to be totally impracticable, with regard to the German Empire.

"Our entire industry is based on our foundation three and a half centuries ago of the Allegemeine Elektricitäts-Gesellschaft. You might as well ask us to deprive ourselves of oxygen. Without electricity, there would be no industry, without industry, no banks, without banks, no finance. We are not an agricultural nation, my dear Minister."

The truth is that the Boche government did not want to renounce the diabolical inventions of an electrical nature that it was holding in reserve for the next conflagration. La Renaudière suspected that, but it was not the time, nor was it his function, to bring that delicate issue to light. He developed the common sense argument that a German exception would entirely undermine the Sidoine scheme of salvation, given that the powerful German electrical organization was sufficient, in itself, to propagate death without remains throughout the entire world—but von Tschuppe was determined not to let go. One of his arguments was not bad.

"How do you know, Monsieur le Ministre, that Maître Sidonie's theory is correct? Does not Monsieur Eustache hold an entirely opposed opinion? He attributes the plague to cinebooks, as you call them—the *cinebiblat*."

"Cinetexts, more precisely."

"All right, cinetexts. Why should it not be him who is right—in which case, civilization would abandon its beautiful electromagneto-telegraphic flowering for nothing?"

"Professor Eustache's theory has been unanimously rejected."

"But there is also that of Professor Ailette, based on the disequilibrium of the cell and cyton. Tomorrow, another explanation more satisfactory still might emerge. We do not understand this haste to destroy the prosperity of the nations of the twenty-third century in the name of what is, as yet, merely a conjecture, and which might appear tomorrow to be a flight of fancy."

I did my best, without insisting too strongly, to support the minister's official thesis, but von Tschuppe's subtle eyes indicated clearly enough that he considered me to be a "Sidoinist by order" and that he did not attach much importance to my assertions. The quarrel sought on the subject of Murmelthier's death was there to mask the firm determination not to give way on the matter of the electrical question. For his part, La Renaudière seemed equally determined.

Mouillemouillard's arrival being belated, the conversation turned to Morrow and the expectant attitude of England.

"It's the ultimate indecisive nation," sighed von Tschuppe, as if that observation pained him. "It's true that there's an immense Empire involved, and that it takes time to formulate a firm decision between Montreal, Bombay Alexandria and London, but it would takes a clever man to ascertain the direction in which the Britannic balance will tip. Only one thing is certain: in three hundred years they've destroyed our war-fleet and annihilated our submarines four times. It will doubtless be the same again this time, if we can't reach an agreement—but it's necessary to hope that we can."

I was beginning to think that we were not making much headway when the usher brought in Mouillemouillard. My laboratory technician was eager to please, increasingly resembling the clown of his region, the priceless Chignol. Von Tschuppe and La Renaudière looked at him benevolently; he did not seem intimidated.

"So, Monsieur Mouillardemule," the Boche began, mangling the name,[12] "you witnessed the sudden disappearance of Professor Murmelthier, in the company of Academician Lepoil. Would you be good enough to tell us exactly how it came about?"

At that moment, the telephone rang. La Renaudiere picked up the apparatus, listened to the communication, and uttered a

---

12. Mouillemouillard combines two derivatives of the French term for "damp"; Von Tshupper's transfiguration makes it more suggestive of "damp mule"—although, in fact, the poor fellow proves to be anything but mulish.

desolate "Oh my God!" He had just been informed of the napusification of his own brother, the French ambassador in Peking. The case was curious, for the dragoman who telephoned announced that there was a residue—a "footprint"—and asked whether he should send it to Paris.

"My condolences, my dear friend." said von Tschuppe, rising to his feet and sketching another military salute. "This plague is truly horrible!"

I wondered whether, while finding the plague so, that von Tartuffe might not be thinking about multiplying the scourge by a war. Overcoming his emotion and grief, however, La Renaudière had resumed his impassive expression and turned to Mouillemouillard as if to ask him to begin his story. I trembled at the possibility that he might become confused, for the German had taken out his notebook and adopted a rather severe expression, like a magistrate on the bench.

"Do you swear to tell the truth, the whole truth and nothing but the truth?"

"I swear!"

Mouillemouillard remained standing in front of the three of us, sitting down, and explained sufficiently what had happened. "Monsieur Murmelthier was already grasping the handle of the second set of doors when there was a *thwock* or *thwack*, as if something soft were being tapped with something hard. Oh, that did something to me when I hard it, because I know what it signifies. And right away, bang!—no more Murmelthier. Right then I said to myself: *That's the Napus*. It was upsetting to see it, though."

"There was someone with you at that moment, Monsieur Mouillardemule?"

"Yes, there was an Academician dressed in green, with a little sword, and whom I knew, since it was Monsieur Lepoil. Oh, he said something...."

"Murmelthier? But he's disappeared."

"No, Monsieur Lepoil. He said something like: *That's frightful*; or, *That's atrocious*. It was enough to make your head spin, if you'll forgive the expression. And he died himself shortly afterwards, but, you know, with his remains—his body, his corpse—while poor Monsieur Murmelthier, it was like Madame Grégeois, Monsieur Baptiste and so many others. They found nothing at all."

"Let's see, my dear Monsieur Mouillardemule," the Boche persisted, "are you absolutely sure that things happened as you have just said? It appears that you were much les affirmative in the beginning, and that you mentioned an altercation between Messieurs Murmelthier and Lepoil."

"Wait a moment," said Mouillemouillard, slapping his forehead. "Yes, that's right—they bumped into one another and cursed at me. It's necessary to confess that I was a bit tipsy, thanks to the six bottles of Beaujolais that I'd been sent from Lyon, and that I wasn't handling the doors very well...I was drunk."

"Oh, you were a little tipsy?"

Von Tschuppe turned to La Renaudière, who grimaced at him, and at my damned Mouillemouillard, who had just destroyed the whole effect of his testimony. What confidence could one have in a drunkard? As for the quarrel between Murmelthier and Lepoil—an uncommonly placid man—I was hearing mention of it for the first time. Mouillemouillard had never breathed a word of it to me.

"I'm obliged to you for your frankness, Monsieur Mouillardemule. Did you notice whether, at any time, Monsieur Lepoil struck Monsieur Murmelthier?"

"Well, you know it's a bit foggy—but if he'd fetched him a slap I wouldn't have been astonished. Oh, there was something!"

"A punch—how long before the napusification?"

"Just before. The *thwock* or *thwack* was immediately after."

I looked at La Renaudière, who did not flinch, The way things were going, Mouillemouillard, who was rather weak-minded and submissive to the well-tempered will of von Tschuppe, was about to confess that Lepoil had murdered Murmelthier and then made his disappear. In the German's arrogant expression one could read the powder-charged words *compensation* and *retribution*.

"Is it not possible," the ambassador continued, "that a violent shock, like that one, might have caused the Napus?"

I replied that, to my knowledge, firstly, there was no need of any shock or trauma to provoke aphanasia, and secondly, that numerous shocks and traumas had not been followed by aphanasia since the advent of the Napus.

"Monsieur Mouillardemule," the German went on, returning to him in great haste, "would you repeat what you have just told me in writing?"

Ink and paper were brought, and my laboratory technician, having become the arbiter of European destiny, wrote a statement in Chignolesque jargon, from which it stood out clearly that Lepoil had sought a violent quarrel with Murmelthier, on the subject of antielectrification and had hit him. Now Lepoil had a sort of official status. The business was getting complicated.

"You can go, Monsieur Mouillardemule. On behalf of my Sovereign, I thank you."

I got ready to leave too, but van Tschuppe stopped me with a gesture. "You must, on the contrary, hear what I have to say, Monsieur Polyplaste," he said. Then, addressing La Renaudière, he continued: "Monsieur le Ministre, in the name of the Emperor, and the brave man in question, I have the honor of demanding from you, for the death of Herr Murmelthier, insulted and struck by the Academician and former Undersecretary of State Lepoil, on the occasion of an official ceremony, an indemnity of five million francs in gold and a formal apology. A delay of a hundred hours is granted, in default of which I shall have the honor of presenting my recall papers to you."

With that, the military gentleman carefully put Mouillemouillard's bewildering narration in his pocket, rose to his feet with a single motion, like a large wooden puppet, made a military salute, shook La Renaudière's hand and left.

Well," said La Renaudière, calmly, "this proves that their electrical devilries have reached the point at which they're looking for a *casus belli*. A cruel alternative: either we allow the Napus to continue its ravages and annihilate without remains the terrestrial population of the Occident, and with remains the population of China, or Germany will make war on us to conserve its electrical and telegraphic position. Who was it who claimed that Science was the messenger of peace among humankind?"

I was stunned by the diplomatic scene that I had just witnessed.

"Do you think," the Minister said to me, "that Mouillemouillard has received a large payment for revising his initial statement in that way and thus representing Lepoil as Murmelthier's murderer?"

I said no, and that Mouilemouillard had manifestly been manipulated by the ambassador. I was not mistaken, for an hour later, having summoned him to my office, looking him straight in the eyes, I obtained an account exactly contrary to the one he had just written out for von Tschuppe, in which it was more obvious than ever that there had been not the slightest dispute or collision between Murmelthier and Lepoil.

CHAPTER FOUR
A DELAY OF A HUNDRED HOURS

On Monsieur de La Renaudière's orders, I immediately apprised Sidoine of von Tschuppe's ultimatum.

Sidoine was the very type specimen of the twenty-third-century scientist and, although not a Polyplast, was animated by sentiments as harsh as mine had been before the walk in the woods at Meudon. In addition, that which he took to be the scientific truth acquired, in his eyes, the status of dogma. He would rather kill himself and set fire to the planet than deny one his "principles," of which the mean duration was between thirty and forty years—for although carp live for five hundred years, and elephants and eagles between a hundred and a hundred and fifty, the best and most seductive medical and biological theories rarely achieve half a century of existence.

At the first word of protest, that brown-haired colossus would cry: "The cause is good! It is that of humanity. The worst enemies of humankind, it is evident today, are electricity, magnetism and wave-transmission. In those infernal machines, which we gladly did without for so many centuries, lurked the Devil of theology. If war has to result from our refusal, never has any holier or more just war been accepted for the salvation of the human species."

Naturally, however, Ailette and Eustache, similarly alerted in their capacity as members of the Great Scientific Council, did not share this opinion. "Sidoine," they said, in substance, "has won, by surprise tactics, a terribly dangerous vote, a vote whose diplomatic and military consequences can now be glimpsed, but whose economic and financial consequences will be no less disastrous, for it is the entire industry that is at stake. Electricity, at the present time, is the very foundation of industry. To renounce it is to renounce all industrial progress, all improvement. A return to steam engine is a return to barbarity, the abandonment of speed, the collapse of civilization. Besides, that is not the true cause of the Napus; it is either the cellular deterioration of cyton or erosion by images."

Thus was thrown as fodder to the passions of crowds and groups a question of pure medicine—which, it is true, contradicted everything we knew regarding the supposed indestructibility of matter.

In case of war the Polyplasts, of whom I was one, could choose between the laboratories of the rear, in which the most modern methods of destruction and homicidal improvements were tried out, or the laboratories of the front, in which new treatments and the latest models of prosthetic apparatus were developed.

In the latter instances, which all relied on electricity, a amendment of the Sidoine law was anticipated, for there could evidently be know question of going back to the wooden legs, mechanical arms, false noses and other barbarities that were the lot two hundred years ago of cripples and the victims of mutilation wounded in the series of Franco-German, Germano-English, Germano-Italian etc. wars that periodically desolate the world. But had Sidoine reflected that the electrical and wave-based mechanisms necessitated by present-day prostheses presumed giant installations, themselves susceptible, according to him, of provoking and bringing about death without remains? The suppression of the latter entailed the suppression of the former.

A telephone call from the Ministry of Foreign Affairs charged Sidoine with summoning to the Aristotle the principal proprietors of scientific and political newspapers, in order to acquaint them with the redoubtable eventuality and to request them to stimulate public opinion. Once again, I was admitted to the meeting of these important individuals in my capacity as the first observer of the Napus and my "special competence." That was how I made the acquaintance of the potentates of the press, who were evidently less ostentatious than their equivalent in the era of democracy and so-called enlightenment, but remained arrogant and quarrelsome beneath their external obsequiousness.

Noirpelat was there, who had formed a monopoly of the dailies of the north and the Parisian region, Tavejus, who controlled the west and center. Tiqueton, who concentrated the press in the east, and Barouille, who commanded the press in the south. The first had the hirsute physiognomy of a wild boar, and pronounced his ss and cs as xs while talking to his deerskin boots. The second was short and thin, as if boneless, with a jaundiced, ferret-like face. The third had a nose like a toucan, set in the middle of a timid face between blinking eyes. Barouille was the most sympathetic, beneath a rain of gray-blond hair, with the face of a satirist, as if carved in spongy wood.

The members of that quartet, on learning of the German ambassador's ultimatum, were not pleased.

Noirpelat, who seemed to be the shrewdest, was in favor of trying to gain time and requesting, to that effect, an extension of the delay of a hundred hours. "It's very little," he said. "A hundred hours, to organize that—it would require at least a week."

Sidoine observed to him politely that such a request might bring forth a refusal that would spoil everything.

Tavejus proposed the request for arbitration that is the resource of all cowards. By comparison with him, England was decisive.

Barouille objected, however, that preliminary hesitation with regard to the Sidoine law, as Morrow and the British government showed, was mere procrastination.

As for Tiqueton, who was incapable of forming an opinion and, for good reason, of putting one into action, he contented himself with giving his astonishing nose different inclinations and articulating nasal sounds. Spending his days in an automobile and his nights in bars and casinos, he was dying for fear at the thought of the Napus, war, death, with or without remains and any kind of responsibility.

There was no situation more comical than that of that poor fellow, placed by destiny at the head of an organ printing three million copies a day. Women said to him: "you're handsome and your nose is driving me crazy; give me ten thousand-franc bills." Men said to him: "you have an astonishing flair as well as an astonishing nose; lend me ten thousand francs." Policemen said to him: "If you don't give us ten thousand francs, we'll put you in prison." Anarchists said to him: "If you don't give us ten thousand francs, we'll blow up your bolt-hole." Magistrates said to him: "If you don't put ten thousand francs on our desk, we'll render judgment against you." Doctors said to him: "If you don't hand over ten thousand francs, we'll let you die in bed." The syndicate of master blackmailers only guaranteed him civil peace against a weekly payment of ten thousand francs to the fund for master blackmailers in need. Tradesmen would only deliver to him for ten thousand francs what others bought for a hundred. Thus was Tiqueton the wealthy taxed, in the midst of a life in glorious bloom and a bush of gilded thorns.

None of these important proprietors ever set foot in his newspaper's offices, Noirpelat for fear of a request of question from his editor in chief to which he would be unable to reply, Tavejus for fear of a slap in the face—he had, it seemed, received a thousand in ten years—Tiqueton for fear of a demand for another ten thousand francs, and Barouille because the press did not interest him and he occupied himself with the art of dentistry to pass the time. He liked putting gold fillings in the molars of his friends, his domestics and his concierge, and he collected stumps.

Sidoine's knowledge of these particularities enabled him to win these powerful interlocutors to his cause. He captured Noirpelat by means of vanity, Tavejus by means of dread, Tiqueton by means of timidity and Barouille by means of flattery.

It was agreed that the German threat would be brought to the attention of the French public the following day, but in a courteous tone that would be maintained until it was absolutely certain that the war could not be avoided. It was also understood that the press, as a whole, would further emphasize the unanimous vote of the conference—apart from Germany and England—with regard to the Sidoine law, which indicated the value attached to the said project by the qualified representatives of all the nations of the world. By opposing such a forceful measure, the only one capable of combating the plague, Germany was once more setting itself up as an enemy of the human species.

Before the conspirators separated, the four proprietors asked me to draft a common note, objective and exclusively scientific in appearance, setting out the facts and the facts alone. I did that right away. This is the note:

> The recent session of the Conference of the Combined Academies and Institutes devoted to the Napus concluded with a plan for an international law drawn up by Professor Sidoine and endorsed by all the nations except two. One of the other two nations, England, simply adjourned its adherence and its signature, for reasons of propriety related to its Dominions. The Sidoine law, considering all electrical, magnetic and wave-emitting installations to be the principal, if not the only cause, of the terrible plague, decrees their immediate suppression. The practical regulation of that law, which thus becomes the charter of the civilized world, will be promulgated one hundred hours from now, under the auspices of the Aristotle Institute— where, of course, Professor Ailette's antinapusic broth can still be purchased.

The "one hundred hours from now" agreed with Minister La Renaudière was simply an indirect response to the German ultimatum.

However, the bankers and financiers independent of banks—who were even more redoubtable—of the two worlds, who had money invested in wave-transmitting and other installations, had immediately rallied to von Tschuppe's German thesis, and their orders to the press trusts, which they controlled to a greater or lesser degree, flatly contradicted those of the government.

Caught between the necessities of the Bourse, linked themselves to the necessity of purchasing immense quantities of paper, and the fear of disobeying La Renaudière, Noirpelat, Tavejus, Tiqueton and Barouille took the course of publishing, pell-mell on the same pages, both sets of press releases. Column two gave the lie to column three, which was itself contradicted by column four.

Favored by the rapidity of means of communication whose prohibition was demanded by the Sidoine law, a deluge of false news began to rain down, soaking the reality and transforming it into a sticky mire of tall stories.

It was in these circumstances that the benefits of the monarchic institution became clear and salutary, as the only one capable of counterbalancing, by means of a fixed axis and continuous action, the zigzags of popular passion and brute interests.

American democracy, however, warned by its war with Japan a century earlier but not cured of its errors, passed more edicts, with a flick of the wrist and in the space of a hundred hours, than it would have been possible to apply in ten years—for it was the habit, in the United States, to replace laws with edicts, and codes by codices of a sort, full of bothersome prescriptions.

It is necessary to recognize, nevertheless, that fear of the Napus was, for the government in Washington, the commencement of wisdom, and that it declared itself ready to break the contracts of all the electrical and wave-emitting companies overnight, just as, three hundred years earlier, it had prohibited all fermented beverages, including wine. The Anglo-Saxons like *tours de force*, moral and otherwise, in whatever direction they present themselves. An individual who drinks seven liters of wine a day—which is the case in vine-growing countries, and not a few of our compatriots—delights them as much as an individual who does not touch a drop of wine or spirits from birth to the age of a hundred.

The independent financiers, whose institution does not go back more than a century, are specialists in matters of monetary exchange, transfer, stabilization and revaluation, which relieve nations in difficulty, collapsing establishments and private fortunes gone adrift with decisive advice. They are, in sum, the physicians of gold, enjoying as honoraria, commissions of thirty per cent on the capital engaged. Freed from all the inconveniences necessitated by the multiple, and sometimes adventurous, operations of great credit institutions, their heads are freed for calculations, ingenious methods and risks that, like currents of thirty thousand volts, pass through the organism without harming it.

There was a case, three centuries ago, of an unphilosophical sugar manufacturer who committed suicide over a loss of a few millions following an imprudent purchase of beets. Before swallowing his cyanide he ate a dish of braised beef, of which he was very fond, and which evidently represented, for him, the finest aspect of existence. But who would now commit suicide over a bankruptcy of five billion, involving the exhaustion of the oil-wells of an entire hemisphere?

One of the arguments developed by the anti-Sidoines of America, Germanic in name for the most part, was that it would be necessary to renounce death by electrocution, to which the American people are very attached. Every people has its genre of execution, which it deems superior to that of its neighbor. We find in the guillotine, although it is disgusting and barbaric, the same charm that the Spaniard finds in the garrote, the Englishman in hanging and the Yankee in the electric chair. The truth is that the Napus, which is ideally proper and prompt, is a form of death far superior to these ridiculous procedures;

unfortunately, it is uncontrollable and defies the skill of the executioner.

It cannot be said that the news of an imminent rupture of relations between France and Germany on the question of aphanasia had an enormous impact on the nation. For one thing, general sensibility and sentimentality, which are the sources of apprehension, had been considerably weakened by the napusian epidemic. Secondly, the rhythm of Franco-German wars, at an average rate of two per century, had reduced that scourge—the one about which human complain more than any other in words, but accept willingly in fact—to banality. Finally, scientific training, to which we owe the curious institution of Polyplasts, resulted in a sort of fatality: "It's the way it is because that's the way it is."

In the nineteenth century, a short lieutenant from Brienne, Napoléon Bonaparte, who had a flat wisp of hair over his forehead, excited general enthusiasm by declaring war on all and sundry, and fascinated the French by enabling them to commit massacres for fifteen years without any kind of valid reason. He came after another wretch with the head of a cat, by the name of Robespierre, who had thousands of heads cut off in order to inaugurate the reign of fraternity. These examples show that hecatombs are easily admitted by nations when the person who orders them has a certain dose of sympathy and enthusiasm, as in a game of chance or angling.

In the laboratories of the Aristotle Foundation we had a few Germans who had come to study our methods, while we were supposed to be studying theirs. The truth is that we each kept to our own; these things are not transmissible. When they discovered what was going on these Germans said: "Damn it! We've going to have to go back to the old routine." No other reflection. Personally, I wasn't sorry to see them go, given that one of them, who was blond and remarkably neat, with a profile as regular as a cameo, was rather attached to my lovely Henriette.

The employees of the Ministry of Foreign Affairs in Paris ensured that in the course of the hundred hours, twelve thousand five hundred communications were exchanged, by wire-less and other means, between the various peoples of the planet, constituting a yellow book of twenty tomes, in which all the questions raised by the Napus and the Sidoine law were treated simultaneously.

The British Empire was in the lead, with three thousand three hundred and one communications, maintaining an uncertainty that lasted until the final minute. It is a prodigy that that great nation has, in the course of its history, taken energetic deci-sions, given the pleasure it takes in not hurrying and "dragging its feet," as the saying has it. We came next with 2,596, on the same footing as the United States (2,507) and Germany (2,610). Italy only had 1,040.

The smallest figure was Spain's, with only seventeen commu-nications. That nation, although struck by the Napus in relatively imposing proportions, seemed to have retired from European life, either because it had succeeded in retreating into its shell like a snail or because it had delegated its historical energy to its descendants in South America. Its example proves that it is not sufficient for a great and beautiful race, as original as the race possessed of the gilded language of Saint Theresa, Cervantes, de Rojas, Calderon, Balmès and Santiago Rusiñol, to produce mystics, writers and painters. It is also necessary to produce military leaders, in the shelter of which the arts, sciences and mores prosper. Although every conqueror is a scourge, there is no greater benefit than a sage and powerful military gift associ-ated with that of a statesman. One such had arrived in Spain in 1924, with a certain General Primo de Rivera.[13]

Around the sixtieth hour, there was a moment of hope that an eventual agreement might be reached. That hope came from a transcription error in a German dispatch to the English govern-ment, which said that no fundamental concession was possible, and which was understood as saying exactly the opposite. For half an hour, until the mistake had been officially established, it

13. Miguel Primo de Rivera, Marquis of Estella, was the Prime Minister of Spain from 1923-30, having seized power in a coup.

was thought that the Boche were retracting their claws.

La Renaudière and the King did not take any rest during the hundred hours, while packets of telegrams were brought to them in baskets. At the Foundation, we organized a rota that permitted us to communicate with the Ministry of Foreign Affairs at any hour of the day or night. The most impassive person of all was Sidoine, in spite of the death threats that were addressed to him by pacifists from all points of the globe.

Remarkably, during that hundred-hour interval, only thirty cases of the Napus were recorded in Paris and seventy-four in the provinces, although the figures had previously risen to five hundred per day. Was it necessary to conclude therefrom that certain mental or intellectual states were unfavorable to aphanasia?

It has been observed that monks, who constantly exteriorized a preoccupation with death, in the midst of extreme privations and frequent mortifications, live for a long time. It was also observed that the Napus afflicted them less cruelly than other social categories, although some of them went as far as imploring it as a celestial grace. It appeared, after extensive research, that the death of an inventor before he had realized his most important invention, especially if the invention in question involved some significant advantage or benefit for humankind. Even with regard to literature, the interruption of a masterpiece by death was rare.

About the seventy-second hour, without anyone being able to figure out why, the conviction was acquired by the public that the new war, dubbed the Napus War, could not happen, by reason of its probable atrocity. People accosted one another, crying: "I swear to you that it's impossible! How can you expect the Germans, or us, to expose themselves to seeing cities like Paris, Berlin, Lyon, Munich, Marseilles, Dresden etc. to collapse beneath bombardments, perpendicular or parabolic?" Those who spoke in this fashion were often the same ones who had declared a few hours earlier that war was inevitable.

We Polyplasts, more complex in our reasoning by virtue of

our mixed blood, objected in vain that in no era had atrocity ever acted as a brake on war. In the wake of our arguments, all weak minds, and a certain proportion of strong but stubborn ones, took up the humanitarian refrain again.

Now, the intensity of killing is not always proportional to the improvement or the horror of the means of killing. The said means being refined, demand extensive knowledge and special conditions; the former are subject to weaknesses, the latter are not always realized. That explains why, in scientifically-organized carnage, more combatants are always spared than one would expect. The battles claimed to be the most murderous of all, even ahead of those of antiquity, are, according to explorers, those of gorillas armed with ironwood clubs.[14]

At the landmark of the ninetieth hour, a petition appeared in the press of the entire world signed by several thousand intellectuals, protesting against the possibility of a war unleashed for a scientific motive over the question of the Napus. On the pretext of averting a certain form of death, the fields of Europe and elsewhere were about to be strewn with cadavers.

The authors of the petition appeared to be under the illusion that absurdity has ever stopped crowds on the brink of stupidity or communal crime. On the contrary, it is evident that the absurd exercises an attraction on human gatherings, as the abyss exercises one on individuals. Where is the resolute alpinist who has not had to struggle, at a bend in a mountain path, against vertiginous magnetism, the call of the gulf? That sentiment, entirely physical, is reproduced in the mental domain. There is nothing more fragile than common sense in the presence of the brutal reactions of instinct. With regard to the impulsion and appetite of insanity, human beings are equipped with few and fragile brakes.

The further the time advanced, dilated and stretched by apprehension, like an elastic band, the more accustomed the public became to the idea of a new conflagration and came

---

14. The said explorers were, of course, lying.

to consider it as an unavoidable fatality, just as they had with the Napus. Human beings, in certain respects, are designed to accept calamities. They begin by resisting, for form's sake, after the fashion of children; gradually, however, the screams die down, the gestures of revolt become more widely spaced and diminished in amplitude. In the face of the tempests that assail them in the course of their brief sojourn in this world, they always seem, to some extent, to be in the process of drowning.

Between the ninetieth and the ninety-fifth hours a phenomenon was produced that had been observed before, but much attenuated, in the run-up to previous wars: a multitude of inventors of technical methods, homicidal or antihomicidal, battered at the doors of the Ministry or the Aristotle Foundation.

The majority of these ingenious devices relied on the very electrical and wave-based technologies banned by the Sidoine law. Others were founded on the employment of a new power-source, extracted from gravity, the sun or the gravity of Jupiter—a power-source that was undeniable, and even industrially employed, but difficult to manipulate in the midst of the tumult of battle.

The employment of "moles," or depositors of subterranean explosives, broadly perfected, apparently ought to play an important role in sieges.

Apparatus productive of intolerable and shattering sounds, capable of causing death at a range of a hundred kilometers, were also greatly commended. Experiments were carried out with instruments of appropriate measure on a small scale using minuscule models, but in which the intensity of the sound was already as dolorous as possible. Rats, guinea-pigs, young dogs and cats could not resist them, and collapsed, agonized, paws in the air, as soon as the strident throbbing machines were switched on. By virtue of a ludicrous exception, snakes did not seem to be inconvenienced; they are animals of a different kind, having original means of communication among themselves and possessing a science that we do not have. It has been claimed that they had been subject to the Napus for a long time—about a century before us—but that is an opinion that has not so far been verified.

Now, of the approximately one thousand inventors of the ninetieth hour, seven hundred and fifty—a considerable number—were to be napusified in the following three months—with the consequence that Henriette, 14,026 and I wondered whether imaginative fertility might not be a premonitory symptom of aphanasia. Have I mentioned that, in the same period, twenty cases of cyclic madness, reputedly incurable, were suddenly cured, without the death without remains seeming to have afflicted the insane more severely than the non-insane?

Remarkably, that recovery from serious mental illness, evidently linked to the mysterious Disease, and which constituted its beneficial aspect, worked in the following fashion: a return not to reason but to the childishness and babbling of the third year, to the zigzags and tremors of nascent thought and to the irreducible obstinacy and impulses of young minds; then, in a phase averaging ten days, a mental replenishment equivalent to the period between the third and twelfth year, a fondness for games and sports and a certain frivolity persisting until the complete return to normality, and even afterwards. It was a recommencement of existence following the sly and rhythmic destruction of the individual struck by madness.

After the ninety-fifth hour, which fell at six o'clock in the evening, while, throughout the extent of the nation's territory, there was already a general mobilization for war under way, crowds began to form in squares and at crossroads, as at the approach of a tragic event. Luminous signs projected in the sky announced, minute by minute, the failure of means of conciliation, the failure of the Chinese intervention, on which people had counted momentarily, the failure of the Australian peace proposals founded on the possibility of an amendment of the Sidoine law—and then, successively, Germano-Austrian mobilization, Russian mobilization, Italian mobilization, Belgian mobilization, Serbian mobilization, Polish mobilization, Rumanian mobilization, Bulgarian, Swedish and Dutch mobilization. England still had not rallied to the call, but the "home fleet" commanded by Admiral Turnship, of the Superior Council of the Admiralty, had returned to its bases and was checking its hypermagnetos.

One would have said that things were moving full steam ahead in the days of coal—a strange phase in human history, that of black bread, when people lived underground like burrowing animals, hammering seams in cadence and bringing down the dark produce of the miserly earth amid shiny or dusty fissures.

What would the initial German strategy be? Would Friedrich-Wilhelm XIII's armies invade Belgium or Switzerland, as in the ancient Franco-German wars, or would they proceed with aerial bombardments of Brussels, Antwerp, Paris, London, Milan and Rome, as in the more recent ones, or with expansions of gas transported by artificial winds, as in the one at the beginning of the twenty-second century, or with electrical thunderbolts? Had they developed a new method of causing irresistible floods and artificial earthquakes, as was rumored? Would they unleash, in the direction of neutral countries, hundreds of wild animals and snakes previously infected with rabies?

Such were the questions that idlers asked one another—for it is remarkable that, in matters of foreign war, as in matters of civil war, the rumors of the last become, with a few variations, the realities of the next. In this domain, there is never any amelioration; things always get worse.

To these macabre anticipations we replied, when questioned, that for our part, we had not been wasting our time in matters of National Defense and that we had at our disposal entirely unprecedented means of annihilating the enemy, extracted from the attentive observation of death without remains.

The truth is that our perplexity was great. Was it necessary to maintain the Sidoine law, so recently voted, at the risk of allowing the enemy the terrible privilege of electro-ondic Archimedism? Was it necessary to renounce that law, as soon as hostilities were opened, when its maintenance was the very pretext invoked by the Boches to start the war?

Sidoine, whose strength of persuasion was immense, affirmed that, without a doubt, the multiplication of the Napus in the German army would rapidly compensate for our losses in consequence of the antielectric law. A redoubtable question mark loomed up, however: what if that multiplication did not occur? What if Professor Sidoine was mistaken? If it is true that in the moment of peril, nothing is graver than the alternative, with its troubling calculations, that one, it must be admitted, was massive!

Just as the ninety-seventh hour elapsed, Mouillemouillard handed me the card of a well-known German physicist, chemist and engineer by the name of Kaninchen, who was, for the year 2227, what Edison had been three centuries before: a father of all invention.

I found myself in the presence of a short bespectacled gentleman, like a gnome in tales of the Rhineland, who began by asking me whether anyone could hear us.

After my reassuring response, he declared, in a musical and well-tempered voice more like that of a Hungarian than a Boche, which I can still hear: "I have discovered, *mein lieber Herr*, not only the secret of the Napus but also the means of providing an admirable system of protection, which consists of always having about one's person this little tupe.[15] I am a humanitarian and a pacifist, *mein Herr*. It is in consequence of my discovery, officially and secretly tested, that the German government has resolved to embark once again, against you, Europe and America, on general and common destruction.

"The Murmelthier affair is merely a vast cover, and you can imagine, being intelligent, that no one in our country believes it. So, in order that the destruction should not be unilateral, at

_____

15. I have reproduced this word as printed in the French text. It is obviously a deliberate misrendering of "tube," but Kaninchen's speech—unlike Murmelthier's, although I have rendered it into ordinary English—is not generally marked in Daudet's text by any kind of eye-dialect supposedly representative of Teutonic pronunciation, so its employment stands out as an oddity.

least with regard to the Napus—there are more than enough other kinds of death—I want you, the French, also to profit from my discovery. Each race requires a particular dosage of the substance, the formula of which, with its ethnic variations, remains my secret and my property. This tupe is only effective on French blood; it only immunizes French blood. I warn you that it would be futile to communicate it to an Englishman. An Italian or a Belgian; it would not provide any protection what-soever. Every type is dosed for the protection of ten thousand human beings."

Kaninchen's physiognomy was too well-known for me to be in any doubt as to the identity of my interlocutor. I was preparing to stammer my thanks when the fatal click was heard and the Boche philanthropist and inventor of an infallible protection against the Napus disappeared, like so many others before him. All that remained was the illusory little tube, which stayed there, within range of my hand, clenched with laughter—for I was laughing wholeheartedly, for half a dozen interconnected motives, as happens to us Polyplasts.

I was laughing at the Boche's galliphilic crisis, doubtless resulting, in his mind, from the identity of contradictions that is one of the pillars of insanity and German metaphysics, the one tending to the other. I was laughing at his naïve confidence in the efficacy of the substance in the little "tupe." I was laughing in anticipation of the laughter at the Aristotle when I told them the story. I was laughing at the incredulity that it would encounter among those who, in spite of everything, remained admirers of Germany—for germanomania is a disease, of a different kind from the Napus, but a disease nevertheless. I was not laughing at the further grievance that Kanichen's death without remains would constitute, if it ever came out that it had taken place in my laboratory, at the ninety-seventh hour of the ultimatum.

What should I do? Should I recommend silence to that imbecile Mouillemouillard, imposing upon him a sugges-tion stronger than that of any examining magistrate or Boche who might interrogate him about Kaninchen's disappearance?

Should I keep quiet, wait, and, as they say, let things take their course? Should I consult Sidoine, or Ailette or Eustache, or my dear Henriette, or 14,026?

I detest perplexity, which does not suit my temperament and makes me feel physically ill. I considered, on the corner of my desk, the little tube that Kaninchen had left me, on dematerializing and vanishing into the ether. The tiny bottle was full of a pink liquid and sealed by a yellow-tinted ground-glass stopper.

Mouillemouillad came in without knocking. He was livid, overwhelmed by the idea of the new war, like a white wax candle meting in front of a fire. Von Tschuppe's interrogation had left him with a prodigious respect, a kind of veneration, for the Boche.

Wide-eyed, he asked: "What's happened to Monsieur Kaninchen?"

Laughing, I replied to him, in the manner of the little girl of yore: "Kanichen *a pati. N'a pus!*"

"Oh my God!" cried Chignol's brother. "What's going to happen to us? What will Monsieur Tschuppe say?"

At that moment, he spotted the tube left by Kaninchen and, with the curiosity of a laboratory technician, before I could stop him, he took out the stopper. This time there was a hissing noise, accompanied by a sudden evaporation of part of the pink liquid, which transported my faithful Mouillemoulliard, to the shoreless land of Catch-me-if-you-can.

Undoubtedly, Kaninchen had discovered a means of artificially provoking the Napus, and he had come, an ambassador of aphanasia, to get rid of the redoubtable masters of the Aristotle Foundation, on behalf of Germany, at the moment of the war's inception. But Providence had determined that either his own product or the spontaneous Napus—the classic Napus—had carried him away before he accomplished his criminal design.

Every cloud has a silver lining: the worthy Mouillemouillard's dispersal dissipated the risk of an indiscretion.

I was savoring that egotistical observation when my delightful Henriette came in, as calm as if the scourge of an inexplicable war were not suspended by a three-hour thread above our heads.

"I'm looking for Mouillemouillard," she said.

"You won't find him. He's just been napusified."

"Oh, the poor fellow! Why, what's this little open tube?"

"Don't touch that!"

I told her the story of the two dramas I had jut witnessed. She confessed to me, in her turn, that they did not intimidate her much, for she was on the track of the fifth magnetic center in the cell, which would doubtless ensure the dynamic equilibrium of tissues.

My preoccupation was quite different. I was wondering how to get rid of Kaninchen's homicidal gift without running the risk of aphanasia. I got an idea. In the laboratory next door 14,026 had a sturdy dog, patched up with thread, that had been used in experiments in vivisection six months before. I went to fetch it, brought it back on a lead and showed it the fatal tube.

"Fetch!"

It looked at me sadly, with an almost human expression of reproach, and meekly approached the object. Scarcely had it sniffed it than it disappeared with a hiss more prolonged that Mouillemouillard's.

"Damn!" said Henriette. "That's conclusive! We mustn't get any closer to that product of Boche malice. But one very serious question arises, my dear Poly 17,177."

"What?"

"Had Kaninchen already delivered his secret to the German General Staff? If he had, induced Napus will become the most terrible weapon of the new war. Shouldn't we at least inform Sidoine and La Renaudière?"

I did not share that opinion. There was a good chance that Kaninchen, who was professionally very discreet, had kept his discovery to himself. I decided to content myself with locking my laboratory and abandoning it, on some pretext or other, until the end of hostilities.

"But how do you know that the residue of the mysterious product in the tube won't pass through the walls, like an omega-ray, and napusify all the professors and Polyplasts of the Aristotle Foundation?"

The fear was justified. The pink substance must be terribly active, since it had aphanased the dog, a member of a species previously immune. I decided to tell Sidoine about the strange succession of complications. He was in mysterious conversation with an officer from the general staff, to whom he was handing sheets of paper covered with figures and diagrams. When the meeting had finished I told him my story briefly.

The decision was rapidly taken.

"There's no doubt that it's a question of an attack on the Foundation. Of all the Boche masked by science, none is more redoubtable than Kaninchen, and his aphanasia is a blessing. We're going to move our laboratory and our archives within the next four hours, on the pretext that they're not safe from bombardments, and we'll retreat to Underground 7, where vast facilities, well-equipped for research, were set up eighteen months ago."

That was done. The abandoned Aristotle Foundation would soon become a center of intensive aphanasia for its surroundings, without anyone except Sidoine, Henriette and myself knowing the reason for that intensification of the epidemic. At the time of writing, however, the virulence of the Kaninchen tube seems to have almost completely disappeared.

From the ninety-ninth hour onwards, the population of Paris, understanding that no conciliation was possible between such opposed viewpoints, waited with mingled curiosity and dread for the first Boche devilment. The general staff of the air force had disposed defensive wave-transmitters around our great cities, especially Marseilles, Lyon and Paris, in spite of the Sidoine law—and rumor of that, like millions of swarms of bees, was already creating an atmosphere of alarm. We knew immediately that it was the same in Germany, where Berlin, Dresden and Munich were protected by other, equally effective waves of a similar kind.

That ensured that the two antagonistic nations avoided

launching their bomber fleets against one another. By contrast, London having continued to remain in suspense, by virtue of the lack of decision that doubtless resulted from unlimited participation in sports, the Lufthansa of the twenty-third century sent a thousand aircraft against the capital of the United Kingdom, which demolished, in advance of any declaration of war, the entire district of Whitechapel, along with Piccadilly and St. James's, which they had targeted. That casual action seemed hardly tolerable to the liberal English government that immediately replaced the conservative cabinet. By way of reprisal, Admiral Turnship launched a hundred hydroplanes that he happened to have in readiness against Berlin, and hollowed out a hole in Potsdam park a hundred meters in diameter and fifty deep.

Thus hostilities commenced, in a manner entirely different from what had been imagined—for there is no example on record of any conflagration, especially a European or German conflagration, beginning in the manner envisaged by the general staff on either side. When one expects a war of battle-lines, there is a war of rapid skirmishes, and vice versa. When one assumes that tanks, aircraft, anti-aircraft weapons, or poison gases will play a preponderant role, it is the converse that happens.

We still laugh when we remember the errors of our French and German forefathers drenching one another with microbial cultures supposed to be the causes of epidemics—in conformity with contemporary legend—which might as well have been cats'-piss. But so powerful is the dogmatization of a scientific hypothesis, and so durable is its tenacity, that it takes time to perceive such things. Then there was talk of the methodical disorganization of cyton, which, being non-existent, was not in danger of being disorganized. But how can one count all the mirages with which so-called civilized humans sometimes imagined that they might cure and protect themselves, and sometimes to attack and massacre one another?

When, at the hundredth hour, no snare became evident—no artificial tidal-wave, no chemico-electrical storm or earthquake, no fulgurant ray, launched by Germany against Belgium or France, there was an atrocious anguish for all the French, as for all the Belgians. Everyone envied the lot of the English, who at least knew what they were dealing with, and, without having wanted to, had entered into battle first.

Henriette, Sidoine and I, the unleashers of Kaninchen's secret, began to reassure ourselves, telling one another that the secret in question had not yet been communicated by the scientist to the Boche High Command and that the maleficent tube was a unique exemplar. Nevertheless, Sidoine was distressed to see his law violated and electro-magnetism employed, as before, with waves, for the propagation of news and the extermination of the human race.

Before shutting ourselves away, for an indefinite time, in Underground 7 and organizing there the intensive Archimedism that decides victory in modern warfare, Henriette and I wanted to take account of the ravages caused by the Napus. It was at Père-Lachaise alone, in the new buildings erected for that purpose, that rows of numbered plaques mentioned, with the names and forenames of the deceased, the place and date of their disappearance: an anthropometric service of a new kind, testifying to the intensity of the most singular and most inexplicable plague of all time.

In Paris, the disease had claimed its eleven thousand five hundred and ninety-fourth victim, with the fateful name of Monsieur Meureblanc, who had disappeared the previous day at the corner of the Rue Saint-Lazare and the Place de Rome, almost opposite the premises of *Action Française*. The curve of the Disease, increasing incessantly since the beginning, indicated a marked fall in the hours preceding the mobilization, but now we were in full ascensional recrudescence.

The old warden, approaching us with a distressed expression remarked, with a sigh: "You can see, Messieurs et Mesdames, that everything is happening at the same time, the war and this. What will become of us."

What would become of us? My God, that which has become

of all human beings since the immeasurable depths of time; that which ordinary, traditional graves indicate to us, whether fresh and covered with a new or nearly-new marble slab, or sunk into the ground and half-disappeared, with their dislocated grilles, or completely covered with stray creepers, nettles and dodder, like images of oblivion.

Never again would the brevity of life, its vicissitudes, its chagrins and its dreams appear to us in such sharp relief, with such a sharp autumnal etching. Never again, either, would that symbiosis of the vegetal and the human, which had become one of the great chapters of human knowledge, after century upon century of darkness, be offered to us with similar clarity and all its horizons. How had it been so long ignored or forgotten, in spite of dryads and Mediterranean or Celtic legends that depict souls captured by vegetation, imprisoned in the hollows of willows, oaks and olive-trees? Innumerable were the sepulchers of hard stone, corroded by the wind, the rain and incessant friction, that had been burst open by the vigorous growth of a seed, at the expense of one or more cadavers, the thrust of an acacia, an elm, an ask, an oak or a linden, and which seemed to have passed on to the tree the substance and the relic of a corpse, or several corpses of vanished human beings.

Here, planted upon an invisible but detectable skeleton, was the wood and the bark of a single jet, translating, or transmuting, in its vegetal impetuosity, that which the speaking being had never been able to yield or produce, mounting toward the heavens with a proud security. Further away, the heavens' response already appeared, with a collapse duplicating that of an apoplexy, or a pulmonary congestion, or a embolism, at twenty-two, or thirty, or fifty, or sixty: the fire of clouds after that of blood. There, before our bewildered gaze, three trunks, green at the base, rusty black higher up, climbed in parallel, and then in a kind of spiral, in the manner of an amorous searching for a perfect embrace, without finding it. One inferred that there were three cadavers there, of various epochs, a perhaps a father, mother and child, henceforth vegtalized, united in that other form of being, and a family, as they had been in the preceding one. With what heart we wished them *bon voyage*, for that new duration of one or two centuries, unless the caprice of a pruner of woodcutter of celestial fluid cut them down.

How evident, among all these symbioticized beings, seemed the sap departed from the opening of the portal vein, or the severed carotid, or even the sclerotized and broken heart, burst forth and remounting from there to the branches, via the sinuosities of the roots, then the verticality of the trunk or trunks. That the sap in question continued the blood or lymph there could be no doubt. That the foliage was itself merely a reprise, greatly increased and multiplied by the new respiratory function of the pulmonary foliage, nothing was more palpable.

One could even ask oneself, on departing from those immediate observations, whether veritable forests might not spring from immense ranks of sepulchers, or ancient battlefields; whether, where the vegetal abounds, the humus might have been fertilized by the cadaver before springing into arborescence.

At least, that view did not seem so absurd to my dear Henriette and myself, moved by the thought of those mute metamorphoses, in the midst of which we were walking. The sky, fresh and gilded, was not at all dramatic. Before serving for carnage, before the doors of iron and steel, the science that we loved opened its silver door there upon clear horizons, which overlook the poetry of logicians.

Doubtless the imminence of the inexpiable hostilities that were about to surge forth, combined with the new and constant threat of the Napus, excited our imagination at the same time as our faculty of reason. What laboratory, however provided by the imagination with apparatus of every sort, could match that vast, calm cemetery, where biologists, anatomists, historians, archeologists, philosophers, botanists and entomologists could, with a little attention and some liberation from current prejudices, work back to the discreet or secret exchanges of life! The chain is there, before our eyes, with its links scarcely separated; and it is laudable for us to reconstitute, at least for an important part of its journey: that which goes from decomposition to renewal.

If it is true, though, that only humans have souls, that only Catholic theology is truly inspired, with a mastery that defies the centuries, what is that spirit distinct from the soul, and also from matter, which associates, by narrow and invisible communications, the animal, the human and the vegetal? In vain we reconstitute in our retorts, cleverer and more sagacious than those of two or three hundred years ago, the substances that are found in living organisms. Those syntheses and syntheses of syntheses, far-reaching as we suppose them to be and grouped in such seductive theories that they give the illusion of truth, are merely a caricature of the animation of their molecules by life. Never is one further away, in our finest methods of research, from the solution of the vital problem than when one believes that one is close to it. There is a mysterious power therein, even more subtle than the Napus, which causes the barely-glimpsed mirage to fade away and vanish.

Until aphanasia, death appeared to be the material dissociation and return to the mould of substances aggregated, fused and hierarchically edified in organs. With aphanasia came the intervention of the unprecedented notion and abrupt passage of components to nothingness, with no intermediary. That was to be, with its recoil, the origin of a new metaphysical system, intermediary between miracle and current fact, which is only distinguished from miracle by the fact that our minds and eyes became used to it. For where is the fact of importance that, in its origin and unfathomable depths, is not miraculous? History, however logical, is merely a tissue of the miraculous that has escaped to the fatal and the expected.

While discussing that, Henriette and I made our way into an elevated sector of the cemetery, as rich in undergrowth, bushes and small trees as a displacement of the forest of Fontainebleau. We followed a path along the side of a hill, bordered by broken and slanting stones, cracked and collapsed marbles and grilles corroded by rust, from which new ash-trees, oaks and elms were launching forth. The bitter file of nocturnal specters that haunt the Parisian necropolis had become Birnam Wood. How many old relatives were there, as in the death of Breton legend, converted into receptacles for chattering, mocking and frivolous birds, re-linked nevertheless to the great and noble mystery of transubstantiation, taking account of it and celebrating it in their songs.

Everyone says and pretends that the nightingale and the blackbird sing for love, and improvise in its honor the symphonic orchestrations that left Henriette and myself breathless, but they certainly do not sing for love. In a different fashion from us, in accordance with a form of knowledge that escapes us, they too are taking account of the vegetalization of the disjointed remains of dead humankind—in a word, symbiosis. They are informing and warning one anther; they would like, being sociable and moderate propagandists, to inform us of it. Who can doubt that there is, in birds, a naturist apostolate of the perpetual transformations of these pockets of fire, water and molds that are living beings, if he has listened to the whistlers and trillers responding to one another, from branch to branch, by vibration and stridulation of a droplet of water in their tiny throats?

From another viewpoint, the cemetery, in the civic and incalculable form of Père-Lachaise, is like a projection of memory. It reproduces its abrupt failures, the collapses, the absences and also the disguises and metamorphoses. We members of the Aristotle Foundation, especially Polyplasts, for whom invention and discovery are everyday affairs, sense its affinities with memory with a particular vivacity. Many a time, seeking a link of cause and effect beneath the ferns and creepers of intuition, as others seek for a word or a date, do we not see that link flee us and disappear with a kind of psychological mischief? Try, then, to decipher, in spite of the encrusted moss and the corrosion of time, the name and date on that slab. The wear and tear is of the same kind, with regard to the past, that of a verbal root or a corpse. Dictionaries are cemeteries, in which few inscriptions remain legible, or even discernible. Here and there, someone erases the signs, and the signs of the signs, only allowing the brief play of light and shadow to subsist, on tombs or in the mnemonic realm.

All of a sudden, the cold gripped my delicate beautiful friend and myself, more coarsely-woven: the cold of the season, of the hour, of all those dead people, of the bellicose circumstances that advertised, once again, such depopulations; the cold of infinite space and of ignorance, around the poor fire of our hazardous suppositions. Death without remains could have surprised us, at that moment, and we would have accepted it in the name of symbiosis, in the name of the birds of the cemetery, and also in the name of that Providence to which it is necessary to come back when one has made, even and especially Polyplastically, the tour of everything.

For, according to what I have just explained, the fact that Our Lord, Jesus Christ, the only possible explanation of the Universe, died on the wood of a cross, called a "particular tree," takes on a precise significance. Among the abysms of light that circum- vent the mystery of the Passion and the connected mystery of the Incarnation, there shines a more blinding certainty. We both reflected upon it as we descended the sinuous slopes toward the threatened city.

CHAPTER FIVE
UNDERGROUND 7

"In an installation improvised by one or more intelligent women, things will find their place and everything will work fairly well. In an installation prepared by men, nothing will work and the most important things will have been omitted."

That axiom, proffered by Henriette Tastepain, lovelier and subtler than ever, was soon verified. Underground 7 had been fitted out by competent technicians. The Polyplasts had been consulted. The great leaders, Ailette, Sidoine, Eustache and the late Madame Grégeois had been consulted. Even I had been consulted. Spies had supplied us with the plans of a termitary analogous to our own designed in Berlin by Kaninchen. The lighting, the electric heating, the laboratories sheltered from all shocks, the superoxygenated ventilation, the indicative and biographical plaques in case of Napus, the cinetext libraries, the files, the magnetic cremation of the dead with remains—everything had been foreseen. Incredibly, however, the provisions had been forgotten, as if scientists would be able to aliment themselves on proteic, chemical and atomic substances or eat one another.

It was Henriette who discovered that enormous omission. "What about the refectories?" she asked, naively.

The architect, Polyplast 15,714, nearly fell over.

In a besieged city there can be no question of anything but preserved foods. Ten thousand cans were immediately ordered from Underground 18, which was that of the grocers, and an entire laboratory was converted into a dining room capable of containing the present personnel of the Aristotle Foundation, which amounted to ninety-two individuals.

Each of us, finding accommodation as best we could, cursed Sidoine, the indirect cause of the war, who was about to live in the midst of an indescribable orgy of the kinds of apparatus that were, according to him, the effective cause of the Napus, and which he claimed to have suppressed. We calculated that our subterranean refuge would be traversed by sixty-three waves and force-rays of different qualities and velocities, in extreme inclinations that were supposedly inoffensive—but that, according to Sidoine, was precisely where the error lay. I ought to say, though, that the author of the unapplied law was much less unstable and absolute than usual, either because the worldwide importance that he had acquired with his sacred law had appeased his immense vanity, or because he was afraid of his responsibilities and wanted to mollify us.

There are scientists like that, who seem to have been predestined to a multiplicity of scourges. Thus, some four hundred years ago, the illustrious Berthelot discovered, or rediscovered, the fabrication and use of explosives, taken since then by the Boches to a formidable degree of power and perfection. Thus, a century ago, the physicist Mab—like the queen of the same name—set out the principles of determined invisibility in a work that was fortunately destroyed, along with his manuscript notes, in the antiscientific revolution of 2114. All that we know about it today is that Mab, studying the principle of hundred-million-volt hyperluminosity, discovered that the maximum point of it was tangential to invisibility. Such a discovery, if it had entered into the order of practical realizations, would have rendered the planet uninhabitable, by virtue of the facility accorded to thieves, murderers, arsonists, profaners, and lunatics of every sort to carry out their misdeeds with impunity.

Although preferring not to have lived in the time of the barbaric revolution of 2114, I am glad that it annihilated the works of Mab, who, like Kaninchen, and very fortunately, had not confided his secrets of manufacture, or even his calculations, to anyone else. It is regrettable that the rioters, all workers or specialized petty proprietors, had not abolished the science of explosives at the same time. That one was, unfortunately, too widespread, and it would have required the extermination of too many people in too short a time.

In the seventy-two hours that followed our move, there was no topic of discussion except the bizarre auspices in which hostilities had been engaged. The excellent Germans, as our pacifists had called them a week before, appeared to be devoting themselves exclusively to the methodical bombing of the British Isles—including Ireland—and English colonies, India and Egypt in particular. Such was the determination of the Emperor, a hereditary revivification of the astonishing Wilhelm II, who had once allowed his entourage of financiers and industrialists to impose the absurd war of 1914-18—which was no more absurd than the anti-Sidoinian war of 2227.

Those Prussian-born princes, prey to the simian rot revealed by the great Tissot[16] of the twentieth century, and which was called, for a long time—when people still believed in microbes—*Treponema pallidum*, or the pale spirochaete, all have a martial mania surpassing that of many Polyplasts. They also have a congenital infirmity, an outflow from the ear, the nose, the navel and shameful parts, which periodically puts them in a bad and reckless mood. The entourage knows that and takes advantage of it. Unfortunately, all of Germany is constructed on an analogous model, with no visible end; after Prussia, it is Bavaria, then Saxony—under another pretext, of course—and then the city of Hamburg, that will pick a quarrel with Europe.

So, for the moment, the Boche spared France, Belgium, Italy

---

16. The Swiss physician Samuel-Auguste Tissot wrote textbooks on the disease of the poor, the diseases of the rich, the diseases of men of letters, migraines, and masturbation (which he treated as a debilitating illness). He was not, however, particularly associated with work on *Treponema pallidum*, the bacterium that causes syphilis, so Daudet's reference might be mistaken.

and Rumania—with what perfidious intention? we wondered—and sprinkled the most beautiful flowers of the English crown with explosives. The latter, after having believed, traditionally and historically, in the good intentions of the *Jas*, set about riposting in a forceful manner. It was generally reckoned, fifteen months later, that the English aerial bombardment equaled, if it did not surpass, the German.

In the meantime, the Indians, Egyptians and Canadians were copiously sprinkled at a rate of two bombs per square kilometer every twenty-four hours. The newspapers controlled by Noirpelat, Tavajus, Tiqueton and Barouille assured us "that it had resulted in great discontent among the population."

The same papers claimed that, if the German general staff had not attacked us, it was because of the atrocious fear they had of the new inventions of the Aristotle Foundation. We laughed among ourselves at that confidence.

There remained America. We were wondering what was cooking there when the wireless transmitted to us, in code, the following surprising news:

> *News from Wall Street seems to indicate that the United States have resolved to confine themselves, whatever the Germans do, to a form of hostility limited to financial warfare. The independent financiers are at work and have already, in a matter of hours, brought the famous Allegemeine Elektricität-Gesellschaft, the center of Teuton resistance to the Sidoine law* (Americans say "the Teutons"—nobody knows why) *to its knees. Four thousand German industrial and commercial organizations are already bankrupt, as well as their branches in Russia and China.*

That affirmation was exaggerated, as we subsequently discovered. A territory of Germano-Russian colonization for more than twelve generations, China had not allowed free rein to the American independent financiers, for its specialists were as good as, if not better than, the Yankees. Since the Chinese, Polyplasts or not, had devoted themselves to banking, with a traditional and millennia-old assiduity, they had caused the wiliest professionals in the entire world to wonder at their mental calculations. While others, in chess terminology, only thought four moves ahead, the Chinese, without apparent effort, went as far as twelve: "He does that, I do that; he ripostes thus, I counter thus; if he goes that way, I go this; if he retreats to there, I pursue from here...." and so on, for twelve alternatives hypothetically resolved. That explains why the merchants of Chinese excrement have all become merchants of paper money.

This information was confirmed by two Chinese scientists who came to Paris by aircraft at the first news of hostilities, one of whom was named Tchi-fao—in Korean, "Root of Exemplary Wisdom Extended to the Fourteenth Generation"—and the other Thou Sing Pe: "Astonishment of the Young Woman before the Cadaver of her Father murdered at Sunrise" in old Manchu. The two yellow men seemed very curious about Underground 7, a form of refuge employed by them, they assured us, as early as the eleventh century, on the occasion of a war caused by a new way of protecting rice from locusts.

We asked them about the progress of the Napus in their homeland, showing them its ideogram. After refined politenesses whose display lasted twenty minutes, they declared that they had been justly struck by the plague and were ready for repentance—they explained, smiling, that their form of the Napus, with the "tiny reeking footprint" had not budged. The people, with the exclusion of the mandarins, had become accustomed to the Disease to the extent that they imagined that the "footprint" had increased, without, however, becoming proportional to the stature of the napusified individual, and that its maker had diminished.

There was nothing to it.

After which, Root of Exemplary Wisdom and Astonishment of the Young Woman visited our subterranean installations—to a depth of three hundred meters, if you please—with all sorts of expressions of wonderment. It was not until later that we learned that they had used almost all the relevant methods of defense eleven hundred years earlier against a jet of exploding and shattering stones projected with incalculable force invented by the scientist-poets of Upper Annam and spread throughout the Celestial Empire. The manufacture of those stones, which were too dangerous to handle, had fallen into disuse in the wake of various edicts of the Dragon. The subterranean laboratory-refuges had disappeared with them.

As indifferent to the war as to the Napus, our Chinese guests seemed to be avid for information about protection by dirt—the Pafenier system—also considered, not so long ago, among them as among us, as disinfectant. Just as they preserved eggs for a hundred years, they conserved dirt scraped from the skins of their ancestors for a hundred and fifty or two hundred years in white porcelain pots of the famous Lao-Mang dynasty. They promised to send us some.

I told them about the adventure of Kaninchen and his little tube. They were delighted by it, being well acquainted with the German scientist, who had stayed for some time in Canton, in order to study certain poisonous mushrooms that only grew there, with a view to the war. In their country, they confided to us, anyone who undertook, by any means whatsoever, to kill his fellow, had to be subjected to "death by general meditation"—which is to say that, for two minutes a day, everyone implored the Dragon for his suppression. An entire school of recent Chinese philosophy attributed the Napus with petty remains to a kind of excess of those communal prayers.

Several of our Polyplasts, who had Chinese blood in their veins—as is my case—became attached to these visitors, to the point that their departure caused us genuine grief. They were, however, charged by their government with tracking the hostilities and the movements of minds throughout the capitals of the world. They wanted to assure us that their hearts "with their dependencies and their thousands of red veins," according to the consecrated formula, would remain in Underground 7.

Tchi-fao gave me a fetish that assures its bearer of the precious indifference of his fellows—for, according to the Chinese doctrine, misfortune comes from the fact that we are sometimes liked and sometimes detested by others of our generation; the fortunate man is the one to whom no one talks or of whom no one takes any notice, who is a matter of complete indifference even to his wife, his children and his parents. "He then rolls like a beautiful pearl over the satin slope of a jewel-casket."

The next day, when the yellow charmers departed, the rumor spread that a dull rumbling, accompanied by grating sounds, could be heard a few hundred leagues away in the direction of the Eastern frontier. Was it some German stratagem?

Equipped with electric ears, which permitted a sound to be identified at a distance of four hundred and forty kilometers, we lay down on the floor of our laboratories, keeping watch until the classifier had eliminated all incidental or accessory auditory communications. In fact, the quivering of burrowing insects can give rise to numerous errors.

Sidoine, clinging to his hobby-horse, tried in vain to dissuade us from putting out temples to the apparatus, which he judged the most maleficent and napusigenic of all. Events appeared to prove him right. The aphanasia of our 14,026 was the first case of subterranean Napus in shelter 7. It was a great loss. Without possessing the inventive faculties of a Sidoine or a Kaninchen, 14,026 was a living nomenclature, a walking bibliography, an incomparable maker of files, such that we would never see his like again. Our regret was attenuated by the observation of the rituals due, on Earth, to the absence of remains. A few prayers, a little commemorative plaque that would be transported to Père-Lachaise at the first opportunity, and that was all.

Eustache, also pursuing his damned hobby-horse, had demanded the transfer into a vast room in the 7, of some two hundred cinebooks, with which he intended to experiment on German prisoners, from the viewpoint of the etiology of the Napus. The whole issue depended on whether, in such a form of war, prisoners were ever taken, and whether the German might not content themselves with crushing the British Empire with explosives. They had already destroyed a third of London, half of Alexandria, a quarter of Bombay, the fortress of Gibraltar and the Suez Canal.

The German newspapers, communicated to us by wireless, made no mention of these events and no longer contained, since the mobilization, any allusion to matters of war. That was by order of the sovereign and was, in fact, the best means of avoiding any indiscretion. The Franco-Belgian and Franco-Italian troops, for their part, had not yet moved forward and were awaiting events. That had motivated a critical question in the Chambre, but, the député who had tabled the question having been struck by aphanasia before being able to develop his theme, superstition prevented the criticism being taken up by any of his colleagues.

After the yellow men came the black. Listening devices signaled that an immense dirigible manned by only two individuals had left the banks of the Tanganyika with an international safe-conduct and was heading for Paris. Shortly afterwards, a negro scientist entirely whitened by the Napus disembarked, who answered to the harmonious name of Gamba-Toto. His pale thick-lipped face bore the marks of two superimposed dreads. One was recent, experienced on discovering from above a Paris deserted and seemingly abandoned, the war-afflicted Paris whose life had taken refuge underground. The other was older and more concentrated, tugging at the lesser-known muscles of the face—which was explained as follows: the maleficent Chinese "footprint" brought back by the first crew some time before had caused trouble in Central Africa and had complicated, in disquieting proportions, the symptoms of the particular aphanasia of the race of Ham, principally the discoloration of the skin. Having heard mention of Ailette's broth, Gamba-Toto, who was a singular mixture of real science and fetishism, had come to ask us for ten thousand jars, at a good price, with which he wanted to fill his dirigible.

That request was welcome; in fact, our funds had run low;

Ailette's broth was a vast commercial hoax, which had never protected anyone from the Disease, and once its initial vogue had passed, we had a remaining stock that was rather difficult to shift. Gamba-Toto paid us in gold bars—a marvelous thing!—for the mixture, which was almost as nauseating as the Chinese "footprints." He also paid in gold for the truck charged with transporting it. He handed over a hundred gold bars, each of a hundred kilograms, to the Foundation on behalf of the Albert Nyanza Academy of Sciences, a rival of Tanganyika's. His eyes shone with gratitude as he did so, and he swore that two whole centuries would not expunge the gratitude of his fellow citizens.

We could never have imagined such a stroke of good luck. A banquet was held for him, as well as his mechanic and pilot Toto-Gamba—a servant's name being formed by reversing that of his master—in our large subterranean dining-room. The menu, entirely composed of tinned food—American, admittedly—regaled our two discolored guests to the extent that they remained at table for three hours, before dishes that all resembled one another, in appearance as well as taste; the lobster resembled the beef, which scarcely differed from the ham, which could easily be confused with the chicken.

On the other hand, the wine was of good quality, being a Beaujolais and, furthermore, from Morgon, furnished more than ten years before by my poor defunct Mouillemouillard, the owner of a vineyard in that fortunate region. Having absorbed more than five bottles of it, Gamba-Toto slid under the table during the toasts. It was Toto-Gamba who listened to them gravely, albeit without understanding a single word, and replying to us in his cumbersome language: "Sera meva, lepto tokani, sera kani, lepto meva." We never obtained a translation of this polysyllabic puzzle, for good reason. Henriette claimed that the meaning would have been indecent, because she had felt herself blushing, but that could have been indigestion.

On that occasion, I took account of the ravages of envy in an organism devoted to science. Sidoine and Eustache, who had no broth to sell, darted glances of hatred at Ailette, who was sitting between two gold bars. Gamba-Toto, not yet drunk, took no more notice of them than the laboratory technicians, and, when he had recovered his senses, he only had eyes for Ailette and the ladies of the Foundation. He went so far as to offer to buy Henriette for her weight in gold and take her aboard as his slave—for the high-ranking civilized Africans had reestablished slavery to the detriment of whites. That was what rendered the aggravation of the Napus discoloration so redoubtable for them. Along with their epidermal polish they lost their civil rights and conjugal authority, as well as the consideration of their entourage. Several generals of the African lakes had been demoted following the accident in question, several admirals relieved of command, several Academicians stripped of their laurels and countless husbands cuckolded.

Since I am recording the events of that historical period here I ought to identify another unexpected consequence of the Napus, doubtless of the same order as the gigantification of mushrooms and the shrinking of elephants. The Australians notified us that the marsupials and other biplacentaries of that eccentric part of the world, comparable to a planetary excrescence, had become monoplacentary. That kind of re-entry into the natural order of gestation was admittedly troubling. Might not the hidden biological force that we called the Napus be comprised of two or three divergent forces, acting differently in different places?

The silence of the German newspapers with regard to the war suddenly ceased with regard to a single point. All the papers in the Empire inserted, on the same day and in the same place, as if marching in step, the following news item:

> Every patriotic German knowing approximately what is involved, and the Ministry of War having an interest in preserving real surprises for our enemies, we have not so far mentioned in our columns that state of general hostility prompted by the French pretention of forcing the adoption of the absurd, unjust and retrograde Sidoine law by the League of Nations.

Nevertheless, it is necessary for us to make an exception with regard to the monetary conflict, or financial war, with the United States of America. We have just unleashed, to our profit and with complete success, a veritable "markian" offensive on the market of the proud nation of the dollar.

It is a matter of the famous Analgesic paper money invented by the late Professor Murmelthier shortly before his murder the French Academician Lepoil at the Parisian Napus Conference. These bills, made of an antidolorous and euphoric—but not addictive—paper with doses of a between a hundred and a thousand hours, and corresponding values, suppress all suffering, mental and physical, by means of a simple application to the skin for the duration inscribed on each one. The first two issues have had a prodigious success, in New York as in Amsterdam and Berlin, and are at a premium on the Wall Street stock exchange, depreciating the dollar by sixty per cent at the day's close. Once again, German science has vanquished the barbaric coalition. This immense victory will certainly demoralize all the nations reliant on the American dollar, and lead them to useful reflections.

We thought at first that it was a joke, one of those vast hoaxes that the race of *Ja*s willingly launch, but having immediately entered into wireless communication with the Boston branch of the Aristotle Foundation, we received confirmation of the news. The Boche had succeeded in the stupendous coup of repositioning the monetary axis on the cessation of all pain, instead of it being based on the capacity of exchange and purchasing power. Pain having recently been multiplied, on the plane of apprehension, as on that of unexpected mourning, by the epidemic of the Napus, the circulation of Analgos—as the new bills were dubbed—was somewhat indefinite and defied inflation.

Evidently, in the same way that gold money is founded on its rarity, analgo was founded on the secret of its antidolorous preparation, but Murmelthier, before disappearing, had been able to confuse its analysis by means of an insoluble cryptochemistry of a special type. The scientist had invented and applied all the *cryptons* currently in usage, which permitted any patent to be protected in any country without fear of any possible indiscretion. The manufacture of substances, or items of covert apparatus, is carried out by assembling components or substances separated by thousand of leagues, which are themselves only designated by combinations of numbers and complex calculations. To be a doctor of *crypton* it is necessary to be a Polyplast of German preponderance and to have spent two years in a school of arcana, in which no pupil knows anything about his comrades or the masters, who are changed incessantly without the course syllabus being modified by an iota.

There was, therefore, no chance of ever extracting the formula for Analgo from the German cryptons, just as there was no chance that the composition of the contents of the Kaninchen tube would ever be divulged. But while Kaninchen had taken his secret into the atmosphere in which he had been scattered without remains, Murmelthier had bequeathed the coating of the antidollar bill to someone else. A veritable financial revolution was under way.

It is curious that the innumerable and prompt means of modern communication realized between peoples has not ended up by fusing them together, and, on the contrary, has accentuated their differences. Within a minute, from our Underground, we could communicate with New York, we could see our interlocutor, we could hear the noises of the street and hear the cries of newspaper-sellers—and yet, it was impossible for us to take account of the effect of the surprise provoked by the launch of Analgo, and the collapse of the dollar before that new rival of an unprecedented type. This is a approximate rendering of a conversation with a Polyplast of our brother organization over there:

"Well, can't the coating be analyzed?"

"No it can't. It's a Murmelthier. That name says it all."

"What color is it?"

"White, slightly tinged with blue, but a blue with red gleams."

"What reagent dissolves it?"

"None."

"Are you sure of that?"

"As certain as I am of your voice. There's panic on the markets here. The dollar's only at parity with the mark."

"And how does it stand against the franc?"

"The franc is no longer quoted. The Analgo's at a premium everywhere; even the greatest patriots here are declaring it admirable and immediately effective. No one any longer has any pain, or any apprehension, from the moment that it's applied."

"Send us a specimen."

That arrived two hours later, by wave-transport. It was a hundred-Analgo bill, which we immediately tried out on Eustache, who was suffering from an intense migraine, accompanied, as I've said, by a sharp crisis of envy. Before commencing the experiment, however, suspicious of Boche "booby traps," always with a double trigger, we slipped an antipithiatic pill into Eustache's right-hand jacket pocket. That remedy against the power of persuasion,[17] discovered some time ago by the celebrated Babinsky, the brother of the master gastronome of the same name, immediately reveals the component of bluff or suggestion in any new method or discovery.

Eustache's migraine persisted, and throughout the time that the application of the analgo lasted, he never ceased slandering Ailette and making fun of his broth, incapable even of recol-

---

17. The author inserts a footnote: "from the Greek *peïtheïn*, or persuader." Crediting the discovery of the antipithiatic pill to someone named Babinsky is a joke, as the Paris-born Polish neuroscientist Joseph Baninski had been a key collaborator of Charcot's in developing the study of hysteria (in which Daudet did not believe) and had developed the concept of "pithiatism," subsequently associated with "shell shock" in his *Hysteropithiatisme en neurologie de guerre* (1917), in that context. Joseph Babinski's brother Henri was an engineer and also a famous cook, who published a culinary guide-book under the pseudonym "Ali Baba."

oring a napusified negro.

Now, we had in the Underground a veritable American patriot by the name of Sterlett, who could not stand the Germans since one of them had got him involved in a disastrous chemical products business and ruined him completely. The fellow in question, very sportive, like the majority of his compatriots, immediately grasped the importance of the trial carried out on Eustache, and resolved to alert his compatriots, thus saving the dollar. It was important to him that the revelation of the deception by persuasion should come from America itself and not France, the sons of Uncle Sam being very ticklish with regard to nationalistic sentiment.

I went in search of the Minister of Aviation, in the midst of his grave preoccupations, and, after having briefly brought him up to date, asked for an ultra-rapid wave-aircraft for Sterlett, which was immediately granted to me. Sterlett embarked full of hope, convinced that he was going to undeceive his fellow citizens and save his nation's currency.

It is always the unexpected that occurs. Four days later, Sterling came back, disconcerted, Murtmelthier's gift of persuasion had continued to act, via the analgo, in such a fashion that the President of the United States and the most important ministers had sent the delegate of the Parisian Aristotle Foundation, who was trying to prevent their ruin, packing. There had been but one cry from the council in the White House: "What is that imbecile trying to do to us?" The most deliberate nation of the twenty-third century—but certainly not the most reflective—preferred the analgesic delusion, with bankruptcy, to disillusionment and pain without.

In the meantime, in Berlin and in the university centers of the Empire, the students celebrated the dollar's funeral with derision. In the Wilhelm XIII-platz a giant statue of Murmelthier had been erected by the syndicate of pharmacists, in compressed and marmorized newsprint, bearing the colossal inscription: *To our Master Murmelthier, treacherously murdered by the French Academician Lepoil.* The enormous sums plundered from the world market by the Analgo coup were devoted to military preparations, of which the crypton has, alas, jealously kept the secret until the present day.

The inhabitants of Paris and large French cities in general who had not yet found places in the Undergrounds had dispersed into the countryside, safer from aerial bombardment, and preferentially into the forests. A significant fraction of the population thus reverted to a primitive and nomadic state, living on roots and abandoning all occupations except hunting, fishing and weaving garments. The fugitives were aggregated in professional groups and neighboring social categories; it was marvelous that, in the midst of such panic and confusion, there were still classes, precedences, masters and servants, pretention and snobbery, braggarts and bigots, determined thinkers and philosophers. Such mobile communities were identified in Artois, in the woods and heartland of Brittany, in the Franche-Conté, the Cévennes, the Forez, on the banks of the Loire and the Garonne, in the solitudes of the Alps and the Pyrenees. Those cinematic and remarkably photogenic scenes, filmed by skillful camera-men, figure today in a large number of cinetexts, which editors refuse to publish, saying: "Oh, please—enough scenes of war anxiety!"

As the Napus continued its ravages, those afflicted with bombardment phobia, scattered throughout rural France, invented ceremonies, initially differing according to region but gradually codified and unified, designed to commemorate aphanasia. The religious element intervened therein, as in the traditional "end of the year," but a biographical remembrance of the career and virtues of the deceased replaced the habitual sermon. It was remarked that the need to make speeches about everything, especially death, so widespread among our compatriots, had not been attenuated or diminished by the Napus, nor by the preliminaries of the new European war, in spite of he anguish they caused. The pronunciation of what was called the *laudatus* or *laudata*, according to the sex of the annihilated individual resulted in a certain vanity—in what strange places is it found!—being attached to the families most tested by the Disease, and a tendency was observed therein to consider themselves as an aristocracy.

In the Undergrounds themselves, the particular psychology of captivity reigned, unmodified by generous supplies of oxygen or by artificial sunlight—whose glare was, in any case, rationed, because of the expense involved. Love took on a melancholy ardor, analogous to that caused by distance between the lovers. Opportunities for Henriette and myself to speak to one another freely, with open hearts, were rare. Polyplasts of both sexes slept in separate dormitories by reason of imminent alerts, in order that everyone could be on their feet at the same time and in a position to take up battle stations. Twice a week we were allowed to retire in couples to the Foundation's thirty bedrooms, and I shall leave it to the imagination what pleasantries, of a rather liberal tone, were born of that regimentation.

Regimentation too is a consequence of captivity, whether it is a matter of a prison, a labor-camp or a ship—navigation is a form of incarceration by the element of water—or the customs imposed on an aircraft, in a railway-carriage, a barracks, a lighthouse, an observatory and, in general, any limited space in which it is necessary to accommodate oneself, with or without companions.

Every morning, in the vast corridors of the mosaic—sunlit, as I have said—every member of the Foundation went to consult the timetable and inform himself, in the most Anglo-Saxon fashion in the world—of things to be done or not to be done, of what was permitted on even-numbered days and forbidden on odd-numbered days. Henriette had a deplorable tendency to defy the schedule and follow her whims, which earned her reprimands from Ailette and the recently-promoted professors.

The declaration of war, even without apparent hostilities— the invisible war, as one Minister put it—had developed a sentiment of hierarchy in all the scientists, provided with the equivalent of military ranks. It was thus that Sidoine declared himself to be Eustache's superior, because he had one golden thread more than him, and tried to forbid him to develop his favorite thesis of cinetext as the cause of the Napus. Eustache refused, of course, which resulted in comical conflicts, in the wake of which Sidoine inflicted on his rival five days' imprisonment, the maximum penalty permitted by the Foundation's War Code. The punishment was entirely Platonic, our subterranean abode already surpassing in rigor all regimental prisons.

Ailette, provided with an intersecting double silver braid—a very rare distinction—by virtue of the famous broth, had the right to a full salute, which had fallen into disuse twenty years before, and which consisted of circling around a superior while raising a hand to the right temple, then to the middle of the forehead and then to the left temple. He started demanding that salute from every Polyplast he encountered in the corridors of the Foundation. Required to carry out that tiresome pantomime, the Polyplast completed it with a regulation thumbing of the nose, which Ailette pretended not to see.

Thus developed rancor, and then hatred—which, like love, is merely the combination of a host of petty impressions instituted by an initial shock. If the shock is voluptuous, there will be love; if it is dolorous, there will be hate, and everything that follows thereafter will be inscribed under the rubric of one or other column. Never will a person you detest do you, in your estimation, any good. Never will a person you love be wrong, in your eyes, in any respect whatsoever. The observation is banal, but gains in savor and accent in the bosom of captivity.

There was no longer any petty gesture or physiognomic change on Henriette's part that did not fill me with morose delight. There were no bad sentiments that were not inspired in me by the memory of the unfortunate Grégeois. Every day exaggerated my rancor against the stupid Mouillemouillard and his mendacious declaration to von Tschuppe regarding Murmelthier's death. Finally, the noxious odor of the Napusian Chinese "footprint" became incrusted in my nostrils to the point of preventing me from sleeping.

The protective role attributed to dirt with regard to the

Napus had caused the suppression of baths, previously imposed as a hygienic measure even on peasant populations. From that originated the institution of "substitutes," who, in many of our villages, took the obligatory bath of a male or female neighbor in return for some favor, thus defrauding the inspectors. It was, in any case, noticeable that the bathing legislation had accentuated, in disquieting proportions, the decline in the birth-rate, although the prohibition of baths fortunately reversed the trend.

An analogous observation, according to Sterlett, had been made in America, where prohibitions changed direction radically every thirty-five years. Periods of obligatory dirtiness are always much more prolific than periods of obligatory cleanliness. It is the same for the periods in which people drink wine and spirits, in relation to those in which it is prohibited. In America, where it is forbidden, under threat of a heavy fine, to urinate more than twice a day—the 2007 edict of President Oldmanner—inflammations of the bladder and urethra are more frequent and painful than in Australia, where President Smith ordered urination at least four times in every twenty-four hours.

As for the concentration of thought claimed to result from captivity and involuntary confinement in a cell—our Underground was a network of cells—that is a joke. Cages are the enemy of thought, which can only take flight in height or in depth, in development or involution, in a straight line or in zigzags, if it corresponds to a free body, which nothing constrains in its expansion or its movement. On the plane of the organism, thought is a prolongation of movement, itself the issue of that ultra-rapid mental action, that imaginative reflex known as the will. There is a circulation within it, as in everything else concerning human beings, inscribed down here like stars of flesh and spirit, under the sign of gravitation.

You might raise the objection of monks, the guardians of Western civilization, maintained by them and their meditations through centuries of darkness, but these cases are different. Monastic claustration was voluntary, designed to concentrate, with the image of the crucifixion, that of the sacrifice accomplished by the Savior of the world. There is nothing of that in scientific claustration in the laboratory, where the indigence of meditation is poorly remedied by the cuisine of experience.

For the second time, a dull and profound sound reached our ears, sensitized by silence as the eye is sensitized by darkness. It seemed to be coming from the entrails of the earth, but no oscillation was recorded by the seismograph, and we did not receive any news or warning from any part of the world with which our wave-transmitting apparatus was in communication of any kind of cataclysm. We were told, in the course of our studies, to beware of communal mirages, a coarse but frequent phenomenon, and the hazardous conclusions that might be drawn therefrom.

That same day, a note reached us from the office of the Minister of Public Information warning us against the mental state of catastrophic expectation that accompanies and follows general mobilization in our era. We were recommended, as was the rest of the population, to distract ourselves and chase away preoccupations by whatever means were available to us, and, in particular, not to remain strictly confined.

That was wise. The fact is that many people, ignorant or semi-ignorant, or scientists, had had recourse to colloidal narcotics, which put people to sleep for three or six months, remaining thus in the insensible torpor of hibernating animals, discouraging those around them and failing in their civic duty, which is to submit to bombardment without complaint. There followed a list of official pedestrian excursions permitted, within a radius of fifty kilometers around each habitation or Underground. By way of an exception, the Foundations and Academies had the right to motorized transport.

Scientists are the most docile of human beings. We might set fire to the universe with our inventions, or be subject to the deformations caused by human malignity, but we never rebel against an administrative decision, even if we estimate it to be pointless, absurd or dangerous. The Aristotle Foundation resolved to set a good example and take a trip as a body in the direction of Corbeil.

Why Corbeil? Because the inhabitants of that pretty location, situated on the banks of the Seine, had erected a statue to Ailette, their fellow citizen, for his marvelous discovery of the antinsapusian broth.

Leaving two guards at the Foundation—which was amply sufficient in view of the multitude of surveillance and autoprotection devices—we climbed into three electric vehicles, each containing thirty people, with sixty cans of food and a large packet of tablets of so-called excursion wine. Only Sterlett encumbered himself with a bottle of natural Burgundy wine, presently obligatory for Americans after the emergence from a period of prohibition.

Since the hecatombs of the year 2110, when, during the vacation period, a hundred thousand French men and women, crushers and crushed, had perished by virtue of the excessive speed of automobiles—that was the time of the two hundred and fifty an hour—it had been forbidden for ordinary mortals to exceed an average speed of thirty kilometers an hour, which permitted the admiration of the landscape and also kissing— something impossible, under the old system, without breaking jaws. The presence of an average of ten Polyplasts, originally intended to keep the peace, for every hundred persons increased the license to a speed of forty kph. That restriction contrasted with the immense amplitude of aerial, ondic, marine or subterrestrial speeds—the last in autoexacavators or autoborers— which Sidoine held responsible for the Napus.

Thus, we departed in a convoy. Seated between my beloved and an indifferent Polyplast, I nestled close to her, and thus displeased the Polyplast, whom I subsequently discovered to be named 4,030 and to be a hybrid of Persian, Arab, Austrian and Parisian. He was the most savagely bellicose individual I had ever met. He never ceased looking forward to the moment when one could reduce an enemy army to pulp just be pressing a button. He seemed to have concentrated within him all the ferocious savagery of the first three blood-lines in his make-up, with a leisurely and debonair accent that came from the quarter of pantruchian origin.[18]

The "legal excursions" whose paths we crossed beneath a cloudy autumnal sky, composed of people of all ages and social levels, gave an impression of anxiety. In order to please the Prefect of Police—who, in order to reassure the public, was wearing a glittering fireman's uniform—the poor pedestrians put on sad little forced smiles.

"Well, Monsieur le Préfet," I said, taking advantage of a pause, "when are you going to visit Underground 7?"

His only response was to point to the sky, where a circular green glow had appeared, reminiscent of that of discolored negroes.

Two hundred years ago, the region that begins at Maisons-Alfort and continues through Villeneuve-Saint-Georges, Dravail and Champrosay was prosperous—which is to say that it was bristling with little houses disposed in a checkerboard pattern, constructed on the sites of the great and beautiful dwellings of previous ages and the parks attached to them. There was a general fragmentation, the consequence of the old law of inheritance and division enforced by the Napoléonic Code. The latter, a military man of genius, after the fashion of Alexander or Caesar, but imbued with democratic, and therefore revolutionary principles, is nowadays deservedly reputed to have been an imbecilic and dangerous legislator.

Monarchical wisdom has once again come into play, and there is no Frenchman who does not think with terror of what the war of the Napus might have produced in a Republic—which is to say, a chronic state of disorder. With the monarchy restored, the indefinite parceling out of property ceased, and, in consequence, forced division and bad finance, and the era of estates with dependencies returned, in which many people live in the family organization most useful to the nation. The fabric

18. *Pantruche* is an argot term that initially referred to a *pantin* [puppet] and then, by a mysterious process of association, became to be applied to Paris.

of the earth is no longer in tatters, fragments of fragments. They form a vestment again.

The return of the estate marked the renewal of an architecture more comfortable than the original, inspired by the eighteenth century and sufficient, likewise, to reawaken painters in stone, who were not merely landscape artists or portraitists. Thus all things hold together, and the amelioration of a small legal text can bring forth beautiful buildings, prevent social convulsions and provoke talents of every sort.

Henriette and I played an innocent game, which consisted of choosing a property for the day of our retirement. In fact, reciprocal love and the prospect of marriage and children had gradually diminished the excessive scientific ardor in our hearts and would end up drying it up. In my composite heredity, a sensible individuality became predominant, whose announcement would have made me laugh—the ironic and distinctive laughter of a Polyplast—had anyone spoken about it to me before. That slow metamorphosis, about which we conversed in our leisure time, proved that any extrinsic scheme with a view to orientating the infinitely malleable being that we are toward one specialization or another, physical or mental, is a chimera.

Sidoine, who was in our vehicle, called the caravan to a halt. The region of Draveil, where we were, had once been littered with factories producing chemicals and other substances that had revolutionized a previously placid population, which had become peaceful again after the disappearance of those houses of hate. That return to normality was not merely a consequence of royalty; it was also due to the antiscientific revolution of 2214, whose excesses Sidonie—a scientist himself—deplored, but which he recognized to have been well-founded in certain respects. Was he not the author of the antielectric and antiondic law, which had just raised Germany against us?

"I'm convinced," he said, "that industrial cycles, with their cortege of social evils, return periodically in different regions of the earth, where they bring, along with indisputable material ameliorations, run, revolution and war. It's also that conviction which unleashed among our forefathers, a hundred and thirteen years ago, that fit of devastating wrath in which the majority of the great enterprises in oil, rubber, paper, cement and others were almost obliterated."

We were scarcely disposed, however, to listen to considerations of that sort. We were observing the green glow on the horizon, whose circular form was that of a ring, darker at the center. Some thought it was an aurora borealis, others that it was a maleficent invention of the Germans.

"It's extraordinary, all the same, that they haven't given any sign of death since the declaration of war, especially since the fall of the dollar and the circulation of the Analgo."

That observation by a Polyplast summarized the general opinion.

Sidoine opined that the Prussians, still the conductors and the champions of the Germanic nation, were experimenting with a state intermediate between war and peace, a kind of armed vigilance permitting brief raids akin to corsair incursions.

Thus engaged in discussion, we arrived at the village of Champrosay, where two beautiful gardens descended a gentle slope toward the Seine. There, in the nineteenth century, had lived the painter Eugène Delacroix, whose entire oeuvre has disappeared, with the exception of a single painting, representing an old peasant, the one who had rented him the house in which he had constructed a studio. Later, Alphonse Daudet, the novelist most widely read today, after an eclipse of a century, lived in Champrosay in three different houses, of which no vestige remains today. It is said that he wrote the scenario to *L'Arlésienne* there. The general farmer Polydore has restored that pleasant town, closer to the bank of the Seine, replanted a grove of poplars, which had the merit of breaking up the frequent storms, and has even put his mark on the beautiful fountains, imitations of Juvisy's, which remained intact after four centuries.

As we were going into the woods of Sénart, reformed by royal edict to remedy the flooding of Paris, which deforestation had rendered periodic, we were surprised by the number of nomads who had taken refuge there. For the most part, they were Parisians and people from the city's immediate suburbs, fleeing aerial bombardments and terrified of not seeing them come. Some of them recognized members of the Aristotle and approached us, their physicians, in whom they had the most touching confidence.

One of them, Monsieur Saint-Fernand, the proprietor of a fine fortune and a racing stable, was clad in a dressing-gown with a floral pattern, which, beneath the trees, made him resemble a huge parrot. A typical specimen of a socialite, a gossip and an idler, and a coward into the bargain, incapable of boiling an egg or roasting a kidney, he was living there in a camp with his wife, a redoubtable tyrant, his mother-in-law, an older version of his wife, three young children ad a forty-year-old domestic who kept the hut tidy and cooked the meals.

"Maître," said Saint-Fernand, addressing Sidoine, "I've suffered a rather unfortunate mishap; I held on to the dollar and the dollar collapsed before that damned analgo. What would you advise me to do?"

"I'd advise you to hold on to your dollars," the scientist replied. "They'll go up again because the German analgesic is a hoax. We've proved that at the Foundation. We carried out a conclusive experiment on that subject."

"Ah!" said Madame Saint-Fernad, delighted by this prognostication. "Can you imagine, my dear doctor, that I have a few shares in the Aristotle, which were part of my dowry. Would you advise me to sell them?"

"Keep them, Mdame. We're presently the most sought-after share."

The mother-in-law came over in her turn. Old and worn out, she had no thought for anything but money, although she could not take it with her into the tomb, and she wanted information about shares in artificial rubber, of which she had been told great things.

Attracted by the tendency of the conversation, other castaways came toward us, in the most unusual costumes, and asked for the latest news of the invisible war. The same anxiety was evident in all of them, combined with the immense frivolity of socialites, reminiscent of a cockroach or a scarab beetle in a tin of powdered rice. There was also a pretty cinema actress in a low-cut dress, surrounded by aging dandies, who never ceased to repeat to a middle-aged gentleman the color of bile, manifestly hepatic: "Oh, how I love scientists. Personally, I adore them. They're my passion! Any man, even the richest in the world, is insipid to me compared with a scientist! Oh, show me a Polyplast...."

"Messieurs," asked one of the beauty's adorers, comically, "is there a Polyplast among you?"

"Present!" I said, although Henriette, already anxious, was tugging my sleeve.

"Oh, Monsieur, I'm a film-star, you're a Polyplast. We're made to understand one another. What do you think of this frightful war?"

"And you, Madame," I replied, in order to avoid such an inconvenient question, "what do you think of the Napus? Have you had many cases here?"

That question appeared to cast a chill. The gracious individual pouted. "It's something we don't talk about, because talking about it brings bad luck. Yes, right here, the day before yesterday, we had a case of aphanasia—which is more polite than 'Napus.' Fortunately, it was only a common person, whose name I don't recall."

"A certain Raoul...," Saint-Fernand interjected, with an expression of disgust. "A chestnut-seller from the Boulevard du Temple. A very slight loss!"

"Raoul...yes that's it. It appears that the epidermis shrinks. Is that what you think? Anyway, it's far less interesting than the war. God knows what the Germans are preparing. Oh well, *au revoir*, Monsieur, for today! I'm going to have a snack with these gentlemen. Can you imagine that we even have muffins here, to take with tea. Oh, my dear, lend me your shoulder; I'm worn out."

She drew away, supported by one of the old fogeys, gazing heavenwards expressively. Saint-Fernand, his wife and mother-in-law were letting their tongues rest in their saliva when an individual of unprepossessing appearance stood up in front of he vehicle just as well were about to move off. In a rude voice, replete with anger and alcohol, he demanded: "Is this really the Aristotle Foundation."

"In person, my friend."

"Is Professor Sidoine here?"

"That's me."

The man had his hands in his pockets, but his tone was threatening. "I'm not sorry to meet you, otherwise than in photographs. So it's you, with your antielectric law, who's responsible for this war?"

"Me, responsible for the war!" Sidoine exclaimed. "Oh, that's a good one! Don't you know that it's the Germans who want war, and that they went so far as to make up Professor Murmelthier's murder? Me, want war...that's insane!"

"It's you who are insane," growled the anarcho. "Well, you're going take back your wretched law, as quick as you can. If not, you'll have to reckon with me, professor at the Aristiotle as you are, and I don't...."

The rest of the threat was drowned out by the roar of the engine. The driver had had the good idea of cutting the ruffian off.

Sidoine seemed anxious, though. It was the first time that anyone had addressed him other than in a tone of admiration and respect. In addition, he had not supposed that his responsibility, which was only apparent—for, in fact, he wanted general well-being—was seen in that way by the public. Henriette and I were also struck by the tirade.

Our companions remained ill-at-ease, and from the forest of Sénart all the way to Corbeil, passing through the woods of Rougeaud, similarly invaded by refugees, we remained under that annoying influence.

The municipality of Corbeil had come out to meet us, rein-forced by those of Melun, Combs-la-Ville, Tigery and Soisy-sous-Etoiles. There were a dozen Maires there with the fine cunning faces of the environs of Paris, with their sashes over their chests and their papers in hand. For his part, Ailette, the inventor of the broth, had prepared—so his foreman assured us—a speech of sixty large-format pages, with all sorts of considerations on the disasters of the war and the means of avoiding them. That vast slash of the razor was in preparation, and there was still that troubling green glow in the sky....

The memory of that scene remains present in my mind, down to its slightest details. I can still see the large head of the Maire of Corbeil, the sweat of his emotion, the houses grouped around the little square, as in a set at the Lyonnais puppet-theater, faces at the windows, the brass band, the ridiculous statue of Ailette holding a bottle of his inconceivable broth, unveiled, and the inscription, in golden letters, on the pedestal of the monument: *To Professor Ailette of the Aristotle Foundation, the vanquisher of the Napus, from his grateful fellow citizens of Corbeil.*

But scarcely had the municipal magistrate, getting up from his red armchair with the gilded arm-rests, opened his mouth than Ailette, flanked by a general in battle-dress, abruptly disappeared, snatched by the Disease that he was supposed to have vanquished.

You will now accuse us of hardness of heart. The initial senti-ment of all of us—I have assured myself since—was: "That will spare us from a speech!"

It is necessary to remember that at the Aristotle Foundation, an official milieu where ministers were continually wiping their feet, we were submerged, inundated and deluged by speeches of every sort; since the fortunate disappearance of parliamentari-anism, there is no official personage who does not have a dozen sonorous turnips to plant.

"*A pati, n'a pus,*" I said to the consternated Henriette.

We witnessed then the absurd spectacle of five mayors in tears and an entire population as afflicted as if they had lost their father. No one was stiff-necked or more indifferent than Ailette, who was a crafty knave into the bargain. As for his inventions, they were all as worthless as his most recent, the broth.

Sidoine, the most senior member of our household after Ailette, stood up then, and made an admirable comment, which was also an explanation.

"Messieurs, in the midst of the grief that is overwhelming us, one consoling—eminently consoling—fact merits the fixation of your attention. Our much-regretted master, Professor Ailette, whose admirable effigy will perpetuate his form and his memory, had stopped taking the protective broth a month ago. Deprived by the invisible war of some of the ingredients indispensable to the confection of the broth, he had reserved the entire fabrication for the poor. He died, therefore, of his devotion, and his spirit of public sacrifice."

The Maire of Tigery had had the delicate idea of asking the leader of the band to replace the "Hymn to the Broth"—a local composition—with Chopin's funeral march, which, since the nineteenth century, has accompanied deceased officials, with or without remains, into the shadows. The music goes as follows:

Poum... poum, poupoum, pou poupoum, poupoum, poupoum.

Hi, hiou, hiou, ou

Hi, hiou, hiou, ou,

Poum poum poupoumm, pou poupoum poupoum poupoum.

The cinema cameras began to roll, collecting both those melancholy tones and the reflections of worthy people. Unexpectedly, a few of the Corbeillois, in spite of being so close to the capital, had never heard mention of the Napus, and remained convinced that they had witnessed a conjuring trick, an incomprehensible scientific *tour de force*, or a kind of prodigy.

The toast of honor that was due to follow was naturally cancelled. Ailette's Napus had hollowed me out; I was dying of hunger.

CHAPTER SIX
IN THE GREEN GLOW

As we arrived at the gates of Paris, after a rather morose return journey, in view of the double specter hanging over us of the Napus and the war, the previously-noted orb of green light suddenly doubled in size, and it was as if the eastern sky were aflame with it.

A dull shudder, seemingly issuing from the depths of the earth, shook the vehicles so violently that we thought they might tip over. No one uttered a cry, however, so highly developed was our scientific mentality, in which all the impulses of instinct were opposed by the powerful brake of curiosity. First find out why; then we shall see.

In any case, the knowledge that we had of the German character, the most indelible and deeply-rooted there is, left no doubt; it was the seismic machination described in the first chapter of von Herzius' *Archimedes* that was announcing itself.[19]

In that famous work, the author, concluding that it is possible to produce cataclysms artificially, promised the palm of victory to whichever of two antagonists could make the earth tremble, rivers overflow, storms, tempests and cyclones burst and unleash tidal waves. Many people laughed at the *Archimedes*, declaring

---

19. The name von Herzius is fictitious, but was presumably coined with the name of Heinrich Hertz, who first proved the existence of electromagnetic waves, in mind. Although Daudet never qualifies the term "*ondes*," radio waves were routinely called "Hertzian waves" before the term "radio" was popularized.

such deliveries incapable of realization, but it is necessary never to laugh at Boche projects, especially in epochs of pacifist propaganda and "intellectual cooperation," like the one through which we had passed before the arrival of the accursed Napus. There has not been a century since the fourteenth, and even before, when such declarations, blowing from the Pomeranian marshes, the Prussian Rhineland, the cities of the Hanse, Saxony and Bavaria, have not preceded mass risings, savage aggressions, massacres, the burning of towns and forests—in brief, the issue of the *furor teutonicus*.

That first artificial quake was not immediately followed by another. It had, however, been powerful enough to make the pale troop of the inhabitants of Paris—less battle-hardened and infinitely less polyplastic than us—emerge from their houses in alarm, fearful for one another and suffering on one another's behalf: parents for children and children for parents; sons and daughters-in-law, no matter what people say, for mothers-in-law, and mothers-in-law for sons- and daughters-in-law; maid-servants for their mistresses and mistresses for maidservants..

All those people thus aroused were interrogating the sky, fearful of the green glow and its oscillations—sometimes it shrank, sometimes it expanded—reassuring one another without reason, becoming vainly indignant, swearing that they had finally finished believing in German promises and repentance and the rabble that stood surety for German good faith.

It is claimed that popular movements make history, but that which is incorrect, aberrant, blindly delivered to successive passions and the extravagant tall stories of the press cannot participate in the confection of that cold mosaic of conse-quences in which each chapter is determined by the stupidi-ties related in the previous one, which is history. In fact, that product of events that have formed, bloodied, enriched and then dispersed, rebloodied and impoverished peoples, shows a few individuals acting on the surface and in the depths—and these figures dominate the fact, dominated themselves by a destiny that the sacrifice of Our Lord Jesus Christ has transformed into

Providence. Such, at least, is my humble opinion, to the extent that the history of the human body through its organs has not obscured in me the history of nations through the inert multitudes and their captains of every sort.

As in the first days after the Napus, people came to the Foundation—in which we had reintegrated out laboratories—in search of information about the green phenomenon, the earthquake and the degree of dread permissible in the wake of that first warning.

So long as people had hoped that the war might be limited to a struggle between the dollar and the analgo—a battle, financial or otherwise between Americans and Germans—hostilities had been imagined in a so-called objective spirit. Now, everyone took account of the fact that his own skin and those of his nearest and dearest were at stake, and that the fatherland was in peril again. Proclaimed an hour after the seismic shock, the state of siege was slightly reassuring, but utterly terrifying from another viewpoint. It was reassuring in promising the immediate execution of every spy caught in the act, but terrifying in threatening the same punishment to anyone diminishing public morale by inconsiderate speech. Stuck on top of the still-fresh posters of general mobilization, followed by general immobilization, large placards instructed everyone, in brief and imperious terms, to keep quiet and be wary. Thus, the attitude of the docile public was one of silence and suspicion.

Our first concern, on disembarking from the vehicle and resuming our respective duties had been the appointment of Aliette's successor. The choice fell upon Cortenaz, a good scientist, but horribly timid, who was known as "the hatpin" by virtue of being tall and thin. He was afflicted by a verbal tic that caused him to reply: "Good, good, that's all right," to any proposal addressed to him.

"My dear boss"—or "My dear Master" or "My dear friend"— "I can't come to the Foundation tomorrow, I'm marrying my sister."

"Good, good, that's all right."

"Chief, I'd be very grateful if you'd increased my salary by so much a month...."

"Good, good, that's all right."

His wife was very pretty and fickle, as un-Aristotelian as could be; it was rumored that when she said: "I'm going to see my lover," he replied: "Good, good, that's all right."

This innocent mania had often made him recognize imaginary debts to the butcher, the baker and others, which dishonest maidservants submitted to his memory: "Monsieur will remember that he owes such-and-such a sum to the butcher...." "Good, good, that's all right."

One of his friends, who had involved himself in a shady deal, having need of capital, asked him point-blank for a hundred thousand francs. Cortenaz bound himself by a "Good, good, that's all right" pronounced in front of witnesses.

The emotion caused him by Ailette's succession caused him to inscribe, in the interval between "Good, good, that's all rights" a new formula, "Put it there," which he applied even when his interlocutor had not brought him anything.

Less than an hour after the inhabitants had emerged from their dwellings, they suddenly went back inside. The rumor had gone around that the German plan consisted of simulating an earthquake shortly before an aerial bombardment; thus the hecatomb would be worse in urban areas.

Meanwhile, New York telephoned us the news that immense bankruptucies were succeeding one another in the United States at a rate of ten per minute, and that a large Boche ship, flying the Dutch flag, had just inundated the States with incredible quantities of analgos. People were snapping up those farcical bills, thus furnishing Germany with fabulous sums for the fabrication of its Archimedisms. In Paris, Antwerp, Brussels, London and Marseilles—not to mention Lyon and Clermont-Ferrand—we had to expect the worst.

My tour of duty appointed me to take this news to Cortenaz. Polyplasts intimidated him more than everyone else, because of their complex ethnicity, inasmuch as he had to deal with several interlocutors at the same time. I discovered him in his office, consulting a cinetext with colored films, which represented an earthquake in Colorado in 2219. On seeing me come in he raised his pale face, which sketched a slight embarrassed smile. I brought him up to date with the American news.

"Good, good," he said, "that's all right."

Those ritual words were pronounced with a desire so intense and so profound that the conversation stopped there, and stood there petrified. At the same time, Eustache arrived, in a state of agitation, holding an ugly-looking diagram.

"All right, put it there."

But Eustache had perceived the fatal book and, instead of "putting it there," he flew into a violent rage, which was nothing but displaced fear.

"So, Monsieur le Directeur, by keeping such works here, bringing them into your office and consulting them, you're exposing yourself and all of us to the risk of aphanasia! Is it necessary to repeat to you, once again, that the statistics are clear, that the ascension of the Napus is in direct proportion to the recent publication of a hundred new cinebooks in the countries afflicted by the scourge. Now the scourges of war and the Archimedes have been added to that of death without remains, and here you are, newly appointed, you, the pilot of the Foundation, setting the worst example and risking the disappearance of all your collaborators!"

"Good, good, that's all right," moaned Cortenaz, trembling all over. He would have liked to close the cinebook again, but that was impossible as long as the earthquake lasted, reproduced with an astonishing exactitude in a tenth of the time. In Colorado there had been four seismic shocks over a duration of ten hours; the book had been on the desk for half a hour. Cortenaz broke into a sweat. Eustache was only restrained from his desire to hurl himself upon the culpable book and annihilate it by his dread of summoning the Napus upon himself.

Brooom, patabooom, grooom, hidigrooom, longpatapom, bobom, broom, bom....

All three of us were thrown to the floor, along with the clock, several bookshelves, a bust of Ailette, five recorders of seismic shocks, sunspots, spots on Jupiter and cyclones in the Îles de la Sonde.

We got up as best we could, observing with pleasure that we had not broken or dislocated anything. The clock had stopped, but by a marvelous circumstance that one might call "homeopathic" that earthquake in Colorado, which had not suffered any damage, continued to unfurl its episodes concurrently with those of its Parisian colleague.

"It's the end of everything!" howled Eustache, who seemed to have lost his mind. Although he was an unbeliever he threw himself on his knees and recited a prayer to Saint Barbara, Saint Helena and Saint Mary Magdalen, which, since time immemorial, has been recited by the men and women of Provence during storms. It is necessary to add, by way of excuse, that he had had a Marseillaise nurse.

Our comrades came running from all directions, demanding instructions. The Archimedic earthquake had done what Sidoine had demanded in vain, stopping all the electromagnetic and other apparatus in the Foundation. The engineers responsible for repairs, always at their posts and ready for action, hesitated over proceeding with readjustments that might perhaps be undone in five minutes if the earthquake recommenced.

For want of electric light, we had a so-called reserve of rosy emanations of elephantium, obtained by the distillation of bison horns treated with the subnitrate of colloidal triniethane of eurhythmine. They had the side-effect, however, of provoking a tendency to drowsiness by bulbary action, which Sidoine saw as a kind of prenapus.

It was reported that a great deal of damage had been done in Ménilmontant and Père-Lachaise, through which the fault-line passed; that numerous houses had collapsed in La Chapelle and La Villette; that there had been deaths in considerable quantity; and that the orb of green light in the eastern sky had been further augmented.

For the timid Cortenaz, that was a terrible debut in his new functions. After two resounding "Good, good, all rights," he slumped as if prostrated by terror in front of his devil of a cinetext, on which the drama of Colorado was fading away to completion.

Giving up on the possibility of obtaining methodical instruction from the distressed director, the Polyplasts, including your humble servant, took the initiative and gave orders in his stead.

My first preoccupation had been to make sure that my valiant Henriette had not come to any harm and that the costly instruments in our cytology laboratory had not been damaged or put beyond use.

Let the Germans come to talk to us about Archimedes again! All our directors of works, surprised by the event accompanying the disembarkation from the vehicles, had remained at their posts without flinching, receiving messages and replying to them, communicating with the Ministers and the Royal Palace, where a cabinet meeting of the greatest importance was being held without interruption. The new German malice once again federated the people of Europe against the enemy of the human species.

Unfortunately, a few hours later, just as we were regaining our confidence, four cases of the Napus occurred simultaneously within a radius of two kilometers, one of which was at the Foundation. There were thirty more in Paris alone, in the quarters where, for lack of electricity and disposable phosphorescence, the pink light of elephantium had been deployed in the aftermath of the earthquake. Sidoine's thesis seemed to be victorious.

The night passed in fear, but without further shocks. As long as the magnetic "geotome," or "earth-cutter" invented by those blackguards did not cut through our 7, and we did not suffer any "fringe" aftershocks, we were almost certainly safe. But there was still a risk, and the annihilation of the Arostotle Foundation, in the present circumstances, would have been an irreparable misfortune. Our fellow citizens were aware of that.

Every city in France and also abroad asked us for confirmation that the catastrophe had not reached us.

From Berlin in Germany, with which communications could not be completely severed, a simple warning reached us by ultra-rapid wireless: "Soon!" That was, in fact, the big question-mark—knowing whether the Boche had discovered a means of orientating their earthquakes in a given direction, over a particular distance. We discovered subsequently that they had made a mistake in operating their controls, and that the giant cutter had gone through the Père-Lachaise quarter instead of ours. In addition, the cost of the maneuver and the risks run by its executors—every artificial quake killing fifty trigger-men and costing two billion analgos—rendered a recommencement impossible. We did not know these reassuring facts at the time however, and the pessimists concluded that there would be an indefinite renewal of the first ordeal.

The day after this excitement, we learned from the newspapers, with joyful astonishment, that the Boche quake had been stopped dead by a counter-quake devised at the Aristotle several years before by its new director, the celebrated Cortenaz. A headline proclaimed in large print:

PARIS SAVED BY THE ARISTOTLE.

The reporter related that the scientist in question, with a exceptional power of realization, compared with whom Murmelthier was nothing but a child, had directed the counter-Archimedes with an unprecedented *sang-froid*, and that we were proposing to set fire, at a distance, to Berlin, Dresden and Hamburg within an interval that would not exceed forty-eight hours. There was no mention of the napusification of Ailette, nor of the Napus in general, and we concluded that a benevolent censorship had already been imposed on the gossip of the press.

That same day, Henriette and I, now officially engaged, set out with the commission charged with assessing the damage to Ménilmontant, Père-Lachaise and other places. I had us added to it quite easily, even though it was not our turn to go out. I simply went to see Papa Cortenaz in his office, to whom I explained my plan, and who replied with the liberating: "Good, good, that's all right."

As I came out I crossed paths with the beautiful Madame Cortenaz, who darted an indefinable glance at me; she was said to be fond of Polyplasts. She was very pretty, but I had sworn to be faithful to Henriette—who had, after all, discovered the fourth magnetic center of the cell and rendered sterling service to cytology.

A first agreeable observation on leaving the Underground was that the damnable green glow was greatly diminished. What remained of it, amalgamated with a pale late autumn sunlight, diffused a light akin to an eclipse, quite appropriate to the day after a catastrophe. This time the inhabitants remained inside their houses, brooding their anxiety. A few, however, reassured by reading the newspapers, stuck their noses outside again and laughed as the alarm passed. Some of them insinuated that the earthquake attributed to the malignity of the Germans had been purely fortuitous. Others, it is true, claiming to be better-informed, announced that there was worse to come, and demanded the conclusion of an immediate, even separate, peace. About a dozen of the latter, mostly nationalized Turks or Bulgars, were arrested and shot.

The cracks, evidently deep, began in the middle of the Rue de Ménilmontant—one of the oldest quarters in Paris—and broadened out on reaching Père-Lachaise. A divergent branch ran from there toward La Chapelle and La Villette. Another, much less significant, extended in the direction of Saint-Ouen. The most formidable spectacle, however, was the great necropolis. A little more than a third of the graves, and the entire Napus quarter, the surviving wardens told us, had fallen into a gulf in the form of a crevasse fifty meters wide and a hundred meters deep. The rest had slipped or folded up, deforming the ground and lifting it up, while thousands and thousands of skeletons were emerging among the broken tombstones and the uprooted trees.

A spectacle of horror! They were the bones of individuals of all sizes, fixed in attitudes of fear—which we attributed to them—and gestures of panic. Tibias fled, metacarpal implored, and the "lanterns" composing the faces expressed, by contrast, hideous laughter. That debris, those fleshless remains—some, even worse, not completely so—seemed to have been rejected by peaceful death into a second existence full of tumult and immodesty. Shrouds fluttered in the gentle breeze like giant butterflies. All that breakage, suggestive of noise, was contradicted by a solemn silence, in which there was a suggestion of reproach.

Old women and pimps from the neighborhood, the former out of compassion and the latter with a vague hope of pillage, exchanged their impressions.

"So long as it doesn't bring bad luck to see all that."

"Don't talk like that—it makes my legs go weak. It seems that the Boche have undermined Paris, and that without the doctors of the Ristole it'd be even worse."

"What do you mean, the doctors of the Ristole?"

But the person "in the know" did not reply.

"Hey, Julot, get hold of that vase on the right for me. Is it gold or imitation?"

"Oh la la! And the silver torch! It's sad to think that it might rot without being able to do honor to anyone."

The numerous busts with inscriptions that ornamented the graves, representing the deceased, were the object of the "gentlemen's" jests, articulated in mocking tones in faubourgian accents that had certainly remained the same since Villon. But the worthy women scolded them, assuring them that nothing brought bad luck like "teasing" in cemeteries.

"It got to them, the bad luck, since they're dead, and thrown all over the place into the bargain!"

"So far as the Boches are concerned, they're men like us. If we were in their place, we'd do the same."

I observed once again that in Paris, the pimps are both humanitarian and pretentious. Henriette, who appreciated the vigor of popular parlance, could have stayed there indefinitely—but a terrible reek, of the same order as that of the Chinese "footprints" began to emerge from the disturbed charnel-house. I glimpsed a series of epidemics that would provide work for cytologists.

Suddenly, a little click resounded, and one of the louts in the process of chatting and philosophizing over the skeletons disappeared. It was a fine case of aphanasia, occurring in an environment in which we had not yet had the opportunity to observe one.

"Well, la la!" said one of the mates, with a gesture of surprise.

"It's the Napus, old chap—must be. Poor Milile, he surely didn't expect that!"

"*Au revoir*, Milile—see you soon!"

"It's still better than getting the chop!"

The man who made the last remark winked significantly. Had Mimile been in danger of "getting the chop"—which is to say, guillotined? I have a keen interest in etymology in all languages, by reason of my polyplasty, and I discussed it with Henriette, each of us forgetting the circumstances. The old women had disappeared, frightened. As for the pimps, they had manifestly got used to the Napus, as to everything inevitable. They're the philosophers of the gutter.

We had taken the road to La Vilette, forgetting the absent committee of enquiry, when a coppery-black cloud of bizarre shape raced rapidly across the sky. What was that further devilry?

We had scarcely posed the question than a jet of warm water, with a reek of wet wool, hurled as if from a bucket, forced us to take refuge in the coaching-entrance of an old nineteenth-century building devoid of any kind of style. The name of the architect was still visible, however, and the date 1899. The avalanche had already ceased; it had not lasted five minutes—but it must have been repeated five times during the day, and ten times in every twenty-four hours during the days that followed.

It was unpleasant, but not terrible. Murmelthier, to whom that damp "Archimedes" was due, had boasted of being able to drown Paris beneath vertical jets a hundred times more powerful than those of American firemen's hoses, which could flatten a man like a pancake. Kaninchen had added a toxic substance to the douche. The effect, as is evident, did not live up to their hopes.

Rapidly informed by their spies, however, of the feeble result of these assaults, the Boches adjusted their fire. That is an accurate description, for, without advancing their armies, whose dispositions we knew, they sent across the frontier flights of tiny bombs made of a new metal, at a rate—as we learned later—of five a minute. These bombs only exploded an hour after landing, releasing a murderous gas over a radius of ten meters. The gas in question was hilarifying, with the result that its victims died in veritable convulsions of laughter.

In fact, the explosions took place during flight more often than not, doubtless by reason of poor regulation, and we only received one bomb per quarter of an hour—which was quite sufficient. The newspaper reportage assured people that the hilarant death, with almost complete remains, was greatly preferable to aphanasia—a difficult choice to determine.

Afterwards, it was the turn of the artificial inundation, very efficiently executed, and which, if it was not very murderous by comparison with the Napus, caused considerable damage in a few rural areas and towns between Paris and Marseilles. It was clamed that the disturbance of rivers and streams was provoked by quakes extended along the watercourses and springs, and that they had been prepared long before. That is possible, but in spite of all our research, we never found out exactly how those Boche animals contrived to make the Seine, the Saône, the Rhône,the Durance, the Isère, etc, suddenly boil, as if they had been placed in a saucepan over an ardent fire.

The boiling was very brief; as soon as it overflowed the river returned to the lukewarm temperature of the artificial rain, spreading out in irresistible sheets, black in hue. It was, of course, undrinkable and, if swallowed, gave rise to the combined symptoms of ulceration of the stomach and goiter.

Two of the Aristotle's Polyplasts heroically sacrificed themselves in order to study the progress of the infection and its lesions in themselves. I can still hear Cortenaz's "Good, good, that's all right," when they announced their resolution and when someone came to inform him of their death.

Bizarrely, certain rivers refused, as was vulgarly said, but as Pascal would also have been able to say, to "play ball." That was notably the case with the Loire, whose depth is admittedly feeble over a large part of its course, but which did not even reach the level of its historical and natural inundations. One wonders whether rivers, by virtue of being involved in the lives of river-dwellers, might not acquire a certain personality, like domestic animals and plants grown in a park, a farmyard or an inhabited area. In many grave circumstances, and twice during the old war of 1914, the Marne appeared to side with the land it waters, and played dirty tricks on the German.

At any rate, neither Blois, nor Amboise, nor Tours, nor Nantes was in the least threatened by the excellent Loire, which continued to flow, as if nothing had occurred, between its banks planted with the most beautiful and most varied species of trees. Admittedly, those same cities were subsequently watered, copiously, by all sorts of German projectiles, filled with the most varied substances, and decimated to the same extent as others by the Napus. Their good fortune was relative.

On the other hand, the Saône rose up like milk boiling over on three distinct occasions, corresponding to three pulses of the mysterious Boche Archimedes. None of the quarters of Lyons, except for Fouvières, was spared. The Lyonnais confronted that veritable disaster, from the viewpoint of damage inflicted, with the centuries-old phlegm that sets them apart from our other fellow citizens and finds its superior expression in the character of Chignol—the phlegm that I admired in my poor Mouillemouillard before he had fallen prey to suggestion and, as they say, "taken for a ride" by von Tschuppe.

With regard to the Rhône, I am convinced that Marseilles and the Provençals are not exaggerating in any fashion when they claim that German sorcery caused it to reverse its course furiously between Saint-Louis and Genève, like someone who, being very afraid of something in a southerly direction, flees northwards, making jokes as he runs. I believe it all the more because I subsequently discovered that the original plan of the Archimedes, already indicated in von Herzius' book, involved the provocation of a reversal of flow in all the rivers and canals in France and Belgium. Here again, things had not worked out as the organizers had supposed they would proceed. If people succeeded in all the criminal enterprises they undertook against one another, the planet would have been depopulated long ago.

The anxiety into which these manifestations of German hatred and industry threw many people in France, England and Italy, was manifest in a singular and simultaneous fashion in many scientists, including the timid Cortenaz. He imagined that the Napus had started out as a Boche invention, an "Archimedes," and that if the Boche had been afflicted by the new plague themselves, that was only to deflect suspicion. It was an absurd supposition, given the amplitude of the statistics of German aphanasia, but those who had formed it did not want to let go of it. In all laboratories, institutes and foundations there are flatterers who pretend to agree with a master's whims in order to gain his favor. That happened at the Aristotle, and we caught one of our cleverest Polyplasts red-handed, coming to the directorial office to supply Cortenaz with false documents supporting his strange mania. "Put it there," the latter said, with a radiant smile that was only slightly embarrassed.

Artificial hail, accompanied by noisy electric storms, only ravaged the départements of the south-west; I have no idea why. There were many attempts elsewhere, but it was along the Garonne, in the valley of the Adour, the Armagnac region, and on the coast as far as Bayonne, that that rural form of the Archimedes, designed to drive agriculturalists to despair, took its toll. The most painful effect, however, was the production of loud noises, projected over various parts of the territory, which could be heard for twenty kilometers around, as if an immense ammunition depot had blown up a mountain containing it.

That which afflicts and wounds the ear afflicts and wounds the mind with particular force, dissociating it into several painful shreds, each of which subsequently becomes an apprehension. The Germans knew that and, at the same time as they made use of silent artillery—which was, in consequence, very difficult, if not impossible, to locate—they produced rackets at will, in selected unusually sonorous locations ranging from drill-like hyperstridulation and screeching to the collapse of an iron monument in a giant bronze basin, which the eardrums could not resist.

When a din attains a certain volume, it is transmitted through the ground as through the air and water, as an echo. Everything is a pretext for it to resound and magnify itself. From the day when that odious procedure was first employed and chronometrically organized by our enemies, laboratory work in our Underground became impossible. Scarcely had an experiment or a measurement begun, a communication been transmitted or received, than the unprecedented, infernal tumult was unleashed, stripping one's cerebral fibers and shredding the nerves all the way to the soles of the feet. It did no good to stick wads of mastic in one's ears and keep them there; the savage din passed through the mastic and, vibrating between it and the shell of the ear, caused atrocious suffering.

One of our people then proposed a chemical composition with an atomic orientation such that sounds of any kind were deflected by the molecular architecture and transmitted away from the individuals coated with the remarkable substance. The first person who tried antinoise no. 110—after a hundred and nine fruitless laboratory trials—no longer perceived any fraction of the devastating bombardment. On the other hand, he was covered, a few hours later, by a multitude of blisters and pustules of a composition that defied analysis, and which caused death within twenty minutes. Everyone thought that the inventor had gone a little too far. The possibility of dismantling the Aristotle and transporting it to an isolated location, sheltered from German attacks, was then seriously envisaged.

What saved us was the knowledge that the Germans must have had of a further considerable emigration of Parisians of both sexes, weary of serving as guinea-pigs for the homicidal fantasies of the land beyond the Rhine. While French soldiers stood by with their arms at their feet, waiting to launch a counter-attack against a Boche offensive that never came, the population behind the lines, martyrized, flooded toward the Ocean and toward the Alps, thus preparing by means of habitat and the transformative mutual contact of children, a sturdy generation of montagnards and mariners. The mental and physical exchanges that are effective in the formative years, turning little town-dwellers into peasants and vice versa, combining hereditary powers beneficially and detrimentally, are in fact, one of the marvels of human nature.

Archimedism no longer knew where to find its victims. It was extremely expensive in all its forms. First, there was a relaxation, and then the cataclysmic era came to an end.

It is also necessary for me to call attention, as a psychological consequence of the Napus, to the exaggeration of the grief caused by absence. What makes absence "the greatest of evils" is that it evokes the image of death, but of a death that might cease. With the Napus, that image was combined with that of the inexplicable, the sudden and the definitive, which Edgar Poe has named so poignantly, the "nevermore."

Whenever Henriette, delayed in a library or a laboratory, was late in joining me, I saw her aphanasicized, dissolved into an impalpable mist of shattered cells. The *angor*[20] was so strong that I could no longer even succeed in reconstituting her delicate features by means of memory, and it was necessary for me to concentrate my thoughts to the extreme of fatigue and exhaustion in order for it to compensate me with a simple reverie.

---

20. The Latin term for anguish; the equivalent of the German *angst*.

La Renaudière convened a conference of military leaders, the professors of the Aristotle and the proprietors of the major newspapers. We were summoned to Underground 22, where the principal administrative services of the Ministries of National Defense were concentrated. Field-Marshal Mugh-Bigfort of the English army was there, Admiral Strummy, the Belgian General Mélevels, and a high-ranking American officer; for our part, there was Maréchal Verve, the conqueror of the previous Franco-German war; Général Levin, to whom we owed the hypersubterranean defenses of Franche-Comté, Lorraine and Alsace, a hundred meters deep; Amiral Duparc and the head of his general staff, whose name I don't know; plus Cortenaz, Sidoine, Eustache and, finally, the four Anabaptists, Noirpelat, Tavejus, Tiqueton and Barouille.

Tea was served in abundance, with artificial jam, preserved muffins and wood-pulp bread, in consequence of the food-shortages brought about by the Archimedean cataclysms. I was impressed by the intellectual appearance of Admiral Strummy and his laconism. From time to time, like a metronome, he uttered a "Good," or a "Right," which made an echo to Cortenaz's "Good, good, that's all right." Field-Marshal Mugh-Bigfort, powerful in his corpulence and meaty in the face, seemed rather drowsy.

Maréchal Verve had a bronzed and wrinkled face like a seasoned amber pipe, and spoke in curt sentences, interlacing and separating his fingers, with a great deal of penetration and optimism. Levin, with the pock-marked and creased face of a male Bellona, seemed a composite image of effort, struggle and success. From his thin and sinuous lips emerged a little voice, softness overlaid on hardness, like oil on trenchant steel. Amiral Duparc, in the twentieth-century of machines and machinery, displayed the cheerful rubicund face of a sea-dog of the times of Surcouf, like a sea-shanty, so much does the element mark the man, as the wind and stars mark the shepherd.

In the name of the King, La Renaudière explained the situation. At times I served as interpreter. Although triply menaced by the Napus, the German Archimedes and the war properly speaking, the allied nations were holding firm. Experience having proved that the best tactic was the counter-offensive, we were waiting at the first barrage, which was the Rhine, for the inevitable surge of the enemy armies. The cities of France and Belgium had been depopulated, of course; America had been virtually ruined by analgo; Japan had just suffered three consecutive earthquakes, which had nothing artificial about them. Aerial bombardments had laid waste to a considerable number of English, Belgian and French monuments. In the meantime, the German press had not breathed a word about the hostilities and reported the misdeeds of Murmelthier, Kaninchen and others briefly, under the various headings of occurrences, accidents and meteorological phenomena.

"That hypocrisy is the worst thing of all," said the high-ranking American officer. "It requires public criticism."

Levin indicated, with a slight sigh, that the moral pint of view was of scant relevance. He stated, in sober terms, that he was only waiting for the order to "come out of his hundred-meter holes" and tear apart the Boche armies, corrupted by the abuse of technology and reduced to the role of mere spectators in the midst of a thunder of inventions.

"All their noise disorganizes them more than us. Whatever sorceries might achieve in that direction, they'll never triumph over military decision, which consists of striking hardest exactly where it's necessary to strike."

Maréchal Verve approved this forthright language—which Mugh-Bigfort and Strummy had difficulty following—with nods of the head. He possessed the exceptional qualities of a great soldier to a high degree, being visionary and quick to act, but he also had the military fault of bowing to civil authority, which permitted democracy to desolate France for such a long time. Bold on the battlefield and in purely technical discussion, he softened in the face of opposition by a Minister of War or the discontentment of a President of the Council. While he explained his arguments with a great deal of logic and force, he followed their effect on La Renaudière's cold attentive face, like that of a chess-player. "Isn't that so, Monsieur le Ministre? What do you think, Monsieur le Ministre?"

Levin's attitude was quite different, as was that of the Belgian general Mélevels, honored with the fine title of Duc de Meuse for having victoriously defended that river, presently overflowing and uncrossable. Both regretted that the intensive bombardment of German cities by aircraft had not commenced immediately. Their criticisms, expressed in a moderate tone, were nevertheless expressive, and an atmosphere of anxious gravity surrounded us in the room, where the eternal drama was being staged of Fatherlands fighting for their independence, or for their preeminence, or—in many cases—for both at the same time.

"Messieurs," said Le Renaudière, eventually, turning toward the newspaper proprietors, "you have your fingers on the pulse of public opinion on a daily basis—have you observed a weakening of the masses, a commencement of discouragement?"

Noirpelat and Tiqueton affirmed that they had, that people had already had enough, and were hoping for peace. Tavejus thought the opposite. Barouille, as throughout his career, had no personal opinion. Noirpelat and Tiqueton were rumored to have gambled on the analgo against the dollar—and, indirectly, against the franc. They spend their sad lives laying traps, denouncing one another, weaving and thwarting financial intrigues and plots. None of the four was capable of writing twenty lines in correct French. Each of them employed and controlled five Academicians.

"Messieurs," said Levin, laughing in a manner that raised gooseflesh, "permit me to tell you that the public is like Monsieur Barouille. "It awaits events before forming an opinion. It's the directors alone who count. Their firmness governs general firmness, their panic sows panic, their hesitation, hesitation. With regard to our adversaries, to which Verve and I have become somewhat accustomed, in view of the periodicity of their aggressions over several centuries, there is only once procedure to employ: to break them at the strongest point, or what they estimate to be strongest. The perfidious and ingenious brutality of the Germans does not survive a well-directed blow. They're wasps, whose nest it's necessary to destroy."

"And you, Professor Cortenaz, what do you think? Have you noticed any weakening in the admirable energy of your Polyplasts, or that of your non-polyplastic professors? I ask the same question of Messieurs Sidoine and Eustache, who have been kind enough to join you for this consultation of the highest importance."

Cortenaz went as red as a tomato. He struggled against the habitual formula, which came naturally to his lips, but whose untimeliness was obvious to him. For want of being able to articulate a sonorous "good, good, that's all right," he lost the thread of his thoughts, and was attacked by an irresistible tic.

It was Sidoine who rescued him from his embarrassment. Faithful to his obsession, the great enemy of electro-ondic installations launched into a host of technical considerations that had no relevance to the question. The English Field-Marshal fell asleep over his cup of tea. Interested at first, Admiral Strummy and Amiral Duparc were no longer listening. The newspaper proprietors had adopted weary and resigned expressions. The American chewed his gum.

Sidoine arrived at his own defense: he had not wanted war; it was an atrocious calumny that imputed the responsibility to him. Anyway, the director of the Aristotle himself, Cortenaz, was inclined to attribute the origin of aphanasia to German Archimedism.

"By the way," he suddenly said, insolently, "why have the allies not provoked rain, thunder, floods and earthquakes in Germany?"

"Because it's contrary to human rights," replied the American observer.

"Because it's too expensive," declared Field-Marshal Mugh-Bigfort.

"Because it's inefficient," added Admiral Strummy.

But Sidoine persited in his remonstrance, determined to ignore the signs of disapproval made by Cortenaz and Eustache. He took as witnesses Général Levin, Maréchal Verve and Amiral Duparc, who were reluctant to support him, against the opinion of the others, or to disagree with him, in his capacity as an official scientist. He forgot the circumstances and the instruction to be brief.

When he had finished, the agenda of the conference appeared to be exhausted, although it was really only our patience that was.

"To sum up, my dear Messieurs, the conduct of His Majesty's government seems to you appropriate to the situation the allies are facing, which is certainly grave but not tragic. In these conditions, there is nothing to do but persevere, always in the presence of the watchword Taciturnity."

Fortunately, La Renaudie stopped on the threshold of that formula, too often repeated, which shows that Taciturnity, in spite of the word's meaning, has a certain tendency to loquacity. Then Cortenaz' incomparable saw was heard, muttered behind his teeth: "Good, good, that's all right"—on which note, we went our separate ways.

CHAPTER SEVEN
SIDOINE'S MURDER

Henriette and I took advantage of the lull in the Boche Archimedes to get married. I had Eustache and a Polyplast as witnesses; Henriette had Sidoine and Cortenaz. My young wife was ravishing, perfectly natural and cheerful. All our friends and colleagues were present. Delicate winter sunlight illuminated the exit from the church.

Suddenly, a man whose silhouette was not unknown to me emerged from the ranks of the spectators, a knife in his hand. He hurled himself at Sidoine and plunged his weapon into the unfortunate professor's neck so precisely that the carotid was cleanly severed. Blood gushed forth over the bride. While the murderer was grabbed, our master rendered his last sight in the arms of the curé.

The event was grave. Sidoine represented the Aristotle, and with it, the National Defense. In the eyes of the country he was, by virtue of his bold conceptions generally crowned with success, someone as important as Tavan might have been in the twentieth century or Pasteur in the nineteenth. His struggle against the Napus, his beautiful antielectric theory, his scorn for the wrath excited by his law, had earned him an enduring popularity that was manifest in all circumstances and made him, in the eyes of the civilized world, the champion of the French intellect. The circumstances in which he died, that tragic passing, added further to the regrets and to his glory.

At the funeral that was held at the expense of the State, along with the entire complement of the Aristotle, there were twenty physicians, writers, journalists and scientists—a respectable number, when one considers that an intensive bombardment was always to be feared in spite of the cataclysmic relaxation. Sidoine's family tomb at Père-Lachaise was inaccessible and impracticable by reason of the recent upheavals, and it was decided that the deceased would repose in a crypt in Underground 7, excavated for that purpose.

At his trial, the murderer, of Catalan origin, named Ramon Mendador, declared that he had killed Sidoine because he was responsible for the war.

"I am," he said, "an antiscientific militant, the son of antiscientific terrorists, and in acting thus, I was only continuing a long family tradition. My father used a revolver to shoot the director of the Barcelona Observatory. My grandfather cut the throat of the President of the Madrid Academy of Sciences. My great-grandfather, employed in the zoological gardens at Antwerp, poisoned the director of that establishment. All the Mendadors have been garroted, broken on the wheel or quartered. I've been watching out for Sidoine for a long time. I met him and threatened him when he got out of a vehicle when the Ailette monument at Corbeil was inaugurated—and if Ailette had not been napusified, I would have stuck a knife in him too."

These words gave rise to the presumption of a cerebral derangement. The judge ordered a mental examination of the criminal by two specialist physicians not belonging to the Aristotle, in order that their independence could not be called into question. One, named Gustave, was a robust fellow, jovial and macabre, known for juggling with the bones of corpses in anatomy displays. The other, by the name of Melchior, had the awkward gait and beard of a fat Turkish letting-agent. Neither of them had the slightest scientific intelligence. The examining magistrate, in thorny cases, outlined for them the thesis in favor of which they were to conclude, or the diagnosis or prognosis they were to deliver. Provided that they could go on the spree together, in a generally crapulous fashion, everything else was indifferent to them.

They recognized in their report, in conformity with orders from the Court, the responsibility of Mendador, attenuated nevertheless by the fact of his murderous antecedents. The claimed to have discerned a few indications of delusions of grandeur; as for active antiscientism, it had been too widespread a state of mind for a hundred and fifty years for it to be considered pathological. The people who had led the bloody revolution of 2114 had not all been insane; there were logicians in their ranks.

The Public Prosecutor, rightly deeming that it was necessary to press on, sent the Mendador file to the Committal Court, which acted diligently. Scarcely a month after the drama, and although the kind of truce that had intervened between the two belligerents was still enduring, the bloody Catalan passed on to the Court of Assizes and collected a well-deserved death-sentence. We immediately claimed him for experimentation at the Aristotle, as if the rule in such cases.

That kind of extraordinary requisition, if the victim is a scientist, dates from the victory of the men of science over the antiscientists in the wake of the great struggle that I have just mentioned. It is destined to inspire terror in those who are still tempted by the impulsive desire for such criminal attempts.

I received delivery of Ramon Mendador on a Saturday. On Sunday the personnel were not at work, so I had to keep the condemned man in a cage for twenty-four hours. He received a can of veal with peas, which he ate with a hearty appetite, and a tablet of artificial wine, which he drank avidly. He was chatty, speaking French with a strong Spanish—or, rather, Hispano-Catalan—accent, and never stopped asking me questions regarding the fate that awaited him. I did my best to avoid his questions.

Our plan was to experiment on him secretly, with regard to his physiological, anatomical, chemical and cellular reactions to the imminent threat and, if necessary, the commencement of realization of each of the modes of execution in use in the civilized nations: the garrote, hanging, electrocution and the guillotine. To those who might reproach us for our cruelty, I would reply that knowledge itself knows neither pity, nor cruelty, nor mercy, nor harshness, but merely measurements and diagrams. We had young experimenters at the Aristotle of exquisite sensitivity, like Henriette. She manifested no revulsion in following the episodes of scientific punishment inflicted on Mendador, and she was one of those who summarized the principal results obtained in a thesis.

Doctors Gustave and Melchior had asked to assist us. That authorization had been granted to them, on condition that they remained completely uninvolved, not touching any instrument or piece of fabric and—an essential point—not laughing. We Polyplasts, laughers ourselves, can bear almost anything, but not the sinister buffoonery of Gustave, obtained by a perfectly hideous contortion of the mouth and eyeballs.

Our "guinea-pig" was calm when he was taken out of his cage by Mouillemouillard's replacement and seated in the garroting chair—an old model equipped with a rusty laryngoclast and a collar whose nickel plating had worn off. He even joked with us, imploring God or the Devil of the Napus to dispose of his executioners. His temperature was 37 degrees. His pulse was beating normally. His Coefficient of Cellular Magnetism (C.M.) of center four was 0.000,000,115. His chemico-nervous coefficient was 12. He marked 7.6 on the thoughtmeter, with images of death and dolor of a wavelength of 4 imagos. Erethism was 40. Heredotension due to congenital memory was 19.

In order to render his internal images visible, he was fitted with a Sidoine helmet, which caused a Balearic landscape to appear, in a flowery spring, with a child playing, doubtless himself. That memory of happy times—for that is what it was—ran along the marrow, then the sciatic nerve, and appeared on the soles of the feet, more visible on the left, leaving a visible mark there in the elephantium sulfhydrocyanide.

The assistant carried out a half-turn of the garrote, producing a commencement of choking and crushing of the cartilages, without excessive bulbary compression. At that moment the operation was interrupted and the patient who had recovered consciousness and was groaning, was given a cup of digitalis broth, to revive his heart, and a tablet of compressed champagne. Then the measurements were carefully taken again. They offered consistent variations of considerable interest.

A whole day and a night's respite was granted before the preparations for the hanging, which the condemned man watched. He was manifestly more depressed and his pride seemed broken. He even implored us in his hoarse speech, swearing—but a trifle belatedly—that he regretted what he had done, and that he was ready to make amends by killing one or more of our enemies, if we would care to point them out to him: a rather ridiculous proposition, given the precautions taken by the senior Boche scientists and Polyplasts since the recent events. Nor could there be any question of spying on those master spies, who knew all the tricks and were perpetually on their guard.

We had some difficulty persuading Mendador to let himself be hanged meekly. The apparatus used in England, notably at Reading, consists of a cord that tightens in response to a trigger, over a trap-door through which the body falls. In this case the fall was calculated in such a fashion as not to kill, while still giving the sensation of death. Doubtless this arrangement was not at all pleasant or euphoric, but nor was it particularly ferocious. The measurements proved that the quality of the anguish differed from that of strangulation by the garrote. The immediate and congenital images had changed completely, and the heredotension was only 8.

The spectators, keenly interested, followed these modifications with sustained attention. We collected and recorded the moans, the cramps, the urine and sweat of the patient.

Another day and another night, and then the Catalan, reduced to the condition of a wreck, was put in the electric chair. Fortunately, dear Sidoine was to longer there to protest against the employment of what was, according to him, napusigenic force. It has never been possible to regulate that form of execution, so practical and so elegant in theory, in an appropriate manner. Sometimes the current passes too rapidly and too strongly, occasioning non-vital disorganizations. Sometimes it passes too slowly and burns instead of striking like lightning, which is not fair play. The use of some kind of clasp caused Mendador's tongue to stick out, bringing with it the buccal floor; it came down as far as the sternum. It was necessary to pause and stick the red package back in and glue it to the palate, all in the midst of spasmodic convulsions that stretched the muscles to breaking point. The two kneecaps burst and the breastbone was detached at the articulation of the ribs. However, the displacement of cellular magnetism in the "Henriette center" was noticed by the whole audience.

The patient merited a reward. It was granted to him in the form of a remission of 72 hours, during which he remained inert and had to be alimented with the aid of liquid conserves of the best quality.

The final ordeal, which was our current and classic guillotine, was to be divided in two: on the first occasion, a section of the parieto-occipital cap by an advancement of the blade. A pause of approximately thirty minutes would follow, permitting the measurement of the tension and sanguinary globalization in the vessels of the base of the encephalum and the principal arterial and venous conduits, up to and including the portal vein, and then the section of the neck and examination of the separated head and trunk, with the aid of records of motricity and sensitivity.

It is well-known that the re-adhesion of the severed head, hemorrhage being avoided by means of a special mechanism, has been carried out successfully in eighteen cases by the English surgeons Hawthorn, Brame and Diwards since 2083. Of those eighteen cases, six patients survived for between sixteen and twenty-four hours, and two were able to articulate a few words. The others only survived for a few minutes, which is already a good result.

I will not hide the fact that the first time was difficult. The knife did not have the ideal trenchancy that removes a segment cleanly from what old executioners call "the coconut." There were saw-like indentations in the blade. Medador did not react any more than a cadaver to external stimuli. The pensograph only gave rough strokes like those in a child's drawing. It was impossible to hazard a guess at the initial date of the homicidal design that had driven him to kill Sidoine, or of its psychic origin. We were unable to get much out of the regulation thirty minutes. As for the re-adhesion, it went awry, but for a reason independent of the determination of the operators. A hiss was produced at the most delicate moment of the operation, and we all thought it was a Napus of the patient, but it was a large vein that was gushing blood. That mishap, which troubled the audience, was injurious to the scientific result.

What I have just recounted here has remained secret until now, by reason of the royal prohibition on conducting such experiments, which once encouraged democracy, but the Aristotle renders services that are too great for it not to infringe the law. With regard to the death penalty, the same principle applies as in war. Every time its abolition has been claimed, it has reappeared, or it has been necessary to reestablish it in another and crueler form, even though it would be exaggerated to claim that "Society rests upon the executioner."

We still do not know exactly what Society does rest on, any more than we know what the equilibrium of our tissues rests on, nor what the unknown force is that disperses and annihilates that equilibrium, and the tissues themselves, in aphanasia. Sometimes, we Polyplasts feel that are these mysteries are minor by comparison with those that will be posed to the humans of the future in the form of scientific discoveries. There is something in the latter akin to the light in Rembrandt's paintings; they reinforce the obscure texture of darkness.

Shortly after Mendador's punishment, I received a visit from Général Levin in my Underground laboratory. He seemed cheerful, rubbing his hands together and then passing them over the short and coarse moustache that shaded his sinuous upper lip. He was a extremely polite man, gallant with the ladies.

"My dear Poly 17,177, I won't ask you for news of your wife; I've just met her at the door of the Underground. She's lovelier than ever. Who would have believed that laboratory life under the ground would provide those fresh colors and that pink tint? It's true that we've adapted to the enclosed life. During the last Franco-German war before this, I was lodged in a bunker without air or light, a little like you here, for eight months. I was perfectly healthy and had an infernal appetite. Air doesn't vivify, it kills—but in the midst of a certain euphoria. Did you know that I've been told that the Boche want to have me assassinated?"

That did not astonish me at all. Levin was a particular target of the German secret service, which has ramifications throughout the international police.

"Don't think that I have delusions of persecution," he continued. "I couldn't care less about my own skin, but my country's is a different matter. Now, there are military services that only I can provide, because, let it be said without any vanity, I have my methods." He emphasized the *my*. "You understand that, as a scientist. That method is untransmissible; it's an aspect of my physical individuality, my corporeality, like my voice or my gaze. I was born, you see, with the knowledge of means appropriate to break through the German front, whatever its disposition for battle might be and whatever general is opposed to me. Others are born to discover magneto-cellular centers, like your wife; others to say 'Good, good, that's all right,' like your new director; others to be napusified. Everyone not only has his own 'little religion' as La Palatine[21] put it, but his own little destiny."

He took an amber pipe out of his pocket, carefully seasoned, and showed it to me. "It resembles Verve, doesn't it? You'll permit me to stuff it and smoke. It won't cause anything here to

---

21. The reference is to the Duchesse d'Orléans, the daughter of the Elector of the German Palatinate, whose letters provide an insight into the court of Louis XIV, and included an oft-quoted comment about seeking "a little religion of my own."

blow up, will it?"

I assured him that it would not, wondering where he was going—for he was not a man to waste his time in pointless visits or ratiocination.

"You've suffered a serious loss, I know, in Sidoine. Ailette was primarily a chatterbox, but Sidoine had guts, intellectual and moral. He was a fighter. Only fighters interest me. You Polyplasts, psychologically and hereditarily, have battlefields for your composite ancestry, so you'll understand me...."

He took two puffs on his pipe, and his gaze took on a remarkable intensity.

"This German Archimedism is a vast feint, which masks something more important than storms or artificial floods. Boche romanticism has always hidden a shrewd and calculating intelligence. Just as the skunk projects a stinking gas to put off its adversaries, the Boche emit complexity, bizarrerie and the baroque. It's a matter of frightening and demoralizing. Well, I believe I've discovered where they're heading. I've talked about it to Verve, but he has an essentially mathematical mind that reality only grips in the intervals of his calculations and logarithms. Wilhelm XIII and his people intend to deliver an almighty shock of an unprecedented type, which will astound and overwhelm us. Don't you agree?"

I replied with a dubious nod of the head.

"I can't be precise, but I'm just as certain of it as I am of breaking through the next German front, no matter what form it adopts—provided that I don't meet my Mendador before then. By the way, the thought of killing Murmelthier never entered Lepoil's head, did it? Murmelthier really was aphanased?"

"There's no doubt about it. My laboratory technician Mouillemouillard was there. Von Tschuppe confused him later, but I knew from the start how things transpired. Besides which, Lepoil was as inoffensive as his Academician's épée."

"In every main square of the major German cities there now stands a statue of Murmelthier. They're convinced that he died a victim of some invention of the Aristotle. It's on me, not you, that they want to avenge him. In sum, if they succeed, I'll be your indirect victim—but I won't hold it against you."

Still speaking lightly, Levin asked me: "Do you believe that, as is rumored, Murmelthier or someone else has discovered a trick, a crypton, for napusifying at will? That, at present, would be annoying."

I told the general, with details, the story of Kaninchen's little tube, to which he listened attentively. I added that the inventor's secret must have disappeared with him, or the German General Staff would have deployed it on a large scale from the very start.

"That's reassuring. If that's the case, and whatever they have simmering, I'm certain that I'll *have* them."

With that point clarified, the conversation turned to the war in general and the means of combating, if not suppressing, a scourge that seemed, in spite of everything, to be avoidable. The perpetual risk, which was its formative element, had given Levin and entirely scientific penetration.

"Avoidable...hmm...that observation astonishes me in an observer of your experience. Have you noticed that the population of Europe has continued to increase considerably since the twentieth century, especially among the Slavs and the Germans? Since the return of the monarchy we're producing as many children as the Italians, in spite of industry, to the point that agriculture has flourished and prospered despite wine tablets. At that rate, there would be crowding in this portion of the planet, if a purgative war didn't intervene from time to time. Yes, of course, there's recently been the Napus, which will take responsibility for creating gaps, if it develops to the extent of a hecatomb without remains, but that's doubtful.

"So, the pretended scourge might be nothing but a precaution of nature with regard to a worse scourge—that of an excessive density of population, with the prospect of famines, and overly numerous elites producing terrifying inventions in almost indefinable numbers. For I don't think you take the view here, any longer, that the elite is always wise and science always benevolent. The collective insanities of the elite are more atrocious and bloodier than those of the masses, whatever moralists may claim. Antiscientism is a self-explanatory fact, which hasn't finished giving rise to battles and murders."

I have often imagined, fearfully, the condition of a Europe populated by men of great worth. The teaching of Our Lord is definitely the only one adapted to all meditations and all circumstances down here, and the precept 'blessed are the poor in spirit' takes on a very great significance in my eyes, in spite of my Polyplasty. The immediate, profound and total accord of his doctrine with all the vicissitudes of our bodies and minds is one proof, among many others, of the evident divinity of Jesus Christ. We have no other example of it.

After a few more puffs on his pipe, Levin took up the brilliant and cutting thread of his thoughts: "Conquerors are necessitated by that threat of European plethora, as laughter is excited as a counterweight by the dull prospect of tragic, or simple painful, vicissitudes unknown to us. The foresight of nature is infinitely superior to ours, and it is pulling us backwards. That is what makes me believe, my dear Poly 17,177, that war is often inevitable. But it can also happen that it overshoots its goal and ends up decimating nations and rendering then anemic, which is precisely what happened as a result of Bonaparte and the Revolution of the nineteenth century, and as a result of Germany and democracy in the twentieth and twenty-first."

"So," I objected, "the foresight of nature doesn't extend beyond the initial intention? That's not much."

"It's not much in your view, because every scientist has acquired the habit of considering nature as the last word of the Creation—but the Bible tells us that humankind is above nature in quality, having come later, and theology informs us that angels are above humans, still in quality."

The pipe was finished. The general got up to take his leave. I had come to understand that he had a universal brain, by the very reason of his exceptional combativeness—which is to say, his exceptional dynamism. He was tormented by the continual need to overcome some obstacle—a dolor, a difficulty, his neighbor, an anguish, a doubt—just as countless others experience a need to submit, to accept, to release, to abandon. His presence had left in my laboratory an atmosphere of rebellion, of zeal, of courage, which remained there, floating like a strong perfume for several weeks.

The relief that had been granted with respect to German Archimedism, producing a slight recovery of the dollar, which was now worth a tenth of a first-issue analgo, a habituation with regard to the Napus, and a rapid and effective clean-up of Père-Lachaise, raised public morale. It is marvelous how rapidly people forget the suffering and anxiety they have endured, returning to their ordinary occupations, their natural idleness, their routines, their faculty of inattention and frivolity. A gigantic street-cleaner and slate-sponger passes over the map of the world, thus permitting new talents, new conjectures and new fatalities to "come together," as they say in the theater.

Then, toward the middle of March, on one of those pre-spring days that have the charm of a precocious flower and the candid innocence of a first communicant, Admiral Strummy, in Plymouth, and Amiral Duparc, at Toulon, were almost simultaneously snatched by the Napus. Admiral Strummy having once had a command in China, during the twelfth war between the north and the south, it was claimed that he left behind a small evil-smelling "footprint" about ten centimeters long, but that might have been a journalistic invention, for such a relic could not have failed to feature in the British military museum.

That double decease of two high-ranking mariners, on whom the allied navies were counting, could not help awakening suspicion of an employment of artificial aphanasia. I immediately received a visit from Général Levin.

"Well," he said to me in his suave little voice, "wasn't I right? I dined with Strummy a few days before his disappearance. He seemed preoccupied—which translated his habitual silence into continual loquacity. No one will ever convince me that the hazard of the Napus could serve German interests like that. Those devilries are about to recommence, or else a properly military attack will be launched—you'll see."

I do not like to refute a single hypothesis twice in the same terms. That's a common trait in Polyplasts. I kept quiet.

The general was full of zest. He explained to me that there are three types or categories of battle: those which happen entirely other than expected, which completely escape science and tactics—in sum, organization; those which proceed exactly as anticipated, organized by one of the General Staffs present; and those which feature improvisation and prevision, which he called mixed. The ignorant only believe in the first type, but their error is considerable.

In any case, according to Levin, the initial battle of a great war, won or lost, is a froth that presumes nothing with regard to subsequent engagements. Naturally, it is better to win it, but if it is lost, it is necessary not to be unduly affected by it. It is the second engagement that is important.

"There was, however, the battle of Poitiers,[22] from which the Arabs have never recovered in the course of the centuries."

"Have no doubt that the battle of Poitiers was foreseen, in its slightest details, by Charles Martel and his generals. It is a third instance. In sum, fundamentally, there is only one permanent struggle, which commands all forms of combat: that of the quantitative and the qualitative. Bonaparte believed in the quantitative; that was what did him a bad turn at Waterloo—but if he had believed in the qualitative and paid more attention to quality, he would have overcome Blücher's arrival. Personally, I believe, in everything, in the qualitative. What is a human being, my dear Polyplast? A continual transformer, and the most perfect known, of the quantitative into the qualitative."

---

22. Because the term "Battle of Poitiers" is commonly used to refer to a major battle in the Hundred Years' War between England and France, the earlier Battle of Poitiers, in 732, in which the Franks under Charles Martel defeated an Arab army, is nowadays more often called the Battle of Tours. Poly 17,177 seems to subscribe to the long-held view that it was a crucial historical turning-point, saving Europe from Islamic conquest, although many modern historians dispute that view.

I assured my interlocutor that science had reached the same conclusion and that all the scientists who had attempted to go in the opposite direction and bring the qualitative back to the quantitative, along with all philosophers of the same inclination, were badly mistaken.

"By the way," the general said, as he got up to leave, "have you noticed that I'm no longer smoking a pipe? Do you know why? I dreamed that the German secret service had succeeded in replacing the tobacco in my pipe and the very substance of the bowl with a hypertoxic combination. It's necessary to believe in premonitions. They're part of the back-and-forth movement that regulates, administers and governs so many natural and moral phenomena."

The death of a man who has a great idea, or a powerful obsession, harms the latter and diminishes their scope considerably. Descartes' vortices were abandoned, along with the pineal gland as the "seat of the soul" immediately after Descartes' death. Pasteur's microbes, Darwin's evolution and Claude Bernard's determinism were reduced to tall stories ninety days after their inventors had been reduced themselves. As for philosophical systems, they are never either entirely active or entirely inert—thank God, for their moral consequences would be frightful—and they float on the surface of time's flow like certain jellyfish, half-dead and half-alive. That was what happened with Sidoine and the explanation of the Napus by electricity, magnetism and wave-emission.

The Sidoine law was not repealed, but it appeared less urgent to the Council of Nations that it should be applied, and German science was suddenly triumphant. "You wanted to impose on us a pretended certainty, which was, in fact, doubtful, and a suppression or prohibition of electricity and waves that no longer seems necessary. Admit that, in those conditions, we were not so wrong to make cataclysmic war on Europe and financial war on America." It was the first time that a state of war, military and otherwise, had been recognized by the German press.

From the moment that hostilities were thus attenuated,

without the Napus relenting at all in its homicidal work, it no longer seemed indispensable for us to remain in Underground 7, where we were much less comfortably installed than in the open air—all the more so because, since we had been operating like moles, public confidence in the Aristotle had diminished and individual legacies had become less numerous. There had only been one really successful publication in the midst of so many events and avatars: my late friend Poly 14,026's thesis on "The Low Frequency of the Napus in Action."

That title referred to the cases of aphanasia relative to drivers at the steering-wheel, mechanics at their post in railways trains day and night, captains at the tiller, and so on. The much-missed Poly 14,026, on examining the statistics, had observed, or thought he had observed that that category of Napus was proportionally less numerous, as if the immediate exercise of an occupation created a kind of semi-immunity. The observation had practical implications, since it spared the doubling-up of technical personnel that the plague had initially seemed to necessitate.

That thesis apart, however, we had made no progress, and had reached the vicinity of the terrible anniversary without yet having the slightest etiological, ethnic, physiological, anatomical, animal, vegetable, symbiotic or chemical precision with regard to that infinitesimal scattering of human being without the slightest residue. Even Eustache seemed less committed to his scarcely-satisfactory explanation by virtue the abuse of cinebooks and reproductive recordings of movement. He now claimed that the most harmful and napusigenic forms of apparatus were transformers of sound into light and light into sound, or into tactile sensations, which are so widely employed today. That passage from one cause to another testified to his uncertainty. According to the vulgar expression, we were "treading water."

As a therapeutic measure, the public—the worthy public, which immediately swallows everything prescribed by people equipped with diplomas, or charlatans, or lunatics—clung to

Ailette's broth and dirt. All bath-houses and manufacturers of water-circulating apparatus had gone bankrupt. All the large hotels and municipal buildings had given up their running water and bathrooms and had returned to the dry toilets of the good old days. The first words that a rich foreigner pronounced on arrival, writing his name in the register, were: "Very little water, and less than very little, or we'll go elsewhere!" All the phrase-books reproduced that sentence in all the languages of Europe, Africa, and Asia. I ought not to omit the detail that, because of fear of the infection of their stinking Napus "footprint," the Chinese were refused everywhere. Rich leprosariums of a sort had been instituted for their usage, with deodorizing rooms, in which they could disappear without inconveniencing or infecting their neighbors. Afterwards, their "footprints" were burned in a special apparatus known as a "celestial."

The news coming by wireless from the great cities of the African lakes revealed that white and yellow emigrants, very numerous by reason of the napusophobic panic, were subject to disappearance as in Europe, and, moreover, became colored by black lines before aphanasia. This observation, which ought theoretically to have slowed down emigration, did not modify its frequency. In fact, black doctors, mischievously, affirmed that after a certain time the specifically tegumentary form of the Napus would be substituted for the total and mortal Napus. It was estimated that their clientele had multiplied a hundredfold thanks to this subterfuge. That was, I think, one of the origins of the rivalry of black and white that is causing torrents of blood to flow in the twenty-third century, and threatens to cause even more to flow.

The personnel of the Foundation sent ten delegates, of who, I was one, to the director in order to discuss the situation and request a return to the surface. Certain routine-bound professors, however, whom had already become accustomed to Underground 7, emphasizing the fears of high-ranking military men, demanded the retention of the status quo. According to them, the suspension of the Archimedes was entirely due to the fact that the principal apparatus, including the so-called Murmelthier-Herzius Giant Geotome, had broken down, and that it was taking time to repair them.

Cortenaz's perplexity, caught between these opposed and irreconcilable requests and demands, was amusing to see. For six days running we went to visit him in the morning, explaining our reasons in exactly the same terms, and he replied with a resolute expression: "Good, good, my lads, that's all right"— but every afternoon, on all six days, he received the recalcitrant professors, including the insistent Eustache, and sent them away, after having nodded his head, with a "Good, good, gentlemen, that's all right" of equal intensity and value.

To annoy him, we went into his office with empty hands, which forced him to renounce the "put it there." He replaced it with a little cough, in which his timidity was manifest.

Finally, it was decided, as in the old song, that those who wanted to go would go and those who wanted to stay would stay—but that decision did not work, for it resulted in a total disorganization of the Aristotle and its complicated services, in particular its dirtiness. In the end, it came down to tossing a coin: heads, open air; tails, underground. The coin came down tails, and I can still hear Cortenaz's sigh of relief. I went toward him as if to remind him that he had forgotten something. Already, extending his hand forward with an expression of keen gratitude, he was saying a final: "Good, good, my lads, all right!"

CHAPTER EIGHT
THE TACIT ARMISTICE

At the time when the singular literary and artistic reaction about which I am about to talk became manifest throughout the world, particularly in Europe and America, aphanasia was continuing its ravages, increasing incomprehensible in its essence and causes. The Germans' invisible war was suspended by a tacit armistice. The analgo was no longer having any but a weak effect on dolor, and had been caught up by the dollar. It was, in any case, a fact that the new kind of paper money, founded on persuasion, had never enjoyed any success in France, where Boche suggestion has very little leverage. The ruins accumulated by the Archimedes over our territory and in our cities were covered over by vegetation, the exceptional growth and extension of which was noted. The mushrooms had begun it, but now, under the influence of an obscure force, certainly linked to the Napus, trees were following the trend and acquiring gigantic proportions in a matter of months. It was thus on the quays of the Saône in Lyon, in the immediate environs of Paris, on the banks of the Loire and the Doubs, and on the Black Mountain in Brittany.

The beginning of that singular Renaissance was the discovery, by a bibliophilic Polyplast at the Foundation, of a work more than three hundred years old, which appeared from a publisher by the name of Champion and was entitled *La Légende de la Mort en Bretagne*. The author, a certain Le Braz, had collected therein, from the mouths of the peasants of old, admirable and simple stories that were appropriate to the general sentiment and sensibility.[23] The book, re-edited as a cinetext, with well-chosen characters and landscapes, full of movement, went rapidly from hand to hand. At the Aristotle everyone seized upon it, in spite of Eustache's protests, threatening us all with aphanasia; people looked within it, and found, concordances with our precarious and menacing situation, and consolations by means of the beyond—a refreshment of the soul. It was more than an infatuation; it was a frenzy.

From our scientific and gossip-ridden environment, the vogue spread into the general public, amid the ignorant and the semi-ignorant and even as far as socialites and idlers. Like a beneficent nepenthe, Le Braz's poem—for it was one, albeit in mosaic—bandaged the wound opened in each of us by the apprehension of death without remains and initiated the almost mystical reverie that is our only recourse and refuge down here, apart from humble prayer before a crucifix. Even the natural hardness of Polyplasts, for which they had been so frequently reproached, was attenuated and softened if not, in some of us, annihilated. Everyone participated to some degree in the state of mind and heart that had thrown Henriette and myself into one another's arms in the woods of Meudon.

That same month of May—the month of flowers, particularly perfumed in 2228, and the reawakening of nature—saw the sudden appearance of a young female Polyplast poet, Marie de Félan, fresh in her inspiration and delightful in her rhythm, whose volume *Occidentales* was inspired by Le Braz, and also by Chénier, Moréas and Virgil; a sculptor worthy of Greek antiquity, Jeanne Ronsin, who had previously been occupied with work in comparative embryology; and a Flemish painter, Van der Seen, in whom was revived, with a more ardent color-

---

23. The folklorist Anatole Le Braz (1859-1926), whose collections of Breton songs, tales and legends includes *La Légende de la mort en Basse-Bretagne* (1893). Daudet wrote a eulogistic obituary of Le Braz in *Action Française*, which called special attention to that book, presumably while he was in the process of writing the present novel.

ation, the great tradition of his compatriots of old, notably the splendid Rubens. A month before taking up the brush where the joyous possessor of the beautiful Hélène Fourment had laid it down, in a ray of blonde light, our Van der Seen had been manufacturing precision instruments and calculating diopters.

The most astonishing case, however, was that of the pharmacist Lehuppe, who, abandoning the drugs to which he owed his immense fortune, wrote, out of the blue, a biography of Leonardo da Vinci, amorous and philosophical, leaving far behind all other enterprises of the same order—a biography that was a perpetual delight, like a revivification, in a clear, fluid, faultless language, which inaugurated the Transparent School, with its enchanting perspectives.

Thereafter, the son and heir of the great company of Spague et Cie, the largest manufacturer of explosives in the Garonne valley—from which a hundred thousand shells an hour emerged in times of war, loaded with toxic gases—Ludovic Spague, at the age of thirty-one, wrote his aphanasic symphony, which recalled, for all eternity, all the terrors, all the anguish, and also all the illusions that had accompanied the debut of the plague. Who would have believed that that young man, trained since childhood for business by a despotic mother and a father of lead with nickel eyes, would exhale, in the most ethereal and idealistic art, the aura of an entire epoch, its mysterious malaise, its moral variations, its frisson?

With Henriette, I witnessed the first performance of Ludovic Spague's masterpiece in the great chemistry hall of the factory, transformed for the occasion into a concert-hall. After an initial moment of glad surprise, which must have been that of the first hearers of Beethoven's Choral Symphony, the entire enthused audience stood up and acclaimed the author, weeping with joy. Tears flowed, charged with genius, over that little simian face, green-tinged and grimacing, whose possessor everyone had mistaken for a degenerate burdened by a celestial curse, crushed by his immense fortune and his sinister exterminator of a father.

There was more to come; everyone knew Madame Tougourte,

the widow of the celebrated financier who had raided half the public fortune and sown France with comfortable but onerous establishments, veritable nets cast over savings. When she tossed her forelock over her face of a bourgeois Gorgon, the Academicians of oakum, straw, dung and sound, invited to her magnificent manger, bowed, smiled and prostrated themselves. She had cultivated a reputation for wit by maltreating and bullying the unfortunate wives of functionaries and employees dependent upon the House of Tougourte, telling each of them her "home-truths" and applauding, with her two short sausage-like arms, outrageously bare, the actors and actresses of her "artistic soirées." Well, that undomesticated Megaera, moved by an epistolary whim, began overnight to write letters worthy of Madame de Sevigné, of a more banal but equally fantastic bent, which were passed from hand to hand and plunged her friends of both sexes, the parasites and spongers of the rich house, into a stupor.

"It isn't possible that that old cow wrote this! She's been napusified and replaced by a double! There's magic behind this! Someone's playing a joke on us!" Such were the amenities that were mingled with the compliments, the former overt, the latter covert, as usual.

One would have thought that, along with the infatuation, individual tendencies, hereditary penchants and moral and mental affinities had passed abruptly from science, mathematics or biology to art, letters and pleasure. Either the metamorphosis was the result of a decomposition of terror, or the necessity of change that universal nature requires, and which humans resist as best they can by means of the image they make of permanence and eternity. Perhaps, too, the hybrid organism, placed between the body and the soul, which permits them to communicate with one another, took account of distant possibilities to escape aphanasia by means of an extension of interior liberty and its adjuncts: poetry, painting, music and sculpture.

Science—who knows it better than me?—is not an escape; it is a chain, whose iron is riveted by reflection. Art, by contrast, liberates the love from sugared lips, warm arms, and tears almost as delicious as laughter. Henriette and I compare it to a beautiful bare-headed girl who opens her window and thrusts back her shutters to the dawning day, displaying her perfect breasts and round shoulders. Undoubtedly, there exists a morose and learned art, which comes in all epochs to cover the gilded fabric of true art with a weave of grey filaments—but that counterfeit cannot diminish the emancipatory role of the sons of the Muses, fecundated by Apollo.

From art, that renewal extended into other crafts, which are the inseparable and indispensable companions of painters, musicians, sculptors, writers and architects. For how could painters and fixers of light and color, extract the admirable forms of nature, and the more admirable ones of womanhood, if they had neither canvases nor easels, nor tubes filled with that special paste that Velasquez, Rembrandt and Goya manipulated? What would become of musicians, without instruments and the makers of instrument, of the reeds of rustic oboes, which are like whistles modulated in water? What would become of the sculptor without his assistant, his rough-hewer, without the person who pours the matter transformed by his genius into the bronze? What would become of architects without masons, writers without typesetters, and without the constructors of the machines at which typographers sit?

When inspiration pulls upon the artist, invention pulls upon the artisan. One is linked to the other by that ardor for improvement and perfection, for beauty and the vanquishing of difficulty, which is half way between amity and love, and no more. It is the passionate conjunction of the master and the thought that permits masterpieces, in every domain, to survive the centuries by means of excellence and the skillful disposition of matter. Thanks to art, the community resumes the appearance of a great family, which would be quickly lost in industry, uniquely directed to the emulation of speed, precision and war.

Sidoine being no longer there to preach hatred and dread of waves, telegraphic instruments, and so on, we used all those means to launch the good news to the world and propagate our artistic renaissance in as many countries as possible. Humans prey to any intoxication, noble or vile, always tend to suppose that their neighbors will share it. It seemed to us that the reaction around us, in response to our appeal, was various.

Strung up by the Germans with analgo, America had conceived a certain respect for those who had temporarily duped and ruined them. Many, on finding that their old ills could no longer be cured by the magic banknotes, murmured: "All the same, it did me good." Doubtless the Napus had sorely tested the populations situated between the Atlantic and the Pacific, but their habituation to non-artificial cataclysms and their taste for fantasy had attenuated the impression of terror and driven the survivors to treat the matter as a joke. People out there use "nevermore" ironically. So the need for artistic reaction was not as violent as it was in France, Italy, Belgium, Holland, Spain and England. Le Braz's book had little success in translation, nothing being more distant from the American temperament and spirit than the Breton temperament and spirit. The United States has replaced the phantom by the medium and the table-turning spiritualist, once and for all.

In England, by contrast, *La Légende de la Mort*, skillfully translated, caused the appearance of a constellation of dramatic authors, of a richness and variety almost equal to that of the Elizabethan period. All of them took some inspiration from aphanasia, and mingled it with adventures and songs of the sea, the colonies, and the open sky, teeming with veritable birdsong. Neither in music nor in sculpture was anything extraordinary observed, or even merely original. Nevertheless, the Scottish painter Southbridge discovered and applied a new color, nap, intermediate between the pale green of napusified negroes and Havana brown, which he employed to represent the London sky during the most tragic bombardments of the Archimedes. That pictorial conjunction of the two scourges was so much appreciated that Southbridge became an overnight success.

As for the dramatic authors, the most famous—I might even

say the most illustrious—of the group was Charles Esbott, who, without making any sacrifice to the baroque, was able to combine irony and emotion in an exquisite and expansive measure, which is generally the privilege of the Latin masters. Without it being possible to equal Shakespeare, the highest and inaccessible summit of the stage, along with Molière, of all countries and all times, one finds in him the mixture of the Celtic and the Latin, the unlimited choice of subject-matter, the complex and brilliant subtexts, and the sure rhythm of dialogue that ensure permanence.

As Shakespeare drew from Scottish and Italian chronicles, from Plutarch, Montaigne, Bandello and others, the substance that, revised by him, would create an imaginative world, so Esbott drew from the work of Le Braz a new type of society, intermediary between reality and dream. He plays with fairies and angels, and thus enchants the earthly sojourn. In replacing us once again with a forward-looking viewpoint projected back in time and equilibrating anticipation, one may wonder what ulterior darkness will be remedied by a ray of light like Charles Esbott.

The German storm, although it had not lasted long on this occasion, had rendered Germany aspirational and porous. During the tacit armistice—for hostilities were never officially suspended—it imbibed Le Braz, translated by Hermann Körper, to the point of extracting a metaphysics from him. It is through metaphysics that the ponderous ingenuity of that belliferous race is exhausted, slicing meaty masses of treatises and dissertations with a sword, as far as the eye can see. That it is a nation of blatant lies can be seen merely by reading Kant, who denies the universal adequation of thought and sense. On that trumpery it has edified a system that turns the world upside down and unleashes chronic war in the name of eternal peace.

The *Gespenstmetaphysik*, or phantasmal metaphysics— which cannot be denied a certain rebellious and brutal originality—thus dated and flowed from the resurrection of a bard and folklorist: a Breton-speaking Breton of the twentieth century. There is in the arts something akin to the fertilization of flowers by the insects, as the poets, the prose writers, the painters and the musicians transport the impalpable pollen of beauty, rhythm and intelligence from one genre to another, from one sense to another, from one category of a sense to another—for there is more than one vision and more than one hearing in the same individual—from one epoch to another and from one nation to another.

In Spain, "Brazism," having become "El Brazio," acted in a fashion that was no longer direct, but indirect, reanimating the legendary foundations that have created, in all ages, the particular savor of a language simultaneously endowed for external life and mysticism, which shines with the same fire in Saint Theresa and Cervantes.

It was, in sum, in Italy, the most original, coldest, most enterprising and firmest people in twenty-third-century Europe, that the impregnation was weakest, not to say non-existent. There was not even a reaction there, nor what we call, for the sake of brevity, a *semen contra*. Italian literature and art pursued their particular involution, in the same way that China had its special and national form of Napus.

The brevity of that Renaissance was to be equal to its intensity. In her third volume of verse, it appeared that Marie de Félan had nothing more to say than what she had said, and that she had exhausted her delicate resources.

Jeanne Ronsin, released by the agile demon of sculpture, returned, after eighteen months, comparative embryology.

The pharmacist Lehuppe, having written a sequel of sorts to his *Leonardo*, or rather, a resuscitation thereof—something one should never do, *non bis in idem*[24]—lost his prestige over the young, the middle-aged and the old at the same time and was considered to be a failure and a has-been.

Charles Esbott, after ten years of resounding success, numerous translations and a few meritorious flops, as savorous

---

24. "Not twice for the same thing"—the legal principle forbidding "double jeopardy."

and fecund as his successes—for they did not result in conces-sions by the public, or any diminution of enthusiasm—gave up the dramatic art, and writing in general, without anyone knowing why, and devoted himself to trading in cereals and playing tennis. Having retired to Alexandria, warming his bones in the sun, he never offered any explanation or any response to the journalists who harassed him except an invariable: "It (meaning his art) disgusted me, and I left...."

Southbridge was napusified in the company of his host Ludovic Spague, after a somewhat orgiastic feast to which they had invited a few friends. It was one of the very few recorded cases of double, or twin, aphanasia. The protestant preachers of the neighborhood lost no time in affirming that it as a punish-ment for their bad conduct and indecent partying—but the most prominent and most eloquent of those preachers was napusi-fied himself shortly afterwards, which lessened the weight of his affirmation.

And what about you and your wife, you ask?

Henriette and I were vigorously touched by that literary, poetic and esthetic epidemic. We dared not admit to one another at first that the cell and its magnetic centers had lost its interest in our eyes since the dawn of our love. That love itself had opened the doors of sensibility and art to our souls, as the aurora opens those of the Orient. Our professors had come to disgust us by virtue of the absolutism of their doctrines, whose ineptitude we suspected or observed. Remorse, a sentiment hitherto unknown, had entered into me after the experiments carried out on the murderer, however execrable, of Sidoine, without my being able to discern whether the said remorse was a consequence of my new internal dispositions or whether it had determined them.

I think, too, that subterranean existence had excited in all of us—the inhabitants of Underground 7, that is—a voluptuous appetite for light, which the most focused and disinterested science could not satisfy. The best-equipped and the best-oriented laboratory remained a penumbra, whereas a simple distich of Virgil or Horace literally inundated us with light—not to mention a painting by Rembrandt!

I have known great inventors, in mechanics and biology, chemistry and physiology, who were always sad and morose, although they were considered as benefactors of humankind and universally honored. I have never known another man as cheerful as a Provençal mariner from Ciotat, who fished for sea-urchins and other fish and shellfish for bouillabaisse and sank from dawn to dusk in his boat. It's true that he too, in his fashion, was a benefactor of humankind.

When anyone asked the inventor, "Maître, why are you melancholy?" he replied, in a choked voice: "The more progress I make, the more the mystery of all things seems to me to be insoluble—that's what afflicts me."

When anyone asked the fisherman, "What is it that amuses you so?" he replied, hauling on his nets: "That I understand almost everything, and that the weather is fine."

Humankind, on the other hand, only had one choice: either to wait, trembling, for a death without remains that was expanding, like a patch of oil, among white people—for, in spite of Pafenier, even the dirty were beginning to pay tribute, in considerable numbers, to the increasing aphanasia—or to seek diversion and entertainment in the emotion of beauty and love, an escape into artistic creation. The majority opted for the second attitude.

For some time, there had been serious discussion about creating an international festival of the Napus, and the intention would have been realized if some people had not observed that the scourge, far from banishing and setting aside, as had been briefly hoped, that of war, had intensified it instead. There was no reason to celebrate the Devil, or death.

Artistic and esthetic conferences having replaced scientific conferences, it was decided to hold in Geneva, in the old Palais of the ephemeral League of Nations, restored in 2160, an amphitheoty of feminine beauty, to which even German women would be invited, in spite of the recent Archimedes and the unstable and indeterminate character of the armistice. Beauty, in the Greek sense of the word, not being complete without intelligence, however, it was decided that the lovely and gracious individuals of the final selection had to emit, after ten minutes of reflection, a remark or and aphorism that would become their motto, and would be transmitted throughout the world.

It seemed that the contest would be a means of bringing people together in a more agreeable fashion than by means of the question of the white slave trade or the distribution of goiters according to the vices and virtue of drinking-water. Alas, it was the opposite that transpired. Ferocious envy, excited among the candidates by the magnificence of the prizes and subsidies, let to a new cause of aggravation in diplomatic relations, less serious at first than that produced by the Sidoine law and the consequent disagreements, but which became terribly envenomed as it was prolonged.

I had convinced Henriette to compete, convinced that she would at least obtain an honorable mention and that she would find a very original and droll rejoinder. We went to ask Cortenaz for authorization. He received us affably, listened to us distractedly, and, wishing Henriette good luck, gratified us with a sonorous: "Good, good, that's all right"—but we found out subsequently that his wife had made an atrocious scene, because she too had wanted to enter the lists.

The journey overland, via the Morvan, the Jura and the Faucille pass, was delightful. The caravan was swelled by charming creatures who were collected on the way, in cities, towns and villages; all of them, being intimidated and then emboldened, took on different shades of pink. I was a guide and chaperone, with a dozen of our colleagues from the Aristotle, five of whom were Polyplasts, who had become disinterested in their work to some degree—without, however, developing the slightest inclination to antiscientism—and were no longer dreaming of anything but painting, music, dancing or love. Imagine how that flowered during the journey, and at meal times!

Calm had rapidly returned to the countries recently laid waste by the Archimedes. The rivers had returned to their beds. The populations chased away by the German bombardments had also returned. Peasants and their wives had resumed agricultural labor and household chores, as if nothing had happened. As for the Napus, although it removed, on average, one of our male or female companions per day, no one paid very much attention to it. The eulogy to the person who had disappeared was only pronounced half-heartedly. Often, it was a matter of a pretty individual whom no one knew, who was going to Geneva without having told those around her, and whose identity remained forever unknown. By tacit accord, no reference to Archimedic war, artificial cataclysms, grave recent events or the Napusian epidemic troubled the determined and general frivolity. When we stopped at inns, those who liked dancing danced; the others chatted or sang. It was a very agreeable existence, contrasting pleasantly with our scientific penal servitude in Underground 7.

Geneva, when we arrived there, in superb weather, seemed like a beautiful white, warm bird, a swan with smooth plumage, posed on the blue water of its adorable lake. It was decked with flags of all nationalities and various sects, those of the worshippers of the Napus, or napusomanes, representing the scattering of a skull on a bright pink background.

The German competitors, who had already arrived, also under the guard of emancipated Polyplasts and former laboratory heads, had retained the best rooms in the best hotels; through the sparkling windows one could see their blonde hair, their rounded profiles and their dream-filled eyes. In Germany, Polyplasts have square faces, entirely clean-shaven in a military fashion, and are clad in white uniforms devoid of braid, which signify consecration to *kultur*. Although the truce was not definitive, the Franco-German meeting was cordial—more cordial, even, than other encounters—and there were a few compliments on both sides before the blushing beauties: "Oh my! Sapristi! Damn! Ach doch, aber was, so so...."

The beauty-cars of Great Britain arrived at the same time as ours, laden with angelic physiognomies and veritable nymphs, who gave the impression of just having emerged from the water, summoned by Amphitrite. Their hair, of a lighter and more vaporous blonde than that of the Germans, as if idealized, was collected and gathered neatly in little baskets in the Greek style.

A physical kinship of sorts was observed between the Bruxelloises and the Lyonnaises, in terms of the solid delicacy of the facial features, as if dipped in honey, legs combining utility with slenderness, and a round but supple waist.

The Provençals and the Bretonnes, although very different in type, were related by the floweriness of the skin, ambered in one instance and blue-tinted in the other, which one might have thought imprinted with rose for the satin quality and variegated carnation for the scent.

How many prejudices there are to rectify, in matters of feminine beauty! For a thousand years, it has been reported, by all authors and voyagers, even more blind than ungallant, that English women have big feet. On the contrary, they have feet of a rare slenderness, and we did not encounter one in Geneva, walking delightfully, as in a play by Esbott, without asking her to take her shoes off—to which she consented amiably. In the same way, it is ridiculous to claim that British women are flat-chested. At the very most, they have a fashion of dressing which gives that illusion to an unobservant person. Finally, it is necessary to recognize that the language spoken on the far side of La Manche is a kind of birdsong adapted to the slender lips of woman and their ironic languor.

Introduced to one another, all these rivals showed themselves to be amiable and courteous, although spiteful individuals had predicted that they would tear one another's hair out. That evening, at the Geneva Opera House, whose orchestra is particularly fine, there was a performance of Ludovic Spague's Aphanasic Symphony, which made all the audience-members of both sexes regret his premature death. The competitors, in low-cut dresses, presented an assembly of European flowers, roses and lilies, carnations and daisies, which would have converted Schopenhauer himself to gynephilia and damned more than one hermit.

The two inaugural sessions, devoted to the definitive selection, gave rise to esthetic discussions between the esthetic artists that nearly degenerated into battle. The female judges did not have the same rules and canons as the males, and their choice went for preference to the less gracious and well-proportioned.

Plump herself, Maman Tougourte, a member of the jury by reason of her recent epistolary authority, eliminated all the slender English "grasshoppers," as she called them, because she had not yet found a publisher in London and only had eyes for Gretchen. Insolent and brutal, she had gained an ascendancy over her colleagues of both sexes, who no longer dared to pipe up when she had delivered judgment and brandished her powerful lorgnette. She led on a leash a celebrated skeptic by the name of Thiberaut, a fashionable writer brushing sixty, with a delicately modeled face terminated by a triangular gray beard, who uttered in regard to everything: "Yes, certainly, isn't it, all the same," and whom she had made into her lap-dog. A juror like her, Thiberaut adjudicated, but a trifle belatedly, on contestants no longer under consideration, and when he recalled, involuntarily and against the orders of his mentor in skirts, a beauty judged "too thin" his eyes accompanied her into the wings full of regret and concupiscence—and La Tougourte, waving her lorgnette, said: "Will you kindly refrain from goggling like a fish; at your age, it's ridiculous."

"She has a noble character" Thiberaut said of her, to excuse himself. "A noble and firm character, and what talent! Yes, but in the end, isn't it always the same: she's suffering—confidentially, it's the menopause."

The final selection included two Germans of very different types, one classically blonde, the other a haughty brunette; two Englishwomen recently flown from Paradise—one searched for wings in the ridges of their shoulder-blades—a Provençale with a Saracen profile, a Bressane reminiscent of a primitive Madonna and an Italian from a painting by Leonardo, endowed with an ineffable and seemingly hemstitched smile. My poor Henriette had been rejected—which did not prevent me from cherishing her with all my might, and experiencing, in her regard, a sentiment formerly foreign to Polyplasts: sensual jealousy.

The competitors, tastefully clad, but with bare arms and the shoulders uncovered, filed before the arbiters slowly, and were each getting ready to pronounce the expected motto when a Protestant pastor appeared, clutching a Bible under his arm. He was from Sweden, where he had miraculously escaped the Napus, which was taking a heavy toll there because of the sportive hygiene and the absence of dirt. He had a long and anxious face, a black frock-coat buttoned from the collar to the knees and a flat black felt hat with a broad brim. He climbed the steps leading to the stage rapidly, and once there extended his free hand—the one without the Bible—in front of him. He began a speech in a hoarse monotonous voice, in which he explained that the implacable Disease was a result of the decay of morals and, in particular, the immodesty of women and beauty contests.

The audience listened with resignation and consternation, without believing a word that he was saying, given that the Napus, presented in that hypothesis as a certainty, would have begun in the terrestrial paradise, where our first ancestors were naked. With wooden gestures, like an unvarnished puppet, the individual—whose name, we were later to learn, was Nysdröm, was continuing his remonstration when a dry click was heard and the Bible fell to the ground. The pitiless Napus had done its work.

The situation was so comical that everyone fell prey to hectic laughter, and the prizes could not be given out that day. They were never to be distributed, in fact, because of a tragic event whose repercussions were about to interrupt the tacit armistice.

The military men of the École de Guerre and the General Staff had been subject, like all cultured Frenchmen, to the crisis of esthetic and literary renaissance that had appeared in Europe and America in consequence of the death without remains and the vogue for Le Braz. Maréchal Verve had taken up playing the cello with ardor—it was no longer Ingres' violin—and it was said that his work on the periodic renewal of subterranean fortifications and mobile troops had suffered in consequence. He had been obliged to move after several complaints from his not-very-patriotic neighbors, who found his musical enthusiasm inconvenient.

Général Levin had been gripped by a taste for cinextual art, in spite of Eustache's campaign, and he had come to Geneva with a company of film cameramen, with a view to making a illustrated text about the esthetic conference. There was general astonishment that the warrior in question should seek, by way of relaxation, such a frivolous occupation, but we were living in baroque times, in which nothing ought to have been astonishing.

Fully occupied with Henriette's disappointment, I had omitted to make contact with the general, when I literally bumped into him at a corner in the Coraterie. His wrinkled and wizened face was lit up with a frank and benevolent smile and he seem to be free of somber internal preoccupations.

"Bonjour, Général! You've come for the beauty contest?"

"Bonjour, my dear Poly 17,177," he said, in his soft little voice. "I have, indeed, made the trip to take account of this interesting manifestation of beauty, and also with a view to the preface of a cinebook. What do you expect? I'm saturated with military plans. There'll still be time to resume the yoke when the Boches attack again. For the moment, 'At ease! You can rest.' I'm resting. And then I read in the paper that the utterly charming Madame Poly 17,177, née Tastepain, had not made the final selection. What an injustice! I'll go to set myself at her feet tomorrow. Where are you going?"

The conversation continued. In the square, people were stopping to look at the glorious soldier, the rampart of the Occident against the periodic fury of the Germans. They, and particularly a Polyplast, recognizable by his white uniform, found his glorious and modest personality curious.

I parted company with the noble soldier in order to go to a

final examination, and arranged to meet him at the banquet that was due to follow the election of the beauty queen.

Two more aphanasias, fortunately of unknown women of indistinct nationality, had occurred within the last six hours. The proportion was tending to increase, which, in view of the immense quantity of magnetic and wave-transmitting apparatus employed in the vicinity of Geneva, supported the late Sidoine's thesis. Everyone was talking about him again, but in low voices, for fear of resuscitating the Germans' Archimedean era.

It was the Bressane who won the prize, and that was justice, in view of the pert animation that heightened her marvelous light-chestnut beauty. Joy erupted in the French camp; we had no suspicion of the misfortune that was to follow.

The banquet, with two hundred places, was held at midday in the stone-paper Palais des Arts, erected in five days at the gates of Geneva by American construction methods, which are the most expeditious in the world. The weather was fine, the rivalries had ceased. The organizers of the grandiose international manifestation were radiant. There was only one shadow over the scene: the Disease—but in sum, that merely increased the shadow of the same kind that everyone bears in being born.

I found myself a short distance away from Général Levin, who was surrounded, and to whom a host of people from al countries, including numerous pretty women, were coming to pay homage. He replied to them all, even the Boches, with the remarkable affability that made such an amusing contrast with the formidable and irresistible shattering and crushing force that was in him.

As the coffee was being poured, after a banal and rapidly-served meal, as is usual at those kinds of feasts, he went pale, put his hand to the pit of his stomach, set down his napkin, goy up discreetly and went to the door. I had noticed his actions because I never took my eyes off him, fascinated by the strangeness of the role he was playing here, even more concentrated, mysterious and decisive that that of Maréchal Verve. I got up in my turn and ran to catch up with him. I did so just at the moment when bent double, he was asking for his kepi and cape.

Stoically, in a faint and halting voice, he said: "My dear friend, I'm suffering horribly. I don't know what's wrong. Could you examine me? Let's go to the nearest hotel."

The vehicles were parked two hundred meters away. I ran to search for ours. It took me twenty minutes to find the driver, who was having his own lunch. When I came back, the general had disappeared. I asked questions. The cloakroom attendant told me that he had left via a small suburban street, narrow but long, into which I immediately hastened.

I ran the entire length of the street, prey to a crazed anguish and making a thousand suppositions. I perceived a hotel of modest appearance, but tidy, as is typical of Switzerland. I went in and inquired. I was told that a general in uniform, who appeared to be suffering greatly, had indeed asked for a room. He had been given number 12. I ran up the stairs. The door was not locked. I knocked. No reply. I opened it and found poor Levin lying on the ground, curled up in the position of a man suffering the torture of being tightly bound. He was dead.

I immediately alerted the hotel manageress, a Swiss woman with an amiable and honest face. She came up to make sure of the death. She recoiled, gripped by horror at the sight of the contorted corpse, and then knelt down. I did the same. The most urgent thing was to inform the police, the conference-organizers and the press, and I took charge of that.

The manageress, whose husband was absent and whose telephone was out of order, came down too in order to notify a funeral director situated five minutes away and to ask a priest for the prayer for the dead. In our haste we forgot to lock the door of number 12. I noticed vaguely, three paces from the house, three individuals of unsavory appearance who seemed to be keeping watch, but I was in too much of a hurry to obtain their description—which I was subsequently to regret.

Having raised the alarm, without lingering over explanations, I ran back to the hotel, accompanied by a dozen compatriots, who did not want to believe in the catastrophe—for it was one—and were already talking about poisoning. On the threshold, the manageress, standing alongside a medical examiner, equally bewildered, was giving signs of bewilderment and fright. She explained to us that on going back up to the room, she had found it empty. The general's corpse had disappeared!

I read in the gazes of the people present that they were all thinking about the Napus, and that the worthy lady and myself had been victims of a common hallucination. That was, in fact, quite plausible—but I was entirely certain, as was the hotel manageress, that there had not been any hallucination: that we had seen, with our own eyes, Levin's twisted cadaver, and that his remains had been stolen, since aphanasia had never attacked a dead body.

It was in these bizarre conditions that the Geneva police and the judiciary identity service—which is the foremost in the world—made their initial investigations I learned later that discreet but serious inquiries had immediately been made by the Swiss police of my wife, my friends and the Aristotle, as to whether I might be subject to visions or nervous troubles, and whether, since the appearance of the Disease and the first case in the Avenue des Champs-Élysées, I had not been a trifle dotty. I recounted the story of the three rogues I had observed. I was assured that investigations would be made, but I could tell from the tone that scant importance was being attached to my denunciation.

By contrast, Levin's comrades, friends, niece and nephew— with whom he lived and who were his only family—not to mention the vast public, were convinced that he had been murdered by the Germans, in accordance with his presentiment. That was also the opinion of Maréchal Verve and, in sum, all of the army's high command. I was told secretly, by an envoy from Minister La Renaudière, that the King did not intend the affair to be hushed up, as so many crimes of the same nature had been in the course of history; that he considered it essential not to give the impression of recoiling before the threats of the unleashed German press, which was already talking about a breach of the armistice; that the necessary money and personnel would be put at my disposal, if the crime really was certain; and that nothing should be neglected in order to make the truth manifest.

Leven's malaise having appeared at the banquet when the coffee was poured, the first point to establish was whether or not he had drunk the contents of his cup. One of his neighbors at the table was a German woman, the other a Belgian. The Belgian, evidently sincere, affirmed that he had drunk the incriminated beverage, the German, evidently schooled, that he had not. The immediate neighbor of the beautiful German—a Frenchman— could not say whether or not the general had drunk, but he had raised the cup to his lips and then lowered it again.

It was impossible to determine which server had poured the coffee on that side, in view of the rapidity and confusion of the staff, recruited at the last minute. In any case, it still remained for us to prove that the body had been removed from the hotel during my absence and that of the manageress. Now, the floor-waiter and the chambermaid insisted that they had not left the servants' parlor at the end of the corridor, and had not heard or seen anything suspicious. The elevator-attendant, however, on the other hand, claimed that he had seen two men coming down, at that precise moment, who had not asked for the "lift." The street was composed of small private houses with gardens, as in every Genevan suburb; no clue came from that direction.

Swiss police cats are justly famous; it was seventy years ago that the first of those animals was revealed, with unexpected success, and climbed up on to a mantelpiece in search of a male-factor's cap, hidden behind a clock. Since then, the velvet-pawed pursuers have made great progress in the new path and five hundred Raminagrobis[25] patrol the streets of the great city night

25. Raminagrobis first appeared as the name of a cat featured in Jean de La Fontaine's fable "Le Chat, la belette et le petit lapin" [The Cat, the Weasel and the Little Rabbit]. La Fontaine later attributed it to the Prince of Cats in "Le Vieux chat et la jeune souris" [The Old Cat and the Young Mouse], and it caught on to the extent of becoming a common noun.

and day, observing, lying in wait and miaowing to attract attention at the first suspect circumstance. In no other place in the world is private and public surveillance exercised as well as in Geneva, thanks to those auxiliaries, a hundred times as skillful and docile as the dogs of old. On the other hand, the exceedingly ingenious and very recent idea of associating them with parrots charged with raising the alarm, had not been successful. The cats had clawed the parrots, which responded with pecks and vociferations, and the burglars made their escape.

Three teams of these highly-reputed animals searched the entire city of Geneva without result. The automatic photographic apparatus that takes silhouettes of passers-by in the less busy streets did reveal the presence of three men at the time I had perceived them, but in an indistinct fashion of no use to the police.

The fact that an occasion like a beauty contest had served to cover up a political assassination was revealing of German psychology. A kind of hypocritical and mocking compassion was observable in the eyes of the Polyplasts in white uniforms. Between them and us the atmosphere had become frosty, and the fragility of the literary and artistic link appeared in the following petty incident.

Thiberaut and Mère Tougourte, who were keen on Franco-German rapprochement, the intellectual fusion of peoples and other insanities, were infatuated with a cousin of Kaninchen's, who spoke French with a terrible accent. The latter recited entire pages from Thiberaut's novels and Tougourte's epistles, calling her "the motern Zévigné"—but when our fashionable couple approached the young and sympathetic Teuton the day after Levin's death, the latter turned his back on them. He blamed them for the general suspicion.

Henriette, who is very intuitive, had a dream in which she saw Levin's cadaver fished out of the lake. In view of the dispersal of the conference, terminated in mourning and dread, and the repatriation of the lovely competitors, the police surveillance relaxed and the feline searchers were freed. I persuaded the Genevan chief of police to entrust two of those animals to us, remarkable in that they had been "hydrophilized"—which is to say that the specific horror of water had been quelled in them from birth by means of appropriate aquatic training. They had accompanied the lacustrian brigades during the epidemic of suicide that had ravaged Switzerland and Savoy ten years earlier, after the disappearance of goiter.

I can still recall the names of those intelligent animals—they were called Tiquart and Frôlant—and the vivacity of their yellow eyes. One might have thought that they could talk.

The problem of the human language of animals was, along with that of invisibility, the great preoccupation of the biological scientists and physicists of the year 2100—who, in sum, were no more stupid than us and might perhaps have had more initiative. One also recalls the great controversy over the question of whether or not parrots had inherited a faculty of elocution inculcated into them a thousand years earlier—whether or not their faculty of speech was the consequence of ancient training. Then, without any appreciable reason, the problem, which had seemed so acute and as close to solution as that of invisibility, had faded into the background, ceased to attract attention and had been forgotten.

Human generations are like children, who become passionately interested in an amusement, an object or a task for an hour or a day, and then abruptly stop thinking about it. Most of the time, the loss of attention is proportional to its anterior tension, and as prompt as the other was swift.

Henriette and I, as lovers and recent deserters of research, joined the search, going along the shore of Lake Geneva amid the blue warmth of the commencing afternoon. Tiquart and Frôlant followed us, the former with dark fur, striped like a little tiger, the second more compact and circumspect, with gray fur that had a silky gleam. They knew why we had brought them, and that we were carrying out an important investigation. Gliding along at the same muscular and furtive pace, they exchanged blinks of their gold-encircled green eyes, replete with images of surprise, surveillance, cruelty and pouncing.

Before the first research excursion we had received a telegram from the Aristotle signed by Cortenaz, evidently instructed by La Renaudière, which gave us authorization to remain in Geneva for as long as necessary. "Good, good, that's all right!" We were both on a mission and in love. Meanwhile, for her part, the lovely and coquettish Madame Cortenaz, already consoled over not having won the prize, was flourishing at some distance from her spouse.

The vaporous and floating azure of the sky was not the same as that of the mountain, seen in oblique perspective, frosted with indigo in the warm light, but the color of the mountain was itself entirely different from that of the water, extended like blue satin cloth and only reflecting the sky and the heights as the splendid midday became distant. They were three blues that opened all the doors of suavity to us at once, as in the immortal sonnet by Keats, but in which, unlike the sonnet, neither the immense sea nor the profundity of a precious stone was evoked.

Accompanied by our small felines, we walked through meadows of delicately tender grass, never trampled, discreetly irrigated: meadows for the feet of elves or Englishwomen—but my eulogy to the latter aggravated Henriette. "Through the conference you only paid attention to Miss Tennhart, and you would have liked her to win the prize. Well, Monsieur, I allowed myself to be courted by the Boche Polyplast Otto 20,014, in his handsome blue uniform." I did not believe a word of it, knowing her to be faithful and hostile to Germans.

Six months before, such a stroll, if any could have taken place, would have steeped us in various considerations regarding the magnetic centers of the cell or the symptoms of the prenapus. Today, our preoccupations were very different. We enjoyed the expansive, immanent, intense blue—the triple blue of that corner of the Earth, whose equivalent is not found anywhere else, not even in Madame de Staël's turban, Voltaire's amethyst or Byron's passionate gaze.

A modulated miaowing resounded—that of Frôlant, who

was going along the edge of the lake. At that appeal, Tiquart came running, and arrived next to his companion with a bound. We drew nearer.

There was an evident disturbance, in that deserted spot, of the water weeds and snaking creepers dangling from the trees on the bank. About two cables out, the emergence of a fragment of gray cloth was perceptible, which appeared at a distance to be part of an elongated parcel.

The two cats came to a stop, purring. Their attitude indicated that their electropsychy—not their sense of smell, which is replaced in that animal by a irritated disgust—had revealed something important. We were immediately convinced that it was the body of the unfortunate Levin.

I went to look for a boatman. After searching for a quarter of an hour I discovered one who was willing to help me. The two of us—Henriette had remained with the cats on the shore—lifted out the floating package, tied up by a broken and fragmented rope, loading it into the small boat and bringing it to shore. There we carefully refrained from touching it.

In spite of its atrocious odor the Swiss and I stayed to guard it. Henriette returned to Geneva. Two hours later—the time of overly long procedural steps—a police commissaire, the head of the identity judiciary and gendarmes arrived, in order to establish that it really was Général Levin, recognizable by his uniform. His face, tumefied by the water, was black.

CHAPTER NINE
BOCHE WILL BE BOCHE

Popularity, which is the opposite of intimacy, had always been something unenjoyable to me, so I was rather disagreeably surprised, on returning to Geneva with Henriette, to be acclaimed by my fellow citizens. Immediately, however, I realized the effect produced by the discovery of Levin's cadaver and the manifest proof of his poisoning. The service of France entails much annoyance and even a few risks. Thus Polyplasty had made of me, by virtue of circumstances, a stalwart patriot, and I thought seriously about taking a name like everybody else, instead of my ridiculous number. A traditional and esthetic spirit had done its work within me without my being aware of it.

Numerous comrades from the Aristotle, with Cortenaz and Eustache at the head, were waiting for me when I got down from the train. The lovely Madame Cortenaz embraced the radiant Henriette and presented her with a bouquet. Cortenaz had prepared a little speech, not badly formulated, in truth, in which he developed the idea that, having departed for Geneva in order to crown beauty, I had crowed Justice there. I had a strong desire to reply: "Good, good that's all right," but I restrained myself.

The murder of our finest general had produced a considerable emotion in all milieux, and had reawakened national fiber, which had relaxed slightly since the tacit armistice. At first people had believed, naturally, in a misinterpreted Napus. Then, as more news arrived, they had concluded that it was a crime.

Now, suspicion of the Germans was such that Ambassador von Tschuppe und Werdenschaft, who had returned to the Rue de Lille—the seat of the embassy since time immemorial—had though it his duty to pay a visit to La Renaudière in order to complain about the perfidy of the Parisian press and what was being said in the street. The step was severely appreciated by the diplomatic corps and the rumor was covertly spread that the British admiralty had secretly given order to the "home fleet" to resume battle dispositions.

Eustache confided to me that a sense of veritable beauty had suddenly taken possession of him, as with all of us, and that he had sold off the paintings, items of furniture and objects of his famous collections, recognized as false, deceptive and hideous. He would only have obtained a derisory sum for them but for an Australian collector who had got it into his head, or had it put into his head, that the heap of rubbish in question was a marvelous opportunity and that Eustache had been afflicted by an acute autodepreciative mania.

"At another time," Eustache told me, "I would have laughed at that stroke of luck, which prevented my ruin, but I've discovered—believe it, my dear friend—that the universal renaissance in art is nothing other than a symptom of the prenapus, the presage of a recrudescence of the plague. No one has listened to me. Cortenaz hasn't listened to me; you haven't listened to me; people have continued to manufacture and publish those accursed cinebooks. We'll learn, and pay dear. I admit that I was convinced of Levin's aphanasia. When I think that he went to Geneva for a company of cinepublishers—him, a glorious soldier! It required the recovery of the cadaver to convince me of the crime. But tell me a little about the beauty contest. The little Bressane is truly pretty, then?"

Eustache, like many others, had become a bizarre mixture of the serious and the frivolous. The disappearance of mental alienation in its classic forms of revendication, dissimulation, persecution, etc. had doubtless been replaced by a shot of liquefaction of common sense and the immediate manifestations of logic and reason. People ripened in the study of medicine, jurisprudence, taxation, general economics, philosophical and biological criticism, and politics were now exhibiting deplorable lacunae from one week to the next, as if there had been a lapse, not in their memory, which remained intact and precise, but in their judgment. It was impossible to determine whether that was a phenomenon of prenapusian preparation or a ravage of internal dread and perplexity, or a consequence of the Archimedes.

One curious phenomenon was a tendency to gather together in order to take the most trivial decision or assume the slightest responsibility. Everything was a pretext for a conference, for assembly, for negotiation, for collaboration. Even though the Armistice of Beauty, as it was called, was precarious, by virtue of circumstances and the reawakening of the ethnic spite of the Germans, there was nothing to be heard anywhere but hymns to peace and eulogies to peace and its benefits; pacifist and pallia-tive figures of speech; declarations of non-aggression and the renunciation of all offensive intention, of the Archimedes, its ostentations and endeavors; promenades of blue flags—blue being the color of peace—altars to peace, flights of doves, reci-tations of poems, sonnets and tiercets to peace.

None of those who devoted themselves to these manifesta-tions believed them to be not only vain but a bad omen—for in all epochs they have signified, by antiphrasis, the imminence of war, in the same way that any project of disarmament invariably precedes the taking up of arms. But there was a kind of vogue, a fad, a psittacism and an echolalia, in which the depression of the public spirit appeared, by reason of the collapse of those who should have been guiding it—which is to say, scientists and writers.

The reaction came from the Sovereign, who insisted to the Ministers that an investigation should be opened in Paris, as well as in Geneva, into the circumstances in which Général Levin had been poisoned, and his cadaver removed and thrown into Lake Geneva. I was the principal witness; I was summoned by the Procureur du Roi, who commissioned a very firm examining magistrate by the name of Séchelard to take my deposition.

As I was going to the magistrate's office I met President Palémon, whom I had not seen since my last visit to the Palais de Justice a few months earlier. He saw me from a distance. "Well," he shouted to me, "wasn't I right?"

Then, as I hesitated, he went on: "What, don't you remember what I said? What is even more dangerous than aphanasia is the simulation of aphanasia. Well, didn't that hit the bull's-eye? Wasn't it spot on? Was I far-sighted? Yes or no?"

Palémon's vanity and self-contentment were legendary. In this instance, however, he had not been wrong, and I congratulated him without reservation. The more compliments I lavished on him, the more he demanded.

"Ha ha—magistrates aren't such cretins as the gentlemen of the Aristotle imagined! Don't deny it! You considered us all to be donkeys, square-hats, like presumptuous marionettes. You judged us even more harshly than we judge those who come up before us in court. Yes, yes, I know, I'm up to date. Père Palémon is nothing but an idiot. But I'm not so easily rolled over—it's me who rolls others over!"

I would have liked to get away from him, but there was no means. He was one of those people who hold on to you by one of the buttons on your waistcoat, your jacket or your overcoat and paw you while admonishing you.

"Can you imagine that Tonqueloque, the Minister of Inventions—the same one who, that other time....in sum, yes.... that fool Tonqueloque—detested Levin? He had, on some occasion, put him in disgrace, for some reason or other. When Tonqueloque found out about Levin's death, he was delighted at first. He's a nice fellow. Then, when the news arrived of the discovery of the vanished corpse, he was heartbroken, because that earned Levin a second wave of posthumous popularity. In fact, congratulations on your great success. What the Aristotle hasn't given you, popularity and a cleverly-conducted investigation will. Where are you going in such a hurry...Séchelard's office? Give him my best regards, and good luck...."

My deposition lasted four hours. I didn't omit a single detail. Séchelard had a symmetrical oval face, the beginnings of baldness, piercing eyes, a small moustache and a remarkable perspicacity with regard to the machinations of the Germans. He was a specialist in such matters, and the Americans had recently commissioned him, discreetly, to clarify the immense State fraud of the analgo, the cause of the perpendicular slide of the dollar. He laughed without opening his mouth, which gave his physiognomy an expression that was simultaneously pinched and radiant.

"What a people!" he repeated, meaning the Boche. "What an astonishing mixture of brutality and hair-splitting, trickery and cynicism, humanitarian jargon and inhumanity! And those cryptons—what a diabolical invention! And that Archimedes and that Murmelthier, and those statues of Murmelthier and that von Tschuppe! You wouldn't believe the extent to which I've put myself in their skin, seeing through their eyes, getting into their evasions and deceptions!"

"Undoubtedly, Monsieur le Juge—nevertheless, Levin is dead, and getting rid of him is a great coup on their part."

"You're telling me! The last time I met Général Levin was at one of La Renaudière's soirées—I took him to one side and told him my fears on the subject. 'Mon general, you're being watched by the German secret police. They want your hide,' He shrugged his shoulders and replied; 'They won't get it.' Well, they have, It's very sad."

I noticed the clerk's admiration for his superior. He was absolutely drinking in his words. When Séchelard went to fetch a file from the room next door, the fellow said to me: "He's the ace of aces. But he has no doubt that he too is in danger. It seems that his name was found in a little notebook that Murmelthier left at the conference before being aphanased."

I was familiar with that legend. I tried to undeceive the clerk, but in vain, and my incredulity seemed suspicious to him.

Séchelard came back with a sheet of paper covered in cabalistic signs, which he showed me.

"It's a Boche list of notable military and civilian individuals that Germany has an interest in seeing disappear. That bottle is Levin, of course. The person in the rebus who's throwing something—*werfen*—is Maréchal Verve. Those six digits are Sidoine. By a bizarre coincidence, Sidoine was murdered too. You can see that their crypton is practical. Believe. my dear Polyplast, that you'll soon be on this blacklist, if you aren't already."

I assured the magistrate that I was armored like Underground 7, and that the permanent threat of the Napus removed much of the acuity of the threat of political murder.

"That's true," said Séchelard, rubbing his hands, as he did every time someone made an interesting remark in his presence. "Can you imagine that there was a time—shortly before your encounter with the little girl and her grandfather in the Champs-Élysées—that the fear of being killed by a Boche trick abruptly entered into me. I kept an eye on my cook. I no longer ate shell-fish, and every time I had a stomach-ache I thought: 'This is it!' For a man who does what I do, that psychosis—that's what you call it isn't it?—was very disagreeable and very inconvenient. My clerk noticed it—didn't you, old chap?—and wondered whether I ought to move house. Then the Napus arrived, and the possibility of suffering aphanasia, at any moment, without preliminary warning, chased away the other thanatophobia. We're strange machines."

From there we went on to more precise points. Séchelard asked me whether I had thought of obtaining the names of the waiters at the Beauty Contest banquet, and Levin's neighbors at table. Yes, I had thought of it, but the Swiss police had wanted to conduct their investigation alone, and hadn't given me the information.

The magistrate picked up his wave-transmitter and contacted the Genevan police. Within five minutes he had his information., rang, and instructed for inspectors, chosen from among the least confused, to obtain information about the people identified, notably a German woman by the name, or pseudonym, of Friede—which signifies "peace" in German.

"A German charged with poisoning a French general takes a pseudonym from the pacifist glossary. That's a clue. Another point: when you pulled the cadaver out of the water, it was in dress uniform, wasn't it?"

"Dress uniform, yes—I can still see the gold braid soiled with mud."

"Had his kepi been placed in the sack?"

"No, the kepi wasn't there."

"Had it been left in the room?"

"No, it had been taken away with the general's body."

"So it's presently somewhere else, and it's improbable that the murderers threw it in the water. They must have given it, as material proof, to the person who had charged them with their sinister task."

"Who's that? Do you have a suspect?"

The magistrate replied, calmly: "Usually, a Beauty Contest attracts a host of procuresses, who go there for provisions, as if to market. Perhaps this Friede is a Frida. We shall see."

When I remarked on the difficulty of pursuing simultaneous investigations in Paris and Geneva, with two different police forces, he said: "The coup was certainly planned in Paris a long time ago; it was carried out in Switzerland, firstly to dichotomize the investigation, and secondly to avoid my investigations with the knowledge I have of cryptons. That careful calculation was made in the German manner. We'll catch up with the gang. I'm convinced, perhaps wrongly, that this lady Friede is presently in Paris."

She was indeed, and the inspectors located her after a week's search. She was living in a furnished house in the Rue Pigalle under the name of Madame della Pace, born in Trieste of a German father and an Italian mother. In a suitcase with a false bottom, a portrait of Général Levin was found, along with an indecipherable crypton. It was decided to arrest the lady.

At the same time the Genevan police got their hands on three individuals, supposedly Polish, one of whom, while drunk, had boasted about taking the general's remains from the hotel and throwing him in the water.

At that moment, Ambassador von Tschuppe intervened—he had returned to Paris shortly before—and declared straight out that the incarceration of Madame della Pace, charged with a secret mission by the Wilhelmstrasse, "a mission favorable to the cause of peace," would be considered an unfriendly action and would lead to the worst consequences.

The Murmelthier coup recommenced. Immediately, as if in response to an agreed signal, all the newspapers in Germany, whatever their political hue, published articles of an extreme violence, exposing French and Swiss perfidy, and the collaboration of the two states in giving Levin's banal murder a "German character." The offence against the Empire was declared to be intolerable.

Thus, the armistice appeared as a mere delay, designed to repair the damage accumulated by the ruinous expense of the Archimedes and give breathing-space to German finances.

That recrudescence of belligerence, which is fundamental to the Teutonic temperament, with its love of string-pulling and confused metaphysics, caught France, England and the Occident in general at a moment of esthetic and literary relaxation. An unfortunate circumstance! People had become accustomed to the irregular depredations of the Napus, which was continuing its work among the peoples of the Earth like a fantastic wood-cutter. They had become unaccustomed to the military heca-tomb, deafening rackets, artificial cataclysms, bombs of every caliber and the tall stories of the press precipitating the masses to the lowest level of imbecility.

We Polyplasts were, in the main, weary of the intellectual and moral tribulations to which our ethnic mixture had subjected us. Supposed pacifists, but actually bellicose, then abandoning science for art and the laboratory for Beauty, we were like a man who has run out of breath, changing direction and goal. In my own personal case, the fact that I had returned to the Catholic faith and my marriage gave me a foundation that my comrades did not have. If France had been a democracy, as in ancient times, submitted to all the gusts of impersonal and discontinuous power, it would have been irremediably lost.

Would that have been a loss to the world? I believe so—all the more so, it seems to me, because the several juxtaposed or interpolated nationalities within me permit me to make an internal comparison, a constant choice. A human being is a composite of clarifying forces and obscuring forces, which are in conflict when one is transmuting the quantitative into the qualitative.

In spite of Séchelard's superhuman efforts to obtain some confession—or, at least, some indiscretion—from La Friede, the latter remained impenetrable, not refusing to speak but drowning herself and the magistrate in a host of irrelevant details. That comedy lasted for three days, and during those three days, at the same time every evening, von Tschuppe came in person to the Quai d'Orsay to keep abreast of the interrogation and to repeat that his government was losing patience and that a resumption of hostilities was imminent. Kept secret in Paris, these steps were published every day in Berlin, and created a real anguish in the chancelleries.

The English ambassador came in person to ask La Renaudière to abandon the investigation in France and release Madame Friede. He affirmed that the Swiss police had for their part, released the Pole who had confessed, recognizing him as a drunkard of doubtful sanity.

In the meantime, we received a visit at the Foundation from a very distinguished German cytologist, Doktor Ochenstein, a mystical pacifist, who was resentful of his homeland for not giving sufficient recognition to his recent study on the shrinking of African and Asian elephants by the Napus. He was a kind of bony Coriolanus, tall and robust, with a hoarse falsetto voice and the square hirsute face of a quadrumane. Introduced into my laboratory, he demanded rather coarsely that I send Henriette away, told me that he was considered in America to be "the frankest man on the world," and explained his compatriots' plan to me.

"I know, confidentially, that the senior general staff are planning, this time, an unprecedented form of battle: mental warfare. The analgo has put money in the coffers of the military budget. It's by the intensification of the war of sound and artillery thunder—*trommelfeuer*—that the high command intends to proceed. No attacks, no gas, no aircraft. It's all about the devastation of the nervous system. Experiments carried out on herds of bison—very resistant animals, as you know—have observed the initial explosion of the cranial cavity after half an hour of that intensified racket. I know that the experiment has been repeated recently on ten Russians, employees in a factory on the Oder, who were claimed to have been killed in an explosion. In fact they were soundblasted, as we say, and dismembered."

"But how will your troops be protected against the effects of the noise that they're unleashing?"

"With the aid of sound-mufflers. It's the latest newly-discovered crypton. That was what determined Levin's murder—for no one back home doubts, any more than they do here, that you're on the right track regarding the murder."

I hastened to make this information known to the French General Staff. Unfortunately, the general who received it, although intelligent, was one of those who make a profession of skepticism and consider as false, *a priori*, any information transmitted by a civilian Polyplast. It is a curious psychological fact that advice concerning Boche dispositions and preparations has always, throughout the centuries, been treated as romances and old wives' tales by the very people who, being in charge of the war, should have taken them most seriously.

Well-versed in that history, and in spite of the strict control I exercised on my senses and their testimony, I had a premonitory apparition, like a simple English or American chemist of physicist: that of Levin in person, who appeared to me soaked in water, livid, without his kepi, terribly sad, as the boatman and I had pulled him out of the lake.

"I have indeed been poisoned," he told me, "with the aid of a cup of coffee containing a Murmelthier product with the German crypton Z 4777. That product leaves traces, contrary to what the Germans believe, but the Swiss judiciary identity service has no means of finding them. As for the arrested Poles and Friede, nothing will be discovered. The war will be resumed by means of sound. The French General Staff, although fore-warned and having at its disposal a system of mufflers as good as the enemy's, will not utilize them at first. Expect tens of thousands of casualties to begin with."

I was streaming with sweat; my hair was stuck to my temples, my feet leaden, my tongue paralyzed. I wanted to ask the general's specter who would be victorious in the end, but at the first word that emerged from my lips he disappeared, twisting his thin lips dolorously.

We were approaching the end of the month of August, which is usually the one in which the Germans invade Belgium or Switzerland in order to penetrate into France after some incident or other, or without any other reason than the perception of cultural differences or the desire for combat: *Kampfsehnsucht*.

More than fifty years ago there was a Polyplast at the Aristotle—which was then called the Plato; I don't know why the Foundation changed its name—who published a thesis on this *Kampfsehnsucht* that generated a great deal of noise. It is particular to Germany, and distinct from simple combative-ness. It has also been observed in a number of animal species, notably the bull and the turkey, where it is manifest either at the appearance of a color that excites the animal's latent fury, or in response to a noise or a gaze judged to be offensive. One Australian lizard takes that impulsive fury to the point of projecting its eyes out of their orbits when it perceives an insect under a certain incidence of light. By night it is perfectly calm.

The Polyplast in question—whose number I no longer remember—had carried out a profound investigation of fifty German immigrants belonging to all the States of the Empire: Saxon, Bavarian, Baltic, Prussian and Hanoverian. In all of them he had found a particular muscular tonus, a certain excitability in response to chemical substances or physical excitations, which permitted thee release of the *Kampfsehnsucht* syndrome into a sort of nascent state. If you bring together ten Germans, you obtain a KS index of seven, giving on the psychomanometer a pressure of Fury of 0.25. The progression rises in twenty Germans to a KS index of ten and a Fury pressure of 0.75. From then on, there is a fluttering in the figures, which tends to the unleashing of a desire for combat among the gathered Germans. But if one Frenchman, Englishman or Belgian passes through the ocular field of an isolated middle-class German, his irritation immediately reaches a level of F 0.90, especially if he pronounces, at the same time, words of forbearance or wisdom. Germans excite themselves for war by talking about peace.

That is the veritable cause of the wars successively declared in Europe by that race of head-breakers and neck-breakers, who do not know exactly what they want or where they are headed, but, like an irritated concierge, incessantly seeks to quarrel with its neighbors, immediate or distant. Besides which, there are other indicators of *Kampfsehnsucht*. Whereas a murderer usually kills one or two people, a German murderer kills a dozen, sometimes with the aid of a club, sometimes with a kitchen-knife or a shard of window-glass, or whatever comes to hand. The representative characters of German legend, with Siegfried at their head, do not fight like the ancient Hercules "for good," against hydras, marsh-dwelling birds, devastating lions or to rescue the wife of a friend from Pluto. They fight for the symbolic possession of a warrior-woman sheathed in fire—which is to say, to slake the inexplicable but irresistible ire that is burning them up.

It is because *Kampfsehnsucht* is working upon them that the Valkyries ride clouds, howling. Wotan rejoices in the din made by his daughters, their thirst for blood and plunder; if he has one regret, it is that they do not do enough of it. If he sees them weary, he becomes blazing mad, and holds out a sword, a spear, a shield and a helmet, and says: "Go, my daughter, and kill more—or at least cripple them!"

This time, the German *Kampfsehnsucht* had, as a pretext, the investigation carried out by Séchelard into the indubitable murder of Levin, just as it had previously had as a pretext the pseudo-murder—in reality the napusification—of Murmelthier. For the highest levels of Ks are naturally found in the senior General Staff, itself supported by the heavy industry of the Ruhr, Silesia and all the metallurgical regions of a land consecrated, for all eternity, to Vulcan. It is the combination of that temperament and that subsoil that has prompted the desolation of the planet for so many centuries. Has not the principal task of the Occident, in modern times, been recovery from the material, intellectual and moral ruins accumulated by *Kampfsehnsucht*?

The rupture of the Armistice of Beauty occurred in the following fashion: Emperor Wilhelm XIII summoned the best-known "Weepers" in Europe to Berlin. That was the name given to those who, imagining war to be a sequence of misunderstandings and failures of comprehension between peoples who are naturally benevolent, generous and honest, set out to drown those misunderstandings in declarations of love and tears, thus bringing back the Golden Age.

The Conference of Weepers took place of the twenty-second of August 2228 in Potsdam, in the midst of an immense display of blue flags carried by charming young women, daughters of the principal manufacturers of asphyxiant shells and Archimedes in Sweden, Norway, Greenland and the Nordic lands in general, where ballistics has nuances of philanthropy. A prize of a million dollars, restored to parity with the analgo, would be awarded to the author of the finest work for peace. It was awarded to General von Herzius, the author of *Archimedes*, the inventor of a mechanical parrot that recited the antiwar sermons of the principal Teutonic preachers. At the banquet that followed, the Chancellor of the Empire made a poignant speech about the benefits of universal understanding and the cruel necessity that sometimes arose of temporarily breaking that understanding in order that it could be better reconstituted thereafter.

Forty-eight hours later, when the Weepers had scarcely got

home, war was declared for "false suspicion of murder." That same day, four hundred cases of Napus occurred in Paris, five hundred in London, three hundred and twenty seven in Rome and a thousand in Madrid. A new growth of monstrous mushrooms appeared in the suburbs of Paris, submerging the forest of Fontainebleau. The news from the great African lakes announced the chromonapus of several thousand black people, who had become pale green in a matter of seconds. In China, however, a nation of pullulation, the Disease assumed vast proportions with statistics—obtained, it is true, from the English and American consuls, who like large totals—of approximately a hundred thousand stinking "footprints" in three days. The result was a veritable infection throughout the Celestial Empire.

Among the notable individuals who disappeared without remains, in Paris and elsewhere, were Mère Tougourte and the newspaperman Barouille. Thiberaut, initially inconsolable about the disappearance of his odious Egeria, apparently never ceased repeating: "Yes, in the end, isn't it, all the same,"—which did not prevent him from departing for Lac Majeur a week late with his young maid, forty years his junior....all the same, isn't it, yes, in the end!

The information that the braggart Ochenstein had given me, dismissed as "romances" by our General Staff, prompted me to look into the new German method of combat for myself. Henriette thought my curiosity perfectly legitimate. It only remained or me to obtain authorization from Conrtenaz. A mere formality, I thought, all the more so as the wife of our excellent "good, good" had departed the day before for an unknown destination with one of her husband's collaborators. I expected to find him prostrate, but, to my great surprise, instead of a sympathetic and resigned cuckold I found an irritable, self-confident, suspicious man, deprived of his verbal tic, who raised a few objections based on my role at the Aristotle, my importance, the Levin affair, etc.

"I need you—and besides, it's important to me to get a fix on the Napusocryptogamy at Fontainebleau; only a Polyplast of your worth, for far as I can see, can inform me."

I objected that my collaborator, Henriette, was just as well-informed and capable of replacing me.

"Oh, women!" he said, with an evasive gesture that signified: *one can't count on them*. All men in his situation tend to generalize.

After many ifs, buts, fors and *verum enim veros*,[26] it was decided that I would make a succinct report on the situation at Fontainebleau, and that it would then be permissible for me to become a spectator of armies. That was, for a man of science who had become smitten with artistic sensations, a fine opportunity to turn, as they say, the taps of nature: that of natural perversity—pullulation—and that of human perversity: *kampf-sehnsucht*.

Henriette and I arrived at the place where Barbizon had once been toward evening. The door of the palace was obstructed by a dozen enormous mushrooms, gigantic boleti, about which the porter complained sadly, for they had driven away the foreigners and admirers of the forest. They had respected the vestibule, though. They gave off a strong, intoxicating odor of damp foliage. One of them rose all the way to the window of out first-floor room.

We dined rapidly; the moon was shining and I wanted to take account of the strange and universal phenomenon that was intriguing the scientists of the entire world. The Aristotle's automobile took us to the chaos of Franchard, to Bas-Bréau, the gorges at Apremont and the ruins of Marlotte. Whether it was a matter of beeches or stones, traced roads or impenetrable thickets, the monstrous mushrooms circumvented, scaled, wound around, slid, insinuated and inserted themselves, individually or in groups, like silent invaders. One might have thought them enormous fat umbrellas, open and gleaming beneath triple Hecate. Their unusual height brought them closer to the animal, and their order of implantation and growth gave

26. All three Latin words can be translated as "truly"; their sum is therefore an unusually emphatic affirmative.

the illusion of movement.

The force that propelled the phenomenal vegetables and annihilated white or yellow human tissues while discoloring those of black people, was evidently symbiotic, composed of two opposed tendencies or directions: one of growth or discoloration, the other of destruction. Undoubtedly, it was a matter of a cosmic force, originating from a heavenly body in fusion or transformation, and which human intelligence, which had had so much difficulty comprehending the similar origin of cancer and tuberculosis—one and the same malady—had not yet succeeded in disentangling. But was it not possible, too, that force X obscured human intelligence as soon as it latched on to it? That is the case, for example, with mathematics, which kill all reasoning that is not applied to their chimerical and logically-deducible formulae.

Henriette, rendered even more subtle by the night, the moon, the imminence of my departure and the war, pointed out to me that the vast sudden fungal display was no more mysterious or inexplicable that the Forest of Fontainebleau itself, a minero-vegetal masterpiece emerged from water and fire to make the esthetic sprit marvel.

"What's prodigiously beautiful here, my beloved Poly, is the proximity of a hidden law, that we can only glimpse in a ray of moonlight. But a Beethoven symphony also moves the *"pulcherrimum"*[27] in us by means of the presentiment of a hidden truth, extended like a golden thread between the human mind and the sound, the human heart and the rhythm. In the same way, when you take me in your arms, when you hold me, when you take me, don't you seek to know as much as to enjoy, and interrogate your avid and curious soul even more than you're burning senses? What is exalting and splendid is perhaps, in all the walks of the life and thought, what prepares one to know everything that is not yet known. The portico of that knowledge

---

27. This Latin term, relating to beauty, is most familiar as a specific designation in the classification of plants; it is presumably cited here because of its use in *Lycoperdon pulcherrimum*, a kind of puffball mushroom.

is always something of a Parthenon."

That lunary night, before the colossal forms of the boleti, the orange-milks, the fly-agarics, the white mushrooms, the puffballs and club-fungi, like vast and powerful corals, took us both to the highest point of conjugal conjunction and communion. Before the Napus, it would have inclined us toward the problem of death, but today that problem, having become too complex, no longer answered the appeal of amorous desire, and the result of that was a serenity of an exquisite softness—which we owed, in the final analysis, to the unknown scourge.

In consequence of these emotions, the report that I drew up at Cortenaz's request was much more of a poem than a scientific document. I don't know what became of it because, on returning to Paris, we learned that the two armies were confronting one another on the plains of Lorraine, where they had confronted one another so many times, and that an engagement was imminent. The *Kampfsehnsucht* was about to break out!

At about nine o'clock that evening I arrived at the Château de Saint-Paterne, on the Hauts-de-Meuse, where Maréchal Verve's general headquarters were located. That dwelling, destroyed by the recent Archimedean inundation, had been reconstructed in a matter of hours according to the American method by Annamite workers. One of the latter having been napusified; his "footprint" had left a disagreeable odor by which neither the Maréchal nor the officers gathered around him appeared to be inconvenienced.

Verve was standing, in a blue uniform and boots, at a table covered with maps. He was absorbed in his reflections and shook my hand distractedly. His subordinates welcomed me affectionately, for the Levin affair, in which I had been involved, was still the object of all conversations. La Renaudière was accused of laxity in pursuit of the truth.

"Weakness in politics is always disastrous," said an officer. "This one, far from preventing the new war...."

"You mean the rupture of the armistice."

"All right, the rupture of the armistice...La Renaudière's

climb-down hastened it. It's unacceptable that, only two and a half centuries after the political education of Maurras, a minister of the King should be so ill-informed about the principles of mastering masters."

But Verve's solid and mocking voice rose up: "Enough criticism, Messieurs, and to action! We've been told"—here the Maréchal turned mischievously to me—"that the enemy is about to deafen us with the aid of a destructive tumult ten times more intense than any unleashed previously. I conclude from that—excuse me, my dear Polyplast!—that what is in preparation, by contrast, is an old-style battle, and what is important is to equip ourselves in advance for an attack by tanks of the latest model.

"I've had two lines of traps dug, hidden under branches and coatings of soft earth. In addition, two anti-tank divisions are ready to set forth, two kilometers from here in Saint-Trigaud. So we're ready. Our counter-offensive will embrace the entire extent of the battlefield, in liaison with the English army— which, incidentally, hasn't yet arrived—but it's been announced, and it's expected at any moment, and we don't have to fear an inverse Waterloo."

I had a strong desire to ask what had been prepared against the noise, just in case, in spite of everything, the Ochenstein information was well-founded, but I dare not raise the question of the mufflers like that.

The young officers were joking about the pretended exactitude and supposed immutability of the English command's timetables: "They're never on time—they've missed the train, forgotten their luggage. They're the most distracted, the most poetic and the least practical people on Earth, and that's why they've conquered it. They're all disembarked mariners and colonizers."

"And in science, Monsieur Poly 17,177, what are they giving us today?" asked a captain with a frank, naïve and joyful face.

"Great visionaries of the universe, in physics and chemistry, who are also skillful and precise experimenters. In biology, they're not as good."

"What do they think of the Napus? What explanation do they give of it? Do they also have Eustaches and Sidoines to develop well-coordinated and compressed fancies?"

I was about to reply but the door opened and, without being announced, Field-Marshal Mugh-Bigfort came in, accompanied by a young interpreter, in whom I immediately recognized a Polyplast of Boche tendency. The significant odor of Germanic sweat-glands, even in a hybrid, is never deceptive. That combined with the odor of the Annamite footprint left by the napusified mason.

"Bonswar," said the British colossus. "The ball's about to start, then. All's well."

"How many men, Monsieur le Maréchal?" asked Verve, elliptically, rubbing his hands—for he had, in fact, been afraid of a delay.

"Sixty thousand this evening, anther two hundred thousand tomorrow. All's well that end well." The Field-Marshal, very literate, willingly quoted Shakepeare and Esbott. He was already drowsy and was yawning as he listened to Verve's explanations.

I remembered Levin's considerations regarding forms of battle, previsions and uncertainty. Would this one belong to the category of combats that happen as one of the antagonists has foreseen, and to whom the decision would be granted?

Tolstoy relates that Kutusov slept sitting down during the preliminaries to Borodino; Mugh-Bigfort was sleeping standing up, smoking an enormous cigar, whose ash, not falling, seemed to have suspended the course of time like a blocked clepsydra. He asked for a glass of whisky of a particular brand, Canadian Club, which could no longer be found in the general quarters, although they were well-enough provisioned. Annoyance gave his face the aspect of a mortified ham. "All" was no longer "well."

At that moment, an agonizing clamor, like the bellowing of a hundred thousand female mastodons having their throats cut, resounded outside, and a large painting hanging on the wall, representing a former proprietor of Saint-Paterne, fell noisily to the floor.

Mugh-Bigfort remained impassive. Verve paled slightly. The officers suppressed a furtive smile. Oschsenstein's bony face suddenly appeared above my silence. It was the great Boche taraboom that was beginning.

As one distributes candy to children, Verve offered each of us wads of perfumed wax, manufactured in Konigsberg, which we swiftly stuffed into our ears in order to stifle the hyper-sound. Taking his blue pencil he wrote in large letters on a blank piece of paper, which I can still see: *It won't last. It's a feint*...for that soldier of high intelligence was prodigiously stubborn. He required two or three errors of prevision to rob him of victory, and when he won he maintained subsequently that it was precisely because of those mistakes.

No underground bunker had been set up, but there were still the cellars of the château, filled with the best vintages in France, and where it was necessary to take refuge. The first effect of the taraboom was to cut and crush all telephonic, wireless and other communications, with the result that we were about to find ourselves, for several hours, in complete ignorance of what was happening.

That was also the case for the Germans, as we learned subsequently. They had thought of everything except for that annihilation of means of communication, which realized Sidoine's desire, but which also, as we shall see, had a result entirely different from the one that Sidoine had expected.

In the cellar—in the depths of the hold, it seemed—we could only record on the manometer the hundredth part of the racket perceived in the apartments of the château. However, and in spite of the ear-plugs, we had the sensation of being plunged in a frying-pan with the dimensions of Lake Geneva., above which a bronze bell was resonating, a sheet of glass continually smashed and reassembled from the height of the towers of Notre-Dame. We communicated in writing, which was not without a certain picturesque quality. The fluid phosphorescence apparatus had not shattered; it was still there; we could see clearly.

I was mistaken, I admit, wrote Verve, *but have no fear. It will work out for the best. It's only a short interval to get through.*

The officers smiled sadly, wondering what would become of the French and English troops. Mugh-Bigfort was still drowsy, standing up like a caryatid dressed in rubber cloth, with the ash of his cigar extinct. His interpreter, leaning phlegmatically on the wall of the cellar in spite of the saltpeter dusting it, blinked his eyes with a muted expression. He seemed fit for a firing-squad to me, for he surely belonged to the secret police and was devoured by *kampfsehnsucht*, but I was the only one who suspected him.

The formidable petard of the Archimedes was joined by the collapse of the paintings, expensive vases, ewers, dressers and other items of the château's furniture. The walls were trembling and vibrating, as if under the urgent blasts of a hurricane that threatened to shred and pulverize them: Vulcan unchained, or irritated by the treason of blonde Venus, jumping and dancing in a metal shell, trampling a mass of cymbals and turning his forge upside-down.

How long did that unexpected ordeal, worse than any kind of bombardment, go on? I don't know. We were told after-wards that we had only gone seventeen hours with nothing to eat or drink, reduced to utter impotence in the cellars of Saint-Paterne. I'd like to believe it—but those seventeen hours were the equivalent of seventeen years.

Even so—and this is one of the mysteries of modern warfare—Verve's personality continued, even living ten feet underground in the absolute impossibility of sending any order to his army, to act and maintain in his heart and his judgment of the French combatants, the certainty of ultimate victory. When all the apparatus, mechanisms and improved systems had bee pulverized by the hypersound, the calculative and warrior emanation of that gentleman with the wrinkled face, as subject to false evaluations as a mother and father, remained intact, transmissible and predominant.

The vastest, most original and most ludicrous of battles are merely a series of duels regulated by the supreme duel of two general staffs and the effluvia of two commanders-in-chief. That seems paradoxical, but is the simple truth. Those two masters of combat each remain seated in his office, meditating on their struggle and concentrating their thoughts, one in Paris, the other in Berlin—of which the final result might be the same as that obtained by the clash of thousands of men, except tht it would not be materialized. The battle is the hectic opposition of two individuals dynamisms, acting on hierarchically-organized hosts. Of those two dynamisms—which is to say, in sum, of those two souls, and not only that of those two minds—the stronger will prevail.

I tell you this, as a Polyplast, not only a metaphysicist but a mystic, floating far above the fields of battle where bloodthirsty crows are feasting.

Suddenly, the fantastic tumult ceased, as it had begun. We thought that it had surpassed the limit that human ears could perceive, beyond which sonic waves destroy rocks and the sphenoid bone without affecting hearing. It was nothing of the sort.

This is what had happened. Not only had the German mufflers not preserved the German army from the rightly-feared counter-shock, but the employment of those mufflers had—at least one presumes so—caused the aphanasia of nearly a hundred thousand enemy officers, non-commissioned officers and soldiers. After an hour, and simultaneously, those hundred thousand Boche had disappeared, napusified, without leaving any kind of trace—not even an *oof!*—taking with them a hundred thousand uniforms, the hope of the Deutschland, their *kampfsehnsucht* and their appetite for rape and pillage: a hundred thousand who would not return, as Baudelaire put it "to eat perfumed soup by the hearth in the evening, next to a beloved soul;" a hundred thousand who would not be there on the day of resurrection, between Wotan and Arminius, Grail in hand, celebrating the superiority of the German Archimedes and the slaughter of a billion Frenchmen and Englishmen in four consecutive wars.

That death without remains of their comrades had, in spite of discipline, thrown a perfectly comprehensible panic into the German ranks. The troops had taken the road back to the "Vaterland," where triumphal arches awaited them and the heroic-symphonic strains of the traditional Schubert march for fifes and drums:

Tim di li li tim tim...tim
Tim di li li tim tim...
Tim di lili tim tim tim tim,
Tim di lili tim tim.
Oum, oum oum, houhou houm, houhou houm
Oum, oum oum, houhou houm, houhou houm
Ti ti di di di deum, deum, deum, deun, deum, deum, deum,
  deum....

You will excuse me for not transcribing the rest of that masterpiece. I have been feeling, for a few minutes, rather tired, prey to a strange malaise. That comes, I think, from the simple evocation of the sonic convulsions that we resisted—I don't know how—at Saint-Paterne.

Thus terminated the redoubtable event known as the Battle of Sound. But it is necessary to add that on our side, if our losses to the Napus were inferior to the formidable losses of the Germans—thanks to the fortunate omission of the French and English mufflers—about eighteen thousand men were torn apart, or immediately crippled, by that tumultuous form of Archimedes. Among the majority of these unfortunates, the skin was hanging down, detached from the bones, and the internal organs were scattered in an unspeakable pulp. The cadavers sent for examination to the Aristotle gave the impression of having been gnawed by myriads of ants and termites. The flesh resembled grains of rice—hence the term "riciform decomposition"—and the blood was black and entirely coagulated.

In accordance with custom, Wilhelm XIII was immediately overthrown and replaced by a Republic, known as the

Archimedes of Peace, of which von Herzius was the president.

"Well, my dear Polyplast," Maréchal Verve said to me, in the midst of the vermicular debris of Saint-Paterne, when we had recovered somewhat from our emotion, "your information wasn't bad."

"No, Monsieur le Maréchal, not too bad."

"I need to tell you something funny. Do you remember that young man who accompanied the worthy Mugh-Bigfort as an interpreter? Well, he was napusified."

"No, Général, he was a spy, and he's rendering an account to the German commandant of what he observed in the cellar."

"Oh, you damned story-teller! What an imagination these Polyplasts have!" the Maréchal said, tugging my ear—as, it's said Général Bonaparte did when he was satisfied. "Do you know what I sometimes say to myself? It's a pity that poor Levin didn't see that! You think, then that he was murdered?"

"I'm convinced of it, Monsieur le Maréchal."

"Hmm! Isn't it cabin fever playing tricks on you again? Bah, at any rate, the Boche are rogues and the Napus has had the last laugh. All of a sudden, there's Sidoine—the late Sidoine—at the pinnacle. It's necessary to recognize that he had seen clearly."

Eustache, by contrast, was furious. The mass napusification of a hundred thousand Boche, if it did a god job of upsetting cryptons beyond the Rhine, also dealt a harsh blow to the cine-textual theory, for it was implausible that the German soldiers thus subjected to aphanasia had all had copies of a cinematically illustrated book in their knapsack.

And now, I ought to explain, as briefly as possible (finally! finally!) the conclusion suggested to Henriette and me with regard to the Napus by the event known to history as the Great Aphanasia of Lorraine.

First observation: the Archimedean hypersound had surely come to the aid of that large-scale Napus, if it did not cause it.

Second observation: the Germans had mufflers, and the Franco-English army, which ought, in theory, to have had them, had not received them. Now, the Franco-English army was not afflicted by the Disease. It follows logically that the mufflers had come to the aid of the hypersound with regard to the disappearance of a hundred thousand men—or, more exactly, a hundred thousand and seventeen, according to the reports of the section commanders.

On that basis, we have concluded, after long reflection, that the Napus might be, or must be, the consequence of an intense din felt by the human organism but not perceived by the human ear; a racket connected with the entry to new spheres of newly-formed heavenly bodies in general gravitation. For if the radiant state to which we owe, among others, radium, is a phase of centrifugal bombardment by the rupture of atomic bombardment and the projection of meteors and bolides, there is another inverse state corresponding to a phase of centripetal effraction[28] by other atoms, or other "imprints" coming brutally to annexe some king of gyratory system. It is to that phase of centripetal effraction, accompanied by an intense interplanetary din, that it is probably necessary to attribute the Napus, just as the phase of centrifugal disintegration corresponds to magnetization and waves. Sidoine had mistaken the effect, or one of the effects, for the cause—which, in science, is quite frequent.

We certainly expected that our thesis would give rise to considerable objections, but we never supposed that the director

---

28. *Effraction* is the term conventionally used in France to describe the crime known in England as "breaking and entering." What Poly 17,177 is suggesting is that the Napus is due to a form of "atomic implosion," an inverse of the process that produces atomic radiation and atomic explosion. He attributes the fundamental trigger-mechanism to the advent of a kind of cosmic radiation, reaching the solar system as the result of some distant cosmic event—perhaps what we would call a "supernova"—manifested, or at least mediated, as sound waves beyond the attainment of human hearing. He believes all diseases to be the effects of similar causes, along with other mental and physical effects, including those manifest in his narration as well as those described by it. The "waves of time" featured in Daudet's subsequent novel *Les Bacchantes* (tr. as *The Bacchantes*) have similarly various and peculiar effects, and clearly belong to the same hypothetical biophysics.

of the Aristotle would beg us to renounce it. That is, however, what the brave Cortenaz did when I went, in the company of Henriette, to submit it to him. After listening to us both attentively, he said:

"My children—for everyone here is something like a child to me—it's possible that you're right, and this explanation of the Napus is, I confess, very seductive. But it's precisely because it's very seductive that I'm asking you to abandon it immediately. Consider, in fact, that discussion of the origin of the Napus gave rise to the Sidoine law, which itself unleashed, within a year, two conflicts with Germany, and, indirectly, a very redoubtable artistic pressure with regard to the division of peoples and their divergences in the presence of the beautiful.

"Yes, yes, I know that people claim the love of beauty unites people and nations—but it's an immense error. It divides them and creates conflicts more atrocious and atrocious than those determined by competitions in science or finance. Quarrels over what one believes beauty and truth to be—which is to say, in the context of eternity, duration and immortality, for the beautiful and the true are interlinked—are of a religious, spiritual order, and involve not only being and mind, but the soul. That is what makes them inexpiable.

"Listen to me: for a long time, already, I've been thinking of creating, here at the Aristotle, a prize more handsome than all the others: one for the abandonment of a true idea, or a legitimate observation or experiment, both of which are susceptible of unleashing Tisiphone or Bellona. Can one imagine a more noble, a more useful, more majestic sacrifice than that of Berthelot, for example, renouncing the publication of his conclusions regarding explosives, or than that of...."

* * * * * * *

Here the narrative of Polyplast 17,177 ends, the unfortunate— who had sensed the approach of the Disease—being suddenly napusified. History does not tell us what became of Henriette, the worthy companion of that excellent observer.

ABOUT THE TRANSLATOR

BRIAN STABLEFORD has translated more than a hundred volumes of French prose into English. His principal interests are the French Romantic Movement and its Decadent/Symbolist aftermath, with particular reference to the evolution of the *conte cruel*, and the evolution of the *roman scientifique* from its origins in the eighteen-century *conte philosophique* to the aftermath of the Great War of 1914-18.

www.ingramcontent.com/pod-product-compliance
Lightning Source LLC
Chambersburg PA
CBHW021241260626
47155CB00004BA/1259